You'll like her. Maggie's words came back to him. Yes, so far, he did like her. He hadn't come to Branding Iron for romance, but if Grace was setting him up with the lady, he owed his sister a surprising vote of thanks.

He did his best not to stare at her, but since she was sitting right across the table, he could hardly avoid taking her in with his eyes. She had a classic air about her—like a Renaissance Madonna or maybe a French fashion model. With her dark hair in a simple twist, a baby-blue sweater set, minimal makeup, and no jewelry except modest pearl earrings that were undoubtedly real, she made most of the women he'd seen in Branding Iron look tacky.

Then as he studied Jess, a more subtle response stirred in him. Something about that unforgettable face was vaguely familiar. Cooper could swear he'd seen her somewhere before. Maybe by the end of the evening, the memory would back to him.

More Christmas romance from Janet Dailey

JANET DAILEY

Somebody Like Santa

ZEBRA BOOKS
KENSINGTON PUBLISHING CORP.
www.kensingtonbooks.com

First Printing: October 2022
ISBN-13: 978-1-4201-5108-4
ISBN-13: 978-1-4201-5112-1 (eBook)

10 9 8 7 6 5 4 3 2 1

Printed in the United States of America

Acknowledgments

This novel could not have been written without the friendship and contributions of my fellow writer Elizabeth Lane.

Chapter 1

Branding Iron, Texas, October 1997

Cooper Chapman stood in the parlor of the eighty-year-old house, surrounded by a forest of stacked moving boxes. He'd tried to convince himself that this move, to a sleepy Texas town, would be good for his troubled teenage son. Now he wasn't sure. They had barely started unpacking when Trevor had announced that he hated this place and stormed outside to sulk on the front porch.

At thirteen, Trevor already had a juvenile arrest record for several acts of vandalism he'd pulled with his friends. Moving from Seattle to Branding Iron, with the court's permission, had been a last-ditch effort to give the boy a new start. But would it be enough?

Something told Cooper that even with the support of his married sister, Grace, who lived next door, he was going to need all the help he could get.

* * *

Trevor Chapman sat on the top step of the low-slung bun-
galow house that was his new home. His dark brown eyes
scanned the quiet residential street. Even the trees in full autumn color, their reds and golds blindingly bright against the
sunlit sky, made him feel like a prisoner, brought here
against his will.

He missed the cool grays and greens of Seattle, the smell
of the harbor, the sound of boat whistles. He missed his
friends, who understood and accepted him. But a thirteen-
year-old didn't have anything to say about where he lived.
His mom had made a new marriage to a man who didn't
want him, so he'd been dumped on his dad, who'd decided
to move to the redneck hell of Branding Iron, Texas.

The place reminded Trevor of that corny old TV show,
Mayberry R.F.D., and not in a good way. He could imagine
Andy, Goober, Aunt Bee, and the rest of the gang strolling
around the corner to give him a neighborly howdy and invite
him to set a spell. The thought of it made him feel sick.

From inside the house came the sound of his dad sliding
a heavy desk toward the spare bedroom that would be his office. Cooper, Trevor's dad, was okay. But his decision to
move to Texas to be near the married sister who was his only
family just plain sucked. As a freelance magazine writer, he
could live and work anywhere. So why did it have to be
here, in the middle of nowhere?

The worst of it was Trevor would be starting school on
Monday—as the new boy in eighth grade. The other kids
would probably be cowboys, riding around in pickups with
the radios blaring country crap instead of cool bands like
Nirvana and Rage Against the Machine. He could count on
being bullied, and if he fought back, he'd end up in the principal's office, just like he had in Seattle.

Through the jagged bangs that screened his eyes, he
could see someone coming out of the house next door. He

watched with mild interest as a little girl in blue jeans, whom he guessed to be about seven or eight, came skipping down the sidewalk. She was trailed by a shaggy brown mutt that looked as big as a grizzly bear. With her bouncy auburn curls, she reminded him of Little Orphan Annie, dog and all, and she was headed straight for him.

Stopping at the foot of the steps, she smiled, showing a missing front tooth. "Hi, cousin," she chirped.

"I'm not your cousin," Trevor said. "I don't even know you."

"You are so my cousin," she insisted. "My dad is married to your Aunt Grace, so that makes us cousins." She thrust out her hand, which Trevor pretended not to notice. "You must be Trevor. I'm Maggie Delaney, and this is my dog, Banjo. Go ahead and pet him. He won't bite you."

The shaggy monster mounted the steps, sniffed Trevor's sneakers, and yawned, showing fangs that looked as long as a Bengal tiger's.

"Scratch him behind the ears," Maggie said. "He likes that."

Trevor hesitated. His mother was allergic to dogs and cats, so he'd never been allowed to have a pet. A couple of his Seattle friends had owned small dogs—little yappers. At least he hadn't been afraid of them, but this behemoth looked big enough to eat him alive.

"Don't be scared," Maggie said. "Banjo's just a puppy. He's not even full-grown yet."

Trevor steeled himself. He couldn't let this pint-sized girl know how scared he was. Heart pounding, he reached out. Banjo's bushy tail wagged in anticipation.

Just then the front door opened. Trevor's dad stepped out onto the front porch. "You must be Maggie," he said, giving the little girl a smile. "I'd know you anywhere. Grace has been going on and on about you in her phone calls. I'm your Uncle Cooper."

"Pleased to meet you, Uncle Cooper." She gave Trevor a glance that clearly said, *See, I told you we were cousins.*

"And who's this?" Cooper held out his hand to Banjo. "Come here, boy."

The bear-sized dog ambled across the porch and leaned against Cooper's legs. When Cooper scratched the furry head, Banjo went into ecstasies of wagging and wiggling, even rolling onto his back for a belly rub.

"My mom—your sister—sent me over here to invite you to dinner tonight," Maggie said. "One of her old housemates will be coming, too. She works for the schools. You'll like her. We'll be eating about six, Mom said, but you can come sooner and visit if you want. I've gotta go now. Mom's letting me make a chocolate cake for dessert." She whistled to the dog. "Come on, Banjo. See you around, Trevor."

Cooper watched the little girl skip back down the sidewalk with the dog trotting behind her. Grace had hit the jackpot with her new, ready-made family. Sam was the former sheriff, now running for mayor of Branding Iron. And his daughter, little Maggie, would win anyone's heart.

He was grateful that Grace had forgiven him for missing her wedding last summer. He'd planned to walk her down the aisle. But that was the week when Trevor had been in a wreck with a friend who was joyriding in his mother's Corvette. Trevor had been hospitalized. His injuries hadn't been serious, thank heaven. However, he'd ended up in juvenile detention for being in a stolen car with an underage driver. This after he was already on probation for spray-painting the front door of the middle school he attended. Cooper had had little choice except to stay in Seattle and deal with the situation.

Not long after that, Cooper had decided it was time to give his son a new start, in a new place. When Grace had let him know that her neighbors' house was for rent and emailed him some photos, Cooper had contracted to rent it sight unseen. Selling his Seattle condo had taken longer than he'd counted on, but at last, here they were. He could only hope the change would be good for Trevor.

They'd arrived with the movers this morning, which was a Friday. Grace, who taught first grade, hadn't been here to welcome them. Neither had Sam, who worked for the county planning commission and was busy with his mayoral campaign. But Grace had mailed Cooper the key and made sure the utilities were on, so they could start moving in.

Grace had popped in after school, apologizing for the parent conference that had kept her late. She'd hugged him, then raced off to shop before dinner. At least the family would be together tonight.

But what was it Maggie had said about Grace's former housemate being invited? *You'll like her.* Those words were a red flag if he'd ever heard one. Was Grace already trying to set him up with a needy friend? He pictured a dowdy schoolmarm in tweeds and Birkenstocks who talked in four-syllable words. *No thanks, Grace,* he thought. *I came here to raise my son, not to find a woman. And if I feel the need, I can find my own.*

Trevor was looking up at him with the usual scowl on his narrow face. "Hey, Trevor," he said. "I could use a hand with unpacking the books. How about it?"

Without a word, Trevor stood and, feet dragging, followed him into the house.

Jessica Graver kicked off her low-heeled pumps, popped the tab on a Diet Pepsi, and sank into a cushiony chair. Most Fridays, after a long, busy week, she'd be looking forward to pulling on her sweats, doing a few yoga stretches, and settling back to watch a rented video.

But tonight she'd been invited to dinner at her friends' house, so the sweats and the movie would have to wait. Jess was tired and not feeling very sociable. But she was lucky to have good friends like Grace and Sam, she reminded herself. Besides, she'd be meeting a young man—a very young man—at dinner.

Even before Grace had called about her nephew, Jess had known about Trevor Chapman. As the youth counselor for the Branding Iron School District, she'd gotten a heads-up from the records office that an incoming student had an arrest record and was on probation. It was part of Jess's job to be aware of such students, keep an eye out for any sign of trouble, and, where called for, to intervene as best she could.

It had been Grace's hope that meeting Jess early, in a non-school setting, would make the boy aware of an adult on his team, someone he could go to if he needed help or just to talk.

Jess was more than happy to oblige. If she could save just one kid from a future tragedy . . .

She closed her eyes. She'd only meant to rest them. But she was tired, and she found herself sinking into the black place that would never leave her—the dark night, the pop of exploding gunfire, the scream of sirens, the blinding flash of press cameras in her face, and the frenzied wails of grief.

"Hey, Jess, aren't you going to Grace and Sam's tonight?" It was Wynette, her pretty blond housemate, who woke her. She'd just come in the front door, one hand balancing a pink box of leftover pastries from the bakery she managed.

Blast, I must've dozed. Jess blinked herself awake. The clock on the mantel said 5:40. She had just enough time to freshen up and get to Grace and Sam's.

She found her shoes and made a quick dash to the bathroom. The mirror above the basin showed deep brown eyes in a pale oval face, framed by dark hair upswept into a twist and showing the first few threads of gray. She was thirty-eight, unmarried, with a past that was nobody's business but her own.

When she returned to the living room, Wynette was hanging her jacket on the rack by the door. "I don't suppose I can offer you a donut," she said.

"No. Save them for Buck. I'm sure you'll be seeing him later."

Wynette's smile sparkled. "We'll be driving to Cottonwood Springs for dinner and a movie. After that we'll probably go to Buck's place. So don't wait up."

Jess chuckled. "I never do. Oh—I almost forgot. The package with your wedding invitations is on the kitchen table. It was on the porch when I got home."

"Great. Wow, this is getting real." Wynette was planning a Christmastime wedding to Buck Winston, Branding Iron's handsome young sheriff. She'd been walking on clouds ever since he'd proposed last spring.

"So you're going to meet Grace's brother," Wynette said. "Lois Harper told me she saw him in town this afternoon. She described him as a smokin' hottie. And he looks to be about your age."

"Oh, no, you don't. I'm not looking for a man—especially if he's hot. They're the kind you can't trust." Jess slipped on her coat, picked up her purse and keys, and hurried out to her car.

When she'd said she wasn't looking for a man, she'd meant it. So what *was* she looking for?

After Wynette's wedding, she would be alone in the small three-bedroom house she'd bought two years ago. Maybe she should wait to advertise for new housemates. The money wasn't an issue, and some time to herself might be just what she needed to clear her head and reset her goals. Maybe she could even get back to the master's thesis she'd never finished.

An autumn wind had sprung out of the west, bringing a chill to the October air. As Jess drove across town, the first fall leaves blew against the windshield. Where had the year gone? Halloween was barely a week away. Then the candy and jack-o'-lanterns would be gone from the stores, and the Christmas glitter would go up.

Jess had never been a fan of Christmas. Too many memories, most of them unhappy. Maybe she should start thinking about a trip to someplace warm and sunny—like Cancún or Hawaii. But of course, she couldn't miss Wynette's wedding, which was set for December 27, the Saturday after Christmas.

She pulled up in front of Grace and Sam's. In the house next door, the porch light was on and an older model Jeep SUV stood in the driveway. But there was no sign of activity. Grace's brother and nephew must be at her house by now.

A smokin' hottie. That was how Cooper Chapman had been described. But it didn't matter how hot he might be. She was here to meet young Trevor.

When she rang the bell, it was Maggie who answered the door. She was grinning. "Look, I lost my other front tooth! Now they're both gone. My mom taught me an old song. It's called 'All I Want for Christmas Is My Two Front Teeth.' Listen." She sang it with a lisp, stopping after the first line. "Come on in. Dinner's almost ready. While you're waiting, you can meet my Uncle Cooper and my cousin, Trevor."

"I hear rumors that you baked a chocolate cake, Maggie."

"Uh-huh. But it was just a mix this time. Come on."

Jess felt her stomach flutter as the little girl led her into the parlor and a tall man rose to greet her.

"This is my Uncle Cooper," Maggie said. "Uncle Cooper, this is Miss Graver. She helps out with the kids at school."

"You can call me Jess." Her gaze traveled upward from

the denim shirt that covered a broad-shouldered torso and muscular arms, to a crown of thick dark hair with a touch of gray at the temples, framing a face that would draw any woman's gaze.

Smokin' hot. Gerard Butler hot.

Not that she was foolish enough to be impressed.

"It's a pleasure to meet you, Jess." Even though she was five-foot-eight, he loomed above her. His startlingly blue eyes shifted to the boy who sat slumped on the sofa, absorbed in a basketball game on TV. Dark-eyed and slight of build, the young man looked nothing like his father.

"Trevor, say hello to Miss Graver," Cooper said.

"Hullo." The boy raised his head, then went back to watching the game. Was Cooper aware of the reason Grace had invited her here? Surely the man's sister would have told him.

"I'm happy to meet you, Trevor," she said. "I suppose it's too soon to ask how you like Branding Iron."

Trevor didn't respond. His attention was fixed on the game.

Cooper motioned her aside. "Getting him used to living in a small town is going to take a while," he said. "For now, I'm just trying to give him time and space."

"That sounds very wise."

Maggie came prancing in from the dining room. "Dinner's ready," she announced. "I made place cards so everybody will know where to sit."

"After you." Cooper stepped aside for Jess to go ahead of him. "Trevor, turn off the TV and come with me."

"Aw, Dad, the score's tied with ten minutes on the clock. Can't we at least turn the sound up so I can hear the game at the table?"

"That's not how it works, son. Now switch off that remote and get off that couch."

"Mom always let me listen."

Jess saw him flinch. "That's enough, Trevor. I mean it," he said.

Scowling, the boy trailed his father to the table. This kind of parent-child interaction was nothing new to Jess. All the same, as they took their seats, she felt as if she'd walked on stage, without a script or rehearsal, into a drama that was not of her making. If this was typical of Trevor's attitude, she was going to have her work cut out for her.

Maggie had made jack-o'-lantern place cards from orange construction paper. Cooper was seated across from Jess, with Trevor on his right.

He did his best not to stare at her, but since she was sitting right across the table, he could hardly avoid taking her in with his eyes. She had a classic air about her—like a Renaissance Madonna or maybe a French fashion model. With her dark hair in a simple twist, a baby-blue sweater set, minimal makeup, and no jewelry except modest pearl earrings that were undoubtedly real, she made most of the women he'd seen in Branding Iron look tacky.

You'll like her. Maggie's words came back to him. Yes, so he did like her. He hadn't come to Branding Iron for romance, but if Grace was setting him up with the lady, he owed his sister a surprising vote of thanks.

Then as he studied Jess, a more subtle response stirred in him. Something about that unforgettable face was vaguely familiar. Cooper could swear he'd seen her somewhere before. Maybe by the end of the evening, the memory would come back to him.

"I hear you're a journalist, Cooper." Jess speared a bite-sized piece of lasagna with her fork.

He took time to butter a slice of sourdough bread. "That

depends on your definition," he said. "I used to be a sports reporter for the *Seattle Times*. But I quit to freelance. Writing my own articles, mostly for magazines, gives me the freedom to choose any subject and to live wherever I like."

Trevor's sullen look spoke volumes. Jess could almost read his thoughts. Of all the places in the country, why did his father have to choose a nowhere town like Branding Iron? And what about *his* freedom?

Maggie spoke up. "Mom says that Uncle Cooper played football in high school, just like my dad did."

"Did you play in college?" Sam had been set to go pro, but he'd blown out his knee in the last game of his senior year.

Cooper smiled, showing a sexy dimple in his left cheek. Jess's pulse skipped. The man was getting to her. *Blast him!*

"I played second string quarterback," he said. "But I wasn't fast enough to be a starter. And I only did it for the scholarship. What I really wanted to do was write."

"Do you like sports, Trevor?" Jess tried to draw the boy out. "I noticed you watching the game on TV."

Trevor shrugged. "I just like to watch. My dad was an athlete, but I take after my mom's family. They only play chess."

"So do you play chess?" At least he'd given her an opening.

"No. It's a stupid game. You win or you don't. I hate it. So I guess that makes me a disappointment to both sides of the family."

"Trevor—" His father's tone carried a warning.

"Well, it's true," the boy said. "Dad, do I have to be in here? Can't I take my plate into the other room to watch the end of the game?"

"No, you may not," Cooper said. "You're a guest. Behave like one."

The boy didn't argue. But his silence and his sullen expression said all that was needed. He hunched over his plate, picking at his food. Jess's sympathetic gaze met Grace's.

"Jess." Cooper spoke into the awkward hush that had fallen over the table. "Didn't I hear Maggie say that you helped out at school? What is it you do?"

So he really hadn't been told why she was here and neither had his son. This wasn't the best time to come clean, but she had little choice.

"I'm the youth counselor for the district. It's my job to work with kids who are struggling, get them the resources they need, and steer them away from more trouble if I can."

She stole a glance at Trevor. He was glaring at her. "So are you a shrink?" he demanded.

"No. I have a degree in psychology, but I'm not trained as a psychiatrist."

"You're a cop, then?"

The question touched a nerve, but Jess kept her voice calm. "No, I'm not with the police. I'm just a facilitator. If a student needs more help than I'm qualified to give them, I refer them to specialists who can offer more. Does that answer your question, Trevor?"

He shrugged. "I guess."

"If there's anything else you want to know, just ask me."

"Yeah, I get the idea." The sarcasm in Trevor's voice was subtle but unmistakable. Jess chose to ignore his reply. He'd guessed why she was here, and he was already defiant. Pushing the boy would only make things worse.

"So how's the campaign going, Sam?" Once again Cooper steered the conversation onto what he hoped was safe ground. At least he'd figured out why Jess had been invited. But it stung a little that it wasn't to meet him.

Sam finished the lasagna on his plate and reached for a second helping. He was a big man with a big man's appetite.

"Funny you should ask," he said. "Something has come up—sorry, Grace, I meant to tell you right away but you were busy with dinner when I came home." He glanced around the table. "What I'm about to tell you doesn't leave this room. That goes for you, too, Trevor and Maggie. Not a word. Got it?"

The two young people nodded. Even Trevor seemed excited about being part of a big secret.

"Here's the thing," Sam said. "I've been running against the man who's mayor now—Rulon Wilkins. Rulon's a politician, and he knows how to work a crowd. But he hasn't done much for the town, so I'd been hoping for a fair chance."

"What's happened?" Grace asked. "Has something changed?"

"I'm getting to that," Sam said. "Today I got the news that Rulon's being investigated for misuse of public funds. In other words, he's been using town money for things like vacations with his wife, dinners, and car expenses."

"That's no surprise," Grace said.

"It isn't. But until now there's been no accounting. Rumor has it that Rulon may resign rather than face prosecution. If he does that, since the election's nonpartisan, and I'm the only other candidate, I might be asked to step in and finish his term."

Maggie clapped her hands. "That would be wonderful, Daddy!"

"Not so fast, Miss Maggie," Sam said. "It hasn't happened yet, and it might not. I'd rather beat Rulon in a fair election, but if he's been using our tax money for personal expenses, he doesn't deserve to be mayor. However, there still needs to be an election next month. Rulon could decide to stay in the race, or somebody else could step forward and run against me."

"But nobody would make a better mayor than you,

Daddy," Maggie insisted. "I love your idea about having a Christmas parade to go along with the Cowboy Christmas Ball. If you get to be mayor early, we could even do it this year."

"That's a pretty big *if*," Sam said. "That's why you have to keep all this business a secret. Do you promise?"

"Cross my heart." Maggie made a make-believe *X* on her chest with one hand. "You, too, Trevor."

"Okay, I promise," Trevor said.

"No, you have to cross your heart, like this." Maggie demonstrated.

"Okay. Sheesh!" Grumbling, he made the gesture.

"You can count on the rest of us to keep your secret," Grace said. "So what do you say we break out Maggie's chocolate cake and have some dessert?"

After dinner, Jess offered to help Grace clean up. Maggie went to fetch her dog out of the backyard, and the two men, along with Trevor, turned on the TV in the parlor to watch what was left of the post-game show. The volume on the set was loud enough that the two women in the kitchen could talk without being overheard.

"So what do you think of him?" Grace scraped the plates and arranged them in the dishwasher.

"What can I say? He's an eighth-grader. Even the easy ones can be hard to handle. Right now all we can do is try to keep him safe while he grows up." Jess frowned. "What is it? Why are you smiling at me like that?"

"Because when I asked what you thought, I wasn't talking about Trevor."

Jess felt the heat creeping into her face. She shook her head. "Oh, no, you don't. I came here to meet a student, not a potential date. Your brother is gorgeous, but I'm not in the market. I get the impression he isn't either."

Grace gave her a mischievous glance before closing the dishwasher door. "Don't be so sure. My brother was checking you out at dinner, and I noticed that you were doing the same with him."

"Wait—are you telling me you set this up on purpose? Was meeting Trevor just an excuse? You may be my best friend, Grace, but I can't believe you'd stoop that low."

"Hey, last year, Maggie staged a sit-down strike in my class so her dad would have to meet with me. And look what happened. The whole year I've known you, Jess, you've never even dated. And now that Wynette is getting married, you'll be alone. You can't blame a friend for trying—and Cooper is a good guy, the best. It was his wife who cheated."

Jess sighed. "Grace, I know you mean well. But trust me, I'm better off without a man in my life. So please, just let this drop. I'll be on the lookout for Trevor at school and try to make sure he's okay. But if your brother needs a girlfriend, I'm sure he'll have women lining up around the block to date him."

They finished in the kitchen. Jess took her leave with a reassuring hug. "It's all right, Grace," she said. "I'm not angry, just making myself clear."

As she crossed the room to get her jacket from the coatrack, Cooper rose from the couch where he'd been sitting. "I hope you won't mind my walking you to your car, Jess," he said.

"It's fine." Her defenses slammed to full alert. Was he going to question her being here tonight? Was he going to talk to her about Trevor? Or should she be preparing to set some personal boundaries?

Whatever he had in mind, Jess sensed that she was about to face a moment of truth.

Chapter 2

Slipping on his leather jacket, Cooper held the door for Jess and followed her outside. She struggled to ignore a spark of awareness as he offered an arm to guide her down the steps. "Watch your footing," he said. "There's a crack in the sidewalk that got me earlier."

The wind had freshened, blowing swirls of autumn leaves around them as the clouds moved in overhead. Jess shivered despite her thin quilted jacket.

"I was hoping we could talk," he said. "But it's getting cold out here. What I have to say can wait a day or two—maybe we can get together over coffee this weekend."

Jess detected a quickening of her pulse. Was he asking her out? For a moment she was tempted to accept. But it would be a bad idea to start something she didn't intend to finish.

"I'll be busy all weekend," she hedged as they reached her aging silver Ford Taurus, which she hadn't bothered to lock. "Climb in. We can talk here and be done with whatever you need to say."

"Got it." He walked around the car to open her door. "This shouldn't take long."

He closed her door, went back around the car, and settled into the passenger seat, his size filling the dark space. His nearness felt strangely intimate. But she'd already set her boundaries, and he had clearly accepted them.

"This is about Trevor," he said.

"I already know about your son. His old school and the juvenile court office forwarded his records, and I was given a copy. It sounds as if the boy is going through a rough time."

"That's the least of it," Cooper said. "He's not a bad kid. But he's hurting."

"I can tell."

"His mother remarried a few months ago, and his new stepfather didn't want him around. His mother chose her marriage over her son."

"I'm sorry. That's terrible." No wonder the poor kid was having problems.

"He feels that I only took him because I didn't have a choice, which isn't true at all, but I can't convince him of that. Back in Seattle, he got in with a bunch of future gang-bangers. I could see where he was headed, and I knew I needed to get him out of there. I just hope I can get him settled in Branding Iron before he tries to run away and get back to his friends."

Jess nodded. In spite of her misgivings, she was warming to the man. He seemed so caring, so worried about his son. She wouldn't mind getting to know him better. But right now, she needed to make sure he didn't expect too much of her.

"I feel for the boy and for you," she said. "I'll do my best to look out for him, and to call you at the first sign of trouble. But I don't have the power to work miracles. He's at an age where a lot of kids, especially boys, have struggles. Mostly they outgrow the problems in time, but you can't count on that. Have you tried to get him professional help? I can recommend some good people in Cottonwood Springs."

"I've tried to get him into counseling. So far, he's dug in his heels and refused to go."

"Then for now, all we can do is try to keep him safe, offer him some choices, and hope he makes the right ones." She reached into her purse and handed him a card with her home and school phone numbers. "I only do this for friends. Call me if you notice anything disturbing, or if you just need to talk. Anything else?"

His silent pause raised a red flag. Clearly, he had something more on his mind.

"Just one thing. Forgive me if it's too personal."

Something tightened in her stomach. She faked a smile. "If it's too personal, I'll stop you."

"Okay, here it is. I've got a pretty good memory for faces. As soon as I saw you tonight, that memory kicked in. I could swear that I've seen you somewhere before. Do you think that's possible? Have you ever spent time in Seattle?"

The question slammed doors that had just begun to open. There was always a chance that he'd seen her on TV or in the newspapers three years ago. As a journalist, he might have paid closer attention to the story than most people would.

But when she'd accepted the job in Branding Iron, she'd locked her past away. And she couldn't risk having this man uncover secrets she'd done her best to bury.

"Jess, are you all right?" His voice jerked her back to the present.

"I'm sorry," she said. "I was just trying to remember where you might have met me, and I came up blank. I'm sure I've never seen you before, and I can't imagine where you could have seen me. I probably remind you of someone else."

"Fine, if you say so. But you're a striking woman, Jess. You have the kind of face a man doesn't forget."

She feigned a laugh. "I'll take that as a compliment. But I'm afraid your memory struck out this time." She started the car. "You should be getting back to your family. I'll do my best to keep an eye on Trevor. My time is divided between schools, but when I'm at the middle school, I'll be sure to check."

"Thanks for your time. Keep in touch." His tone was neutral, in the manner of a man who's just been shown the door.

After he left the car, she watched his tall, broad-shouldered frame move up the sidewalk, mount the porch, and disappear into the house. He was a lot of man, just not for her. Too bad, she thought as she shifted into drive and headed home.

Soon after Jess left, Cooper thanked his hosts and took his son home, along with enough lasagna and cake to last them through the weekend.

The hour was too early for bedtime, so Cooper set himself to wiping down the fridge and put Trevor to work stacking the boxed dishes in the kitchen cupboard. He was hoping the boy would open up on his own and talk to him. But Trevor was as sullen as the black clouds that had spilled across the moon outside. If Cooper wanted a conversation, it would be up to him to start it.

"I know you've never been around family much," he said. "What did you think of your aunt and uncle?"

"They're okay, I guess. The little girl's kind of a pest."

"Her name's Maggie, and she made that chocolate cake you ate so much of."

"That other woman, though . . ." Trevor paused to set a stack of saucers in an empty space. "She's a fake. I can tell. I don't like fakes."

Trevor's assessment of Jess struck Cooper like a dash of ice water. "What do you mean by fake?" he asked.

"You know. Like when she said she wasn't a cop. But she had cop written all over her, even if she wasn't wearing a badge. And I could tell she was there to let me know she'd be keeping an eye on me, and that I'd better not mess up. She reminded me of the people at my old school. They acted like they cared about me, but they didn't. They were just doing their jobs. Nobody really cares about me."

He stopped working and studied Cooper with insightful eyes. "You liked her, didn't you?"

"I guess so. She was pretty, and she seemed nice. But don't worry, I'm not looking for a girlfriend. Too many complications." He finished the fridge and tossed the sponge in the sink. "Hey, tomorrow's Saturday. We can check out a place to get lunch and get you a haircut."

"Haircut!" Trevor swept his long bangs out of his face. "No way. My hair is just the way I like it."

Cooper sighed. "Trevor, this isn't Seattle. Folks around here are more conservative. You won't fit in at your school with long hair."

"Tough. I'm not cutting it."

"Fine. But if you show up at school looking like a punk rocker, you're asking to get picked on. I want you to be happy here, Trevor. I want you to make friends."

"I know. But I won't do it by pretending to be somebody I'm not." Trevor finished stacking the dishes, then left the kitchen for the living room, found the remote, and clicked on the TV. The power came on, but there was nothing on the screen but static.

"What the—" Trevor cursed as he switched off the remote.

"Watch your language. I called the cable company today. But they can't get here till next week. Until then you'll just have to find other ways to entertain yourself."

"That sucks! Why did we have to move? I was happy in Seattle."

"That's enough, Trevor. I'm tired and so are you. Go to your room and make up your bed. If you're not sleepy, you can unpack your clothes and put them away. If you've got any dirty laundry, put it on top of that washer and dryer in the hall. The machines are old but they're supposed to work. We can do the wash when we buy some detergent at that grocery store we passed on the way into town."

"You still haven't told me why we had to move."

"I don't need to tell you. You know. Now go."

Cooper sank onto the sofa as his son disappeared down the hall. Why did the boy have to fight him at every turn? It was exhausting. He could only hope that school would turn out to be a good experience for him. If not, this whole move could prove to be a disaster.

He would give it a little time, maybe till Christmas, Cooper resolved. If by then, Trevor was still getting in trouble, he would start checking out other options. Perhaps a small town had been the wrong choice. Trevor might be happier in a city setting—not Seattle, but maybe someplace like Austin or Santa Fe.

But he didn't want to reward his son for misbehaving. And there was a lot to be said for toughing it out in Branding Iron. If they stayed here, he'd have Sam and Grace to lend support—and maybe Jess, too.

Jess's influence could be good for Trevor. But how could she help him if the boy refused to trust her? And, as Cooper reminded himself, he hadn't exactly broken the ice with her either. In the car, she had been cool and distant, especially after he'd mentioned that she looked familiar.

But it was too soon to throw up his hands and walk away. Something in him wouldn't let go of the hope that he might get to know Jess and discover the secrets hiding in those mysterious dark eyes.

He would try again, at the first opportunity.

As the only grocery store in town, Martin's Market had plenty of customers. The crowded shelves carried all the basics, the produce was fresh, and the owner, Max Martin, was a master butcher who processed his own meats. When the new Shop Mart at the south end of town opened up in the spring, Max and his wife, Cloris, would probably close up and retire. That would be a shame, Jess thought as she perused the narrow aisles for the few things she needed—coffee, onions, Drano, tampons, and two bags of Halloween candy. There was something to be said for a place where the owners greeted you by name.

With her shopping basket full, she headed for the single checkout counter. Since the store would be closed the next day, there was always a line on Saturdays. Jess was resigning herself to a ten-minute wait when a cart with a faulty wheel clanked into line behind her, giving her a slight bump.

"Sorry." The masculine voice was familiar. She turned to see Cooper, with Trevor in tow, pushing a loaded cart. "We're stocking up," he said. "At least, with this wheel clunking along, folks can hear us coming and get out of the way."

"Well, it looks like you two are settling in." She was making lame conversation, far too conscious of his piercing blue eyes and the dimple that deepened when he smiled.

"We're trying."

"Hello, Trevor." She made sure to acknowledge the boy. "Have you seen much of Branding Iron yet?"

He shook his dark head, the hair badly in need of a trim. "I must've blinked and missed it."

"Give the place a chance," she said. "I'm a city girl, too. But this little town has grown on me. Lots of good people."

"A city girl, you say? What city?" Cooper's curiosity was clearly roused. She remembered what he'd said about having seen her before. Her defenses sprang up.

"Chicago." She knew better than to lie. It would only get her in trouble. Scrambling for a diversion, she glanced into the packed shopping cart. "I see you bought some candy. You'll have plenty of little goblins coming around, and they'll go for those miniature candy bars. Are you going to dress up, Trevor?"

His look told her she'd asked a stupid question. "That's kid stuff. I'll probably just stay home and watch TV—if we get our cable hooked up by then."

"Patience, son," Cooper said, turning back to Jess. "Say, I hear that the best restaurant in Branding Iron is Buckaroo's on Main Street."

Jess chuckled. "Buckaroo's is the *only* restaurant in Branding Iron, unless you count Rowdy's Roost, the bar out by the old railroad tracks."

"So how's the food at Buckaroo's?"

"If you're in the mood for burgers or pizza, it's pretty good. And they have great pie. They get it from the local bakery."

"We were going to stop by there for lunch on the way home. Why don't you join us? You could tell us about the town and the school."

Trevor rolled his eyes.

Remembering her resolve not to encourage this compelling man, Jess almost declined his invitation. But helping kids was her job, and Trevor was going to need all the help he could get. "Sure, I'd be glad to join you," she said.

"Thanks. Maybe you can even help me talk this young man into getting a haircut."

Trevor's expression froze into a stubborn scowl. At that moment Jess could have punched Cooper for putting her on the spot. She settled for giving him a disapproving look. If

Cooper wanted her to make friends with his son, he was going about it the wrong way. Maybe it was time to step back.

She glanced at his grocery cart. "You've got some frozen things in there that'll thaw if you take time to eat. Maybe another day would be better."

"No problem. We've got a cooler in the back of the Jeep. So, we'll meet you there?"

"Fine." The checkout stand was coming up. Jess got her purchases through fast and carried the plastic bags to her car. The thought nagged her that she was getting in too deep with this charming father and his needy son. But barring a sudden emergency, it was too late to back out.

She drove to the restaurant, parked in the side lot next to a battered farm truck, and waited. A few minutes later, Cooper's SUV, an older model Jeep, pulled in beside her.

She climbed out of her car. "It looks like we got here ahead of the lunch crowd. Let's go inside."

Buckaroo's had been a Main Street fixture for as long as anyone in Branding Iron could remember. Like the redchecked oilcloth table covers and the string of lights above the counter, the menu had changed little over the years. Only pizza had been added in the past decade. But the food was always good, and the little café was a gathering place for everyone from teens to seniors.

They chose an empty booth and gave their orders to the waitress, a plain young woman with a warm smile and a tiny diamond sparkling on her ring finger.

"So when's the big day, Connie?" Jess asked her.

Connie's smile glowed, lending beauty to her pale, thin features. "Sometime next spring. Right now Silas has all he can do getting his new garage ready to open. We don't plan on a fancy wedding, just family and a few friends."

"Everybody in town is your friend, Connie. And we're all grateful to have a good mechanic in Branding Iron. Silas's garage is going to get plenty of business." Jess turned to Cooper. "Silas learned his trade in the army. He's one of those mechanics who can listen to an engine for a few seconds and tell you everything that's going on with it."

"I'll remember that next time my Jeep breaks down," Cooper said.

Connie bustled away and came back with their orders a few minutes later—a deluxe pizza for Cooper and Jess to split, and a jumbo burger with a chocolate shake for Trevor.

An older man with a sad face sat in the booth across from them, finishing his coffee and apple pie. Abner Jenkins, who was in his mid-sixties, owned a small farm south of town. He'd raised his family there, but now that his children were grown and his wife had passed away, he was alone.

As he finished eating and rose to leave, Jess gave him a smile. "Hello, Abner. How's it going?"

"Fair to middlin' now that the hay harvest is done. Don't know what I'll do with myself till spring, but I'll figure it out, I guess." His eyes took in Cooper and Trevor. "Have we got some new folks in town, or are you two just visitin'?"

Jess made a quick introduction before Abner excused himself and left.

"You seem to know everybody here, and their business, Jess," Cooper said.

"In a town this size, it doesn't take long. But people look out for each other here. You won't find that in a big city."

Trevor shook his head. "This place really is Mayberry. One garage, one café, and everybody knows everybody else's business. The kids are probably a bunch of rubes, with cow shit on their boots and straws hanging out of their mouths."

"They're just kids, Trevor, all different kinds," Jess said. "Don't judge them before you've given them a chance."

"But are any of them like me?"

"And what do you think you're like, Trevor?"

"Like . . . you know, cool."

"There are different kinds of cool," Jess said. "Give the kids a chance—and they'll give you a chance."

Trevor slumped in his seat, slurping the last of his chocolate shake. The lady sounded like she was reading from a script for a Mr. Rogers show. She didn't have a clue what it would be like for him on Monday, walking into a new school with everybody staring at him.

At least he was smart. He didn't always turn in his homework, but he'd aced every test he'd ever taken. But for a new kid, being smart was liable to count against you. Playing dumb was less likely to make enemies.

"Dad," he said as they drove home from the restaurant. "What about homeschooling? You could get me some books or some computer software, and I could do classwork at home. Heck, if I got a lot done, I could even graduate early."

"Nice try," his dad said. "But what if you don't stick with it? You need school. You need to be with people. Now about that haircut . . ."

"No. No way."

"Suit yourself. We should've asked Jess whether long hair was a dress code violation."

"I guess I'll find out, won't I?"

"I guess you will if you insist on being stubborn. Let me know if you change your mind. Remember, the barbershops won't be open tomorrow."

Cooper sighed as he pulled the Jeep into the driveway. He would rush into a burning building or dive into a sea full of sharks to save his son. But this constant battle of wills was wearing him down. Sooner or later something would have to break. He could only hope the change would be for the good.

At least things had gone all right with Jess today. But her manner had made it clear that any involvement with him and his son was professional, not personal. Too bad. It was hard to watch her sitting across from him, sharing the pizza, without wondering how she would feel in his arms, and how those soft lips would taste against his.

But a Branding Iron romance wasn't in the cards. He was here for his son, and nothing else could be allowed to distract him—not even the gorgeous, mysterious woman who haunted his fantasies.

At work in the small school district, Jess usually spent her mornings at the high school, her afternoons at the middle school, and was on call as needed for the two elementary schools. This was her second year in Branding Iron, and she liked her job. But how long she would stay remained to be seen.

Yesterday, a Monday, she'd arrived at Branding Iron Middle School during the lunch hour and had taken a walk down the main hallway. She'd noticed Trevor, dressed all in black with his hair hanging in his face, leaning against a bank of lockers—all alone. Had he even eaten lunch? Or had he been too afraid that nobody would sit with him?

She knew better than to single him out. The last thing he'd want was to be seen talking to an adult, especially the adult in charge of problem kids.

In the school office, she checked her mailbox for any reports on students. There were some routine slips, but nothing that involved Trevor. As she recalled from the comments on his record, he was never disruptive in class. His acting out mostly took place after school hours.

Today, a Tuesday, Jess arrived about the same time as usual, when the hall was crowded with students. At first, she didn't see Trevor. Then she spotted him, walking between two ninth-grade boys. They were laughing and joking with him. He looked almost happy.

But this wasn't a good sign. The boys, Skip McCoy and

Cody LeFevre, were known troublemakers who'd been on report so many times that Jess knew their records from memory. They wouldn't have befriended a young loner like Trevor unless they were planning to take advantage of him in some way.

It might be wise to alert Cooper to the situation. But right now she was scheduled to administer a standardized test to the seventh-graders—also part of her job description. She needed to set up the room before the students arrived. Besides, the last time she'd spoken with Cooper, he was still trying to get a home phone installed. He might have had a cell in Seattle, but there was no service in Branding Iron or even in Cottonwood Springs. For now, the problem would have to wait.

Cooper had spent most of the day in Cottonwood Springs, arranging for the internet service that was vital to his work. After years in Seattle, he hadn't realized how complicated some things could be. But by early afternoon the landline phone and internet installation had been arranged for the end of the week, the earliest date that was open. Hungry, he wolfed down a drive-in burger and headed home to Branding Iron. He wanted to be there when Trevor came home.

Cottonwood Springs and Branding Iron were connected by a two-lane paved road. The road ran through the outskirts of Branding Iron with a connection to Main Street and continued south, through open country dotted with farms and ranches.

Lost in thought and enjoying the clear October day, Cooper was ten minutes past Branding Iron before he realized he'd missed the turnoff that would take him home. He was headed south, away from the town.

He was watching for a wide spot on the shoulder where he could make a U-turn, when he saw the hand-lettered sign:

FOR SALE: 60-ACRE RANCH, WITH HOUSE, BARN, AND WELL.
LIVESTOCK AND EQUIPMENT OPTIONAL.
DISCOUNT FOR CASH SALE.

The address and phone number were written in smaller letters at the bottom of the sign. Interesting, Cooper thought as he jotted them down in his memory. He'd gotten good money for his two-bedroom Seattle condo, in a city where real estate prices were over the moon. Could he afford to invest in a small ranch?

But what was he thinking? He and Trevor were still getting settled in their rented house. To buy property when he had no idea how long he'd be staying here would be insane.

But he could at least satisfy his curiosity by making a phone call and having a look at the place in the next few days. Maybe Trevor would even like it. At least, it wouldn't hurt to keep his options open.

Still thinking, he swung off the road, turned around, and headed back to Branding Iron.

Chapter 3

Cooper was still mulling over the idea of the ranch when he drove up to his house and pulled into the driveway. Trevor was sitting on the front steps, a sour look on his face.

"I didn't have a key to get in," he said. "If you're not going to be here after school, you need to give me one."

"Sorry. I've got a spare. We can figure out a place to hide it." Cooper glanced at his watch, wondering if his son had skipped last period. "It's early. How long have you been home?"

"Not long." The boy shrugged. "I'm starved—what is there to eat?"

"There's plenty of that good lasagna left. We can warm it up in the microwave. Come on in." Was Trevor skipping lunch? Cooper wouldn't have been surprised, but he'd let it ride for now.

He took a small helping himself and let Trevor fill his plate with the rest. "Hey, Dad," Trevor said between bites, "I made some new friends. They want to take me hunting with them on Halloween night. Can I go?"

"Hunting? At night, on Halloween?" Cooper's instincts

sprang to full alert. "What kind of hunting is that? There'd better not be guns involved."

"No, no guns. We'll be hunting these little birds. They're called snipes, and they're supposed to be really good eating. Have you ever heard of them?" Trevor's dark eyes shone with excitement.

Cooper stifled a groan. "Tell me more," he said, hoping the boy might figure out the truth for himself.

"The snipes come out at night, and they run along the ground, sort of like quail," Trevor said. "To hunt them, one person stands at the end of a field with a big gunnysack, holding it open. Two other people drive the snipes down the field toward the sack. Sometimes they jump right into the sack to hide. If not, the sack holder has to grab them and toss them in."

"Let me guess," Cooper said. "You're the one who gets to hold the sack."

"Yup. My friends say it'll be a lot of fun. And afterward, we can build a bonfire and have a snipe roast."

Cooper sighed, knowing he was about to shatter the boy's trust. "Son," he said, "I hate to break this to you, but snipe hunting is a joke—one that's been around for years."

Trevor stared at him, heartbreak creeping around the edges of disbelief.

"The snipes aren't real," Cooper said. "And the kids who've promised to chase them down to you will just go off somewhere and leave you there, holding the bag. If you've heard that expression, now you know where it came from."

Trevor slumped in his chair. "That's a stupid trick. And it's mean."

"I know. Somebody played it on me when I was about your age. I stood there in the dark, holding that bag until my arms felt paralyzed. Sometime after midnight, I gave up and went home. The next day at school, everybody had heard the story. They all made fun of me."

Trevor sat silent for a long moment. "So those jerks aren't my friends after all."

"I'd bet against it. Who are they?"

"Skip and Cody. They're ninth-graders. They dress and talk like cowboys, but they're probably fake, like a lot of other people around here."

"It sounds like you need to find some friends your own age," Cooper said.

"The kids don't like me. They think I'm weird. I wasn't weird in Seattle. I had real friends there. Friends like me."

Cooper had been down this road before. He didn't have the patience to go down it again. "Trevor, you've got a brain. Use it to solve your problem. That's all I'm going to say. Now load the dishwasher while I run next door and use your Aunt Grace's phone. When I come back, I want to see you doing your homework."

"I did it in class."

"Then do something else. Read a book."

At least Trevor liked to read. Currently he was into fantasy. He had read all three volumes of Tolkien's *Lord of the Rings* and had started on *The Hobbit*. Testing had confirmed that the kid was extremely bright. But that creative intelligence and energy had nowhere to go. Maybe coming here had been a mistake.

Faced with a wall of frustration, he needed to talk things out with someone who understood what he was dealing with. That was why he wanted to use the phone.

"So when will we have TV and a phone and internet like normal people?" Trevor demanded as Cooper opened the front door to leave.

"Believe me, I'm as anxious to get connected as you are. I've paid the deposits and made the appointments. With luck, we'll have everything by the end of the week."

"I'll believe it when I see it—kind of like the snipes."

At least the kid hadn't lost his sense of humor, Cooper

told himself as he strode down the sidewalk to his sister's house next door. Just as he was mounting the porch steps, Sam swung his pickup into the driveway, switched off the engine, and climbed out.

"Come on inside with me, Cooper," he said. "I've got some exciting news to share."

Cooper followed his brother-in-law into the house. Grace and Maggie were in the kitchen, but Banjo came wagging out to greet them, tongue lolling as he drooled on Cooper's shoe.

"Hey, in there!" Sam called out. "Everybody come in here and meet the new acting mayor of Branding Iron, Texas."

Maggie burst out of the kitchen, followed by her step-mother. "So Rulon actually resigned?" Grace asked.

"He did. He promised to repay the money he'd spent in exchange for the town not pressing charges. The town council accepted that and named me acting mayor."

Maggie flung herself into Sam's arms. "This is wonderful, Daddy! Now we can have the Christmas parade."

"Whoa," Sam said. "Not so fast, honey. We still need to have the election. And even if I win, there won't be time to plan a parade."

"I'll help," Maggie said. "I helped plan the Cowboy Christmas Ball last year, and it turned out great. We can have a great parade, too, if everybody does their part."

"We'll see," Sam said. "But I don't want to hear about it until after the election."

"Where's Trevor?" Grace asked. "Didn't he come with you, Cooper?"

"He's home," Cooper said. "Actually, I just came over to borrow your phone. We'll get ours in the next few days, along with cable and internet. Then we'll be out of your hair."

"Don't be silly," Grace said. "You don't get in our hair. We love having the two of you around."

"There's another game on tonight," Sam said. "Why don't you and Trevor come over and watch it with me. The pre-game show starts at six."

"Thanks, Trevor would love that. Whether I can come, too, will depend on the phone calls."

"You can use the phone in Sam's office," Grace said. "And you're welcome to come to supper before the game starts. It's just chili, but it'll fill you up."

"Thanks, we just filled up on your lasagna—but I'll ask Trevor if he wants to come. A growing boy's stomach is a bottomless pit." Cooper stepped into the spare bedroom that served as Sam's home office.

He remembered the number to call about the ranch, but at the last moment he changed his mind. If the place wasn't suitable, calling now would waste his time and the owners'. He would drive out and look the ranch over from a distance first. Maybe by then, he would have decided that his interest was nothing more than a whim.

Now for the other call . . . Still hesitant, he fished Jess's card out of his wallet. She'd invited him to call her if he needed to talk. But maybe she was just being polite. Would calling her at home be an imposition? Would he be taking advantage of her friendship with Grace?

But no, he was genuinely worried. Hungry for acceptance, his son had fallen in with a couple of bigger, older boys who'd meant to exploit him. As a father, he needed enough information to deal with the issue.

And—*face it*—he wouldn't mind hearing that low, sexy voice over the phone. But this was no time to get distracted by a stunning woman. His problem was real, and he needed real advice.

His pulse quickened as he punched in the number and heard the phone ring on the other end.

"Hello?" She sounded just the way he remembered.

"Jess, this is Cooper Chapman."

"Oh, hi." Jess put down the glazed bakery donut she'd grabbed after arriving home and changing into her comfy sweats. Something about his voice made her heart race, but she was a sensible woman, she told herself. The reaction meant nothing.

"Sorry to bother you at home," he said. "I hope I didn't catch you at a bad time. But you invited me to call you if I had a concern, and I actually do."

"Not at all." She remembered what she'd seen earlier at school. "In fact, I would have called, myself, if there'd been a way to reach you." She paused. "Since you brought up a concern, you go first."

"All right. I don't know where you grew up, but do you know what a snipe hunt is?"

She chuckled at the long-forgotten memory. "Heavens, yes! Doesn't everybody?"

"Not quite, I'm afraid. Trevor came home all excited because these two ninth-grade boys had invited him to go snipe hunting. I set him straight, but I could tell he was hurt that they'd tried to play a trick on him. The reason I'm calling is to find out more about those boys."

"Skip McCoy and Cody LeFevre, right? I saw him in the hall with them today."

"I take it they're bad news."

"Not the best, I'm afraid. They've been written up at school for bullying and truancy and hauled in by the sheriff for underage drinking. Trevor needs to make some different friends."

"That's easier said than done. At least he knows that the boys were planning to prank him. But that doesn't mean he's learned his lesson, or that they'll leave him alone." She heard him take a breath. "Do you have time to talk? We could get coffee or something."

Jess's pulse skipped. He wasn't really asking for a date. Or was he? And how should she handle it?

"For coffee there's only Buckaroo's, and it's noisy at this hour," she said. "You could come here, but my housemate will be making dinner for her boyfriend. I know you don't want to wait, but—"

"Hear me out—I've got another suggestion," he said. "There's a property for sale south of town. I've been wanting to drive by and check it out. You could come with me for the ride. That would give us a chance to talk on the way. It's not far, and the drive won't take long, but if we go, it'll need to be soon while it's still light. Would that work for you?"

Jess hesitated. She could always say no. But she cared about Trevor and the father who was worried enough to ask for her help.

Was this a ploy to ask her out? She dismissed the thought. He sounded too concerned for that. Turning him down because she was on her own time would be insensitive, even cruel.

"That would be fine," she said and gave him directions. "I hope you don't mind seeing me in sweats and sneakers."

"I wouldn't mind a bit." *Sweats, sneakers, or less, maybe a lot less.* Cooper banished the inappropriate thought from his mind. They were meeting to discuss his son, nothing more.

He drove to the address she'd given him, a small frame home with a dead cottonwood tree in the front yard. When he rang the bell, the door opened to reveal a petite blond woman with a face that reminded him of a blooming pink rose. Delicious aromas wafted from the kitchen behind her.

"Hi," she said, greeting him with a grin. "I'm Wynette. And I know you're Cooper. Come on in and have a seat. Jess will be out in a jiffy."

"So you're the bride-to-be," Cooper said. "Whatever you're cooking in there tells me your groom will be a lucky man."

"He'd be a lucky man even if I couldn't boil water." She gave him a saucy grin. "Jess is a good cook, too, when she has time—just in case you're wondering." With a wink, she turned away and vanished into the kitchen.

Seconds later Jess emerged from the hallway. Black sweats, with a denim jacket, her long, dark hair caught back with a scrunchie. She looked fresh, relaxed, and damned sexy. But again the sense of déjà vu slammed him. He'd seen that haunting face somewhere before—unless she had a twin.

But that wasn't why he'd called her.

"How's your son?" she asked as he opened the door of the SUV and lent a hand to help her climb onto the high passenger seat.

"All right for now. He'll be at Grace and Sam's watching a basketball game for a while. They've been good to him. And little Maggie is determined to be his friend, even though he thinks she's a pest."

"Maggie's a jewel. And she's not one to give up. She'll win him over."

She settled back and fastened her seat belt as Cooper pulled the vehicle away from the curb. "These boys I told you about," he said. "I gather you know them pretty well."

"I'm afraid so. Neither of them has a good home life—Skip especially. His father has been arrested countless times for beating up his wife. Every time it happens, Ruth comes in the next day and refuses to press charges. He's broken her nose, blackened her eye, dislocated her shoulder, and the bruises . . ." She shook her head. "Skip's her son by her first husband, who died. He has two little sisters. You can imagine what seeing that kind of brutality could do to a young boy."

"And the other one, Cody?"

"It's just him and his mother. The father's long gone.

They live up in that trailer park on the last street in town. She takes in boyfriends. They stay for a while and then there's a new one. Again, you can understand why the boy gets in trouble."

"And I understand why Trevor might feel a kinship with those two, after his mother's choice," Cooper said. "But that doesn't mean I want him palling around with them. They've already shown that they want to make sport of him, and aside from that, they don't give a damn. But unless Trevor figures that out for himself, anything I say to him will be blowing air. And forbidding him to see them will only feed the fire."

"I agree. For now, all we can do is keep an eye on him and hope he comes to his senses—or better yet, makes new friends. I'll do my best to watch the situation and to keep you informed. But until he learns to trust me, trying to get close will only push him away."

"For now, I guess that's about all we can do." Cooper had turned onto the main road out of town and was watching for the spot where he'd noticed the sign.

"So where's this property you want to check out?" she asked.

"It's not far from town. I saw a sign that pricked my interest—a small ranch for sale. I wasn't looking for anything like that, but it made me curious. If I like what I see from a distance, I'll call the seller and get the asking price."

She didn't reply.

"What?" he asked. "Do you think I've lost my mind?"

"I had you pegged for a city boy, that's all. You're full of surprises."

"I am a city boy. But one summer my college roommate got me a job on his family's ranch. I learned to ride, fish, and even rope a little. It was great. I didn't want the summer to end. Right now, I'm just looking. But for years, getting back to a life like that has been a fantasy of mine."

"What about Trevor? Does he know what you're thinking?"

"Not yet—and if nothing comes of this, I don't plan to tell him. We've got a good situation, living next to Grace and Sam. But it's occurred to me that Trevor doesn't have anything to do except watch TV, play video games, and read. He hates playing sports, but he needs something to keep him active."

"So you think you can turn him into a cowboy?"

"You never know. I'm desperate enough to try anything." As he spoke, Cooper spotted the sign, attached to the corner post of a barbed wire fence. A dirt lane cut off from the road, leading west along the fence line. There was nothing in sight but a dozen Black Angus cows grazing in the pasture.

"I know where we are," Jess said. "Abner Jenkins, the older man you met in Buckaroo's, lives out this way."

"Do you think he might be the one selling the property?"

"Maybe, but I don't think so. He would have said something about it, especially knowing that you were new in town. But we'll see."

After a few minutes of slow, bumpy driving, they saw a second sign with an arrow pointing left to where a rough driveway led toward a long windbreak of tall Lombardy poplars, standing like sentinels against the sky. Through the trees, Cooper could make out a low house, a windmill, a barn that wanted paint, and a scattering of corrals and outbuildings. A sign lower on the fence said, PRIVATE PROPERTY. NO TRESPASSING.

Cooper stopped the SUV, idling the engine. "I guess this is as far as we go."

"This isn't Abner's place," Jess said. "He lives in the other direction, to the right of this road."

"So who lives here?"

"I have no idea. But look, somebody's coming."

A red tractor, looking like a relic from the 1950s, was

coming down the lane toward them, driven by a man in overalls and a broad-brimmed straw hat. A black-and-white dog raced ahead of him.

"Well, I guess I won't need that phone call." Cooper switched off the engine and climbed out of the Jeep. "You might want to stay inside, in case he plans to drive us off with a shotgun."

But Jess was already out of the vehicle.

Cooper waved to show that he was friendly. The man on the tractor waved back. But the dog, a border collie, was still protective. Stopping a few feet away, it raised its hackles and barked.

"Hello, boy." Cooper spoke in a soothing voice and held out his fist for the dog to smell. "It's okay, boy. I won't hurt you."

The border collie edged closer, sniffing cautiously.

"I think she's a girl, not a boy." Jess came up even with Cooper and held out her hand. "Hello, girl. My, aren't you pretty!"

The farmer, past middle age, with the look of a man who'd spent his life working in the hot sun, stopped, shut off the noisy engine, and climbed down from the tractor seat.

"Her name's Glory. She won't bite. Just not used to strangers, that's all. Come on, girl. Get back here." The dog trotted back to her owner. He scratched her ears before he spoke again. "Now what can I do for you folks? Are you lost?"

"I hope not." Cooper introduced himself. "I was curious about that For Sale sign and thought I'd drive by the place and take a look before I troubled you with a phone call."

The man's eyes, pale blue beneath the brim of his hat, took Cooper's measure. "Well, now that you're here, you might as well take a closer look. Clem Porter's the name. And you—" His gaze shifted toward Jess. "I take it you're the missus."

"No, just a friend," Jess corrected him swiftly.

"Too bad. You two make a right handsome couple. Anyhow, you can follow me back to the house. I'll give you a look-see and answer any questions you might have. I'm anxious to sell. Got my eye on a little beach place in Mexico—good fishing, good beer, and friendly señoritas."

Cooper cleared his throat. "Before taking any more of your time, could you tell me your asking price—with the discount for cash? Mind you, I'm not making an offer. I just want to know if the property's affordable before I see it."

"Sure." Clem Porter nodded, pausing to scratch the dog, who was dancing around his legs. "With or without the livestock?"

"That depends on what it is," Cooper said.

"The steers I was raisin' have been sold off for beef. But there's a couple of good horses with tack, this old tractor, and a wagon. You'll see some hens, too, but they're already spoken for. I'll throw the other animals in for free. And I'll shave another two hundred dollars off the price if you'll take Glory. She's a great dog, but I can't take her to Mexico with me. And you said cash, right?"

"If I decide to make an offer, which I haven't. Right now, I don't need an exact price, just a ballpark figure."

"I understand." He was silent, figuring in his head. "For cash, here's my asking price."

The figure he gave Cooper was about half what he'd gotten for his Seattle condo with a view of Puget Sound. Cooper could buy this place for cash, use some of the left-over money to fix it up, and maybe sell it for a profit if he decided not to stay.

But what was he thinking?

He and Jess climbed back into the Jeep and followed the tractor to the house. "I can't believe you're doing this," she said. "Are you usually so impulsive?"

"Not at all. I'm just curious." Cooper steered the Jeep

around a deep pothole. "And it sounds like a good deal—an amazing deal, compared to real estate prices in Seattle."

"You may change your mind when you see the place close up," she said. "Take a look."

Chickens scattered across the weedy yard as Cooper pulled up next to the tractor and parked. The single-story frame house stood a few yards away, screen door hanging ajar by one hinge. A cracked front windowpane had been mended with silver duct tape. The wood siding bore the last peeling traces of white paint.

But most of the damage was just wear and tear that could be fixed. Looking beyond its dilapidated condition, Cooper could see that the house had good lines and was solidly built—no sags in the roof or walls. But he'd need to inspect the frame for termite damage and make sure the plumbing and wiring were in decent shape, before . . .

But what in blazes was he thinking? For all its attractive price, this rundown place could turn out to be a money pit.

"Come and have a look." Porter shoved the broken screen door aside and opened the front door. "My wife ran off and left seven years ago, after the kids were grown, so the place could use a woman's touch. But fixed up, it would be great for a family. The school bus stops out there at the end of the lane."

"That's good to know, since I have a thirteen-year-old boy," Cooper said as they entered through the front door, the dog tagging behind them.

"Well, he'd have plenty of playmates out here. Most of these ranch families have kids. The McCoys on the next place over have a boy a little older than yours."

Skip McCoy. One checkmark in the negative column.

The inside of the four-bedroom house showed signs of long neglect—the stained, worn carpet; the cheap, peeling linoleum in the kitchen; the grease-spattered stove; and the old-fashioned sink piled with dirty dishes. The place probably had mice or even roaches. But the stone fireplace topped by a beautifully carved mantelpiece looked good, as did the moldings and well-made cabinets. Lifting up a loose corner of the carpet, Cooper saw good quality oak flooring underneath.

"Did you build this house?" he asked.

"Nope. Bought it off this lady whose husband had died. He was some kind of craftsman—had a workshop out back where he made stuff like tables and cupboards. The place could be right nice if it was fixed up."

Yes, it could, Cooper thought. *Almost nice enough to make up for having Skip McCoy's family as neighbors.*

"How's the plumbing?" he asked.

In answer, Porter turned on a faucet. A stream of clean, clear water shot out. "The water's from the well outside. In all the years I've been here, it's never run low. And I've kept the windmill working fine. Bathroom's down the hall. It ain't too clean right now, but there's some nice tile on the floor and around the tub and shower. Everything works."

"I'll take your word for it," Cooper said. "How about the barn?"

They went outside, Glory wagging her tail behind them. The barn was a small one; the two big geldings—a grulla and a pinto—were past their prime but gentle. Trevor would like the horses, Cooper thought. He might even learn to like the dog.

"You say you raised cattle here?" he asked.

"Yup. About fifty head of Hereford steers. Bought 'em as calves and sold 'em to a feed lot. You could grow hay, too. But if you just want the country life without all the work, you could lease out the pastures. There are plenty of folks who need more grazing room for their stock or a place to grow more hay. They'd pay for the use of your land, and you wouldn't have to lift a finger." His eyes narrowed. "So what do you say, Mr. Chapman? Do we have a deal?"

"Whoa," Cooper said. "I'll confess I'm interested, but I need time to think about this."

"Take all the time you want. But I can't hold the place for you. If somebody else comes along with the money, it'll be gone."

"I understand. I've got your phone number. I'll let you know."

"No need. You'll come back or you won't," he said.

"Well, that was interesting," Jess commented as they drove back toward the main road.

"What did you think of the place?" Cooper glanced at her. "Be honest."

"Since you asked, it looks like a lot of work to me—and a lot of extra expense."

"But for Trevor. Do you think he'd like it better than living in town?"

"My guess is that he'd either love it or hate it. But you can't just drag him out here. You've got to give him a say in your decision. If you're serious, you'll want to drive him out here and show him the place."

"What about having Skip McCoy for a neighbor?"

"I can't tell you what to do. Skip's had a hellish home life. But no boy is all bad at that age."

He was silent, as if weighing her words. Jess studied his rugged profile as he drove back toward town. He was a compellingly attractive man—and a good man, she sensed, desperate to save his son from a destructive life. It would be easy to fall for a man like that. But she'd be a fool to get emotionally involved. She could already feel herself caring more than she should—and she sensed that the attraction was mutual. The last thing she wanted was to get between Cooper and his vulnerable boy. It was time to cut and run.

The silence between them was growing awkward. "What are you thinking?" she asked.

"I've been thinking that you already know a lot about me. But I know next to nothing about you. So why don't you tell me a few things?"

"Let's see . . . I'm thirty-eight years old, never married, have a degree in psychology, and I make pretty good chow mein. How's that?"

He frowned. "Fine, so far. But where's the rest? You're an intriguing woman, Jess Graver. I want to know more about you."

She faked a laugh. "Why spoil the mystery with boring facts when you can imagine anything you want to? Maybe I'm a princess in hiding, or a foreign spy, or a movie star. Take your pick." She'd spoken in a teasing tone, but she could feel the tightening in the pit of her stomach. Cooper was a curious man—maybe too curious. Was he just making conversation? Or was his journalist's mind sensing a story?

"Seriously, I'm a very private person," she said. "I'm never comfortable talking about myself. Good luck with the ranch if you decide to buy it. And good luck with your son. Now please take me home."

Chapter 4

Trevor wasn't looking forward to confronting Skip and Cody at lunchtime. But he couldn't have them thinking he was dumb enough to fall for that stupid snipe hunt prank.

He was walking down the hall after fourth period when they caught up to him, flanking him on either side. "Hey, pal," Cody said. "Are you excited about that snipe hunt? It's going to be a blast."

"It sounds like fun," Trevor said. "But I want you to hold the bag, Cody, while Skip and I chase the snipes down to you. How does that sound?"

Skip snickered. "I think he's on to you, Cody. Smart kid we got here."

"I'm too smart to let you play that dumb trick on me," Trevor said. "So I guess you guys don't want to be friends with me anymore."

"Heck, we like you for being smart," Skip said. "Maybe you can even help us with our homework."

"Anyway, that snipe thing was just a test," Cody said. "You know, like an initiation, so you can join our club."

"You've got a club?"

"Uh-huh," Cody said. "But before you can join, you'll need to pass one more test. Can you still come with us on Halloween?"

"I'll have to fib to my dad." Trevor knew how much his father hated lying. But sometimes it was the only way to get around him.

"Have you got a bike?" Skip asked.

Trevor shook his head. He'd had no place to keep a bike or ride one in Seattle. His dad had promised him a real grown-up one if he behaved himself until Christmas. But that was a long time off—almost two months.

"That's okay," Skip said. "I can pick you up close to your house. You can ride behind me. So, are you in?"

"You bet." It felt good to have cool friends, and even better to belong to their club. He could hardly wait for Halloween.

When the thirty-first arrived, Trevor seemed restless as nightfall approached.

"Dad," Trevor said, "I've got a new friend. His name's Michael. He wants to go out trick-or-treating tonight."

Cooper stopped working to give the boy some attention. The technicians had arrived earlier that day to install the phone and internet, and he'd finally got his computer set up and working. At last he could finish his article assignments and get some money coming in. Between that, the undecided question of the ranch purchase, and thoughts of Jess, he'd almost forgotten it was Halloween. At least he'd remembered to buy candy. But the kids coming by would make it hard to get much writing done.

"I thought you said trick-or-treat was for kids," he said.

"I did." Trevor was doing his puppy-eyed thing. "But

Michael knows the houses that have the best candy. We'd just be going to those. He lives over in the next block. I can walk to his house."

"Well, at least you won't be going snipe hunting with those two ninth-graders," Cooper said. "What'll you do for a costume?"

"Michael's got some Halloween makeup. I'll just smear some on my face and go as a hobo. I'll be back by ten thirty. Okay?"

"Fine. You know our new phone number. If you need to be picked up, you've got change for a pay phone. Call me."

"I will." He was out the door and gone.

Heart pounding, Trevor crossed the porch, flew down the steps, and raced along the sidewalk. Fallen leaves crunched under his sneakers. The risen moon cast the bare branches into eerie shadows on the ground. The air was chilly but not too cold. Perfect Halloween weather.

He was out of breath by the time he reached the corner where he'd agreed to wait for Skip and Cody to show up on their bikes. Little kids in costumes, some with their parents, were trooping from house to house, their sacks open for treats.

What could he expect from his new friends tonight—a treat or, more likely, another trick? He didn't fully trust them, but no one else had come forward to offer their friendship. And he did like the idea of being in a club.

He waited, kicking at the leaves. Maybe the boys weren't coming. Maybe this would be like the snipe hunt, where he would end up waiting for someone who had no plans to show up. But no, here they came down the street on their bikes, laughing and waving as they saw him.

Their bikes were the old-fashioned kind with thick tires. Cody's bike was missing the bar between the handle and the seat, like a girl's bike. Until now, Trevor hadn't realized that they were probably from poor families. The slick new racing bike his father had promised him was something he'd assumed most kids had. But he was still learning how other people lived.

Skip braked to a halt. "Climb aboard! Let's have some fun!"

There was a narrow platform mounted over the back fender of his bike. Trevor sat on it, gripped Skip's waist, and they were off.

Cody's bike had a wire basket on the front. In the basket was a plastic grocery bag with something inside. As they turned down a street in the nicer part of town, the boys stopped their bikes. Cody reached into the bag, pulled out an egg, and handed it to Trevor.

"This here's part of your test. See that red brick house? That's where Mr. Millsap, the middle school principal, lives. When we ride past, you throw the egg at his front window. If the egg hits the window, you pass. Got it?"

"Got it." Trevor held the egg carefully, afraid of humiliating himself by breaking it in his hand. He sucked at throwing, but desire lent his arm strength. As Skip sped along the sidewalk past the red brick house, Trevor flung the egg so hard that he almost fell off the bike. The missile struck the window with a hideous yellow splatter. The boys whooped and cheered as they flew down the street, pedaling like crazy.

A few blocks away, they stopped to catch their breath.

Skip was laughing. "Yee haw! That was awesome!"

"I got more eggs," Cody said. "How's about trying for two out of three?"

They continued their wild dash through town, lobbing eggs at the homes of teachers and other folks that Skip and Cody viewed as enemies. Trevor missed the target once but connected one other time before the older boys took over. At last, out of eggs and laughing until their sides ached, they stopped to rest outside a convenience store at the south end of town.

"Who's thirsty?" Cody asked.

"All of us," Skip said. "But who's got any money?"

"I've got a couple of quarters my dad gave me for the phone," Trevor said. "But that isn't enough to buy sodas for all of us."

"Never mind," Cody said. "I've got an idea. Trevor, there's one more thing you need to do before you can be in our club, okay?"

"Okay. What is it?"

"Go into this little store with us behind you. Get yourself a canned soda with your money. While you're at the counter, talk the clerk up and distract him for a few minutes until we leave. Got it?"

"Sure." Trevor's instincts were tingling, as if trying to warn him that something wasn't right. But these boys were counting on him. If he let them down, they wouldn't be friends with him anymore. He couldn't chicken out now.

Without looking at his companions, he sauntered into the store, studied the cold drink case, and picked out a Dr Pepper. With the ice-cold can in his hand, he took his time meandering back to the counter.

"Fifty cents." The clerk, a gray-haired woman, had sharp, knowing eyes that seemed to look right through him.

Setting the can on the counter, Trevor fished the two quarters out of his jeans, grateful that he had the right amount. "So how's your Halloween going?" he asked. "Do a lot of kids come in here trick-or-treating?"

"A few," the woman said. "When they do, we let them take a candy from this bowl. Here, have one." She held out a plastic bowl half filled with cheap, cellophane-wrapped hard candies. Trevor took his time making a choice, trying not to think about what his friends might be doing.

At last he settled on a red-and-white peppermint. As he thanked the clerk, unwrapped the candy, and popped it into his mouth, he heard the door open and close. Skip and Cody had made it outside. Trevor turned away from the counter and hurried after them.

"Wait!" the woman called after him. "You forgot your soda!"

But Trevor kept going. He could see his friends climbing onto their bikes. A sick feeling came over him. Were they about to ride off and leave him here?

But no, Skip was waiting for him. Cody glanced back through the window of the store. "She's on the phone!" he said. "Probably calling the cops! Let's get out of here!"

Trevor leaped onto the back of Skip's bike, and the three of them sped south along the paved road out of town.

"Hold this for me." Skip reached back and thrust something at Trevor. Trevor's hand closed around the cold, wet beverage can his friend had shoplifted from the convenience store—with his own help, Trevor reminded himself.

He was expecting a soda. But something about the can felt different. Its shape was a little narrower and slightly taller than the pop cans he was used to.

Damn! It was beer—had to be. Trevor felt sick. Shoplifting was bad enough. But underage drinking was real trouble. And if they were to get caught, he'd be blamed along with his friends.

As the bikes flew along the road, a faint sound reached Trevor's ears. It was the wail of a police siren, coming from the direction of the store, and now, coming up fast behind them. Red lights, still small with distance, flashed in the dark.

Trevor clutched Skip's belt with one hand and the beer can in the other. He'd be smart to lob the beer into the bar ditch, but it was as if his hand had frozen around the cold can.

Not far ahead, a dirt road turned off the asphalt. Skip swung his bike onto it, almost throwing Trevor off the back. Cody followed. "Are we going to your place?" he asked as he caught up with his friend.

"Hell, no. My dad would kill me," Skip said. "There's a barn on the neighbor's place. We can hide in there. The old man won't even know we're around."

Trevor glanced back to see the police car making a turn onto the dirt lane. The bumpy surface had slowed them down some, but they were still coming. "Hurry!" he said. "They're getting closer!"

With Skip in the lead, they flew through the open gate and into the moonlit barnyard. Trevor saw an old-looking two-story house. About twenty yards away stood a weathered barn. The door, which faced at an angle away from the house, was open at one end. The boys wheeled their bikes inside and laid them in the shadows. Trevor, who'd jumped out of the way, paused to look around.

He'd wondered whether there'd be animals here, but there appeared to be none. The moonlight that fell through the cracks between the shrunken boards revealed a tractor and a hay wagon, with other machine parts stacked against one wall. In the far corner of the barn, an object about the size of a compact car was hidden beneath a large canvas tarpaulin.

"Do you think those cops saw us come in here?" Cody asked.

Trevor peered through a space between the boards. He could see the police car approach the open gate and turn in. One of the windows must have been open, because he could hear the chatter of the dispatch radio.

Suddenly, as if summoned by an emergency call, the black-and-white car revved its engine, made a screeching U-turn in the yard, sped out the gate and back down the road, flying over the bumps and potholes.

"Give me that beer!" Skip laughed, took the can from Trevor, popped the tab, and took a deep swig.

Cody did the same with his can. "Want a sip?" He held it out to Trevor, who shook his head. He'd tasted beer in Seattle and hadn't liked it all that much.

"So am I in your club now?" Trevor asked.

The two older boys looked at each other and grinned. "Sure, kid," Cody said. "Hell, you can be in any club you want. You can even be president."

Trevor was still digesting the words when Skip put a finger to his lips. "Listen. I think somebody's coming."

From the direction of the house came the sound of a door closing. When Trevor peered between the boards, he saw a flashlight beam dancing in the darkness, still distant but coming closer. Then another sound froze all three boys with fear. It was the bark of a good-sized dog.

"Quiet, Butch! Get back here." The man's voice had a gravelly tone, as if he might be old. "Who's there?" he called. "I've got a gun, and I know how to use it. Come on out with your hands up—now."

Skip and Cody grabbed their bikes. "I know a back way out of here," Skip whispered. "Come on, let's go!"

Dropping the beer cans, they leaped onto their bikes, shot out the door and, still hidden from the stranger's view, disappeared into the night—leaving Trevor alone in the barn.

"Come on out! I know you're in there!" The man was still outside but getting closer. Trevor could hear the dog growling and chuffing. Maybe he should do what the man said—come out of the barn with his hands up. But no. The man had a gun, and he had the right to shoot an intruder on his property. All he'd have to do was pull the trigger, or sic the dog on him and let it tear him to pieces.

He could even be crazy, like the villains in horror movies—the kind of villains who kidnapped kids and tortured them to death, or held them for ransom.

Even if the man were to just call the police—or Trevor's dad—this story was bound to have an ugly ending.

With terror pumping adrenaline through his body, Trevor made a wild dash for the canvas-covered object in the corner of the barn, lifted the edge of the tarp, and dived underneath.

Maybe, if he kept still enough, the man would shine his light on the beer cans and bike tracks and think that all the intruders had gone. Hopefully, he would stop looking and leave before coming into the barn.

But what about the dog?

The space under the canvas was pitch dark, the ground smelling of earth and moldy straw. Thinking that the hidden object might be a car, Trevor groped for tires to hide behind, but he found none—just concrete blocks where the wheels should be.

Why hadn't he run when his friends left on their bikes? But they weren't his friends and never had been. He understood that now. They had used him, and when danger had shown up, they'd left him to face it alone.

The man had come into the barn. Trevor could hear him talking to the dog. "What do you think, Butch? Are the little bastards gone?" He kicked one of the beer cans. "I'll wager they were up to no good. Take a good sniff around to make sure. If you don't find anybody, then we'll go back to the house and have some ice cream."

The dog was nearing Trevor's hiding place. Trevor could hear the big animal sniffing the ground. He shrank between the concrete blocks, expecting to be found and attacked any second.

The dog yipped, scratching at the edge of the tarpaulin. "Good boy," the man said. "Come on back now. I can take it from here." He raised his voice, speaking to Trevor. "Better come out now, before I shoot this tarp full of holes and you with it."

Trevor lay still. The man was probably bluffing. But what if he wasn't?

"I'll give you to the count of three—one . . . two . . . three!" He grabbed a corner of the tarpaulin and yanked it away. The flashlight beam caught Trevor in the eyes, but he could make out an old-looking man with white whiskers, a pistol in his hand, and a huge, shaggy dog at his side. The dog looked a lot like the monster that trailed little Maggie around. Maybe the two animals were related.

The man lowered his gun. "Come on out, you damn fool kid. I won't hurt you, and neither will Butch, here."

Trevor crawled into the light, scrambled to his feet, and stood there, shaking.

"Well, I'll be swanned," the man said. "You're the kid I saw in Buckaroo's the other day with your dad and that Miss Graver. You'd better have a damned good story to tell, especially about these beer cans."

Trevor knew he was in big trouble now. "Please," he begged. "I'll tell you anything. Just don't call my dad."

He turned away to hide a surge of tears. That was when he saw it—the flashlight beam shining on the object that had been under the canvas.

He'd assumed it was a car. But it wasn't a car at all. Except for the missing runners, it was an honest-to-goodness Santa Claus–style *sleigh*.

Trevor hadn't believed in Santa since he was in first grade. But he was so stunned by the sight of that sleigh that for a moment he almost forgot he was in trouble.

"What are you staring at, boy? I told you to come with me."

"Sorry. Just kind of surprised me, that's all. I've never seen a real sleigh."

"Well, help me cover it up again. Then we'll decide what to do with you." He glanced at the two beer cans on the floor of the barn. "Are those yours?"

"No, sir." Trevor remembered his manners. "My friends left them."

"And where are your friends now?"

"They left on their bikes."

"They don't sound like very good friends to me." He picked up a side of the tarpaulin. "Here, take the other corner and slide it back over the sleigh. Then follow me to the house."

"Yes, sir." Trevor did as he was told, reminding himself to be cautious. The friendly old man could still be a psychopathic serial killer.

The dog sat back and watched, his shaggy head cocked to one side, as if trying to decide whether Trevor was friend, foe, or food. When the old man opened the door of the small farmhouse and motioned Trevor inside, the dog came, too.

For Trevor, entering the roomy, well-used house was like stepping back into the 1970s. A wood-burning stove warmed the living room, where a well-worn overstuffed sofa and a La-Z-Boy recliner faced an older-style TV. The set was running a pro rodeo event.

Through an archway, Trevor could see through the dining room and into the kitchen. His gaze roamed from the avocado-green stove and refrigerator to the flowered oilcloth on the small table and the wildlife calendar on the wall. The blended aromas of beans, bacon, and corn bread lingered on the air.

All in all, the place didn't strike him as the home of a serial killer. And what about that unfinished sleigh in the barn? The old man even looked a little like Santa, although with less of a beard.

Maybe he was dreaming.

The old man turned off the TV and ushered Trevor into the kitchen. "Have a chair," he said.

The chairs were like the ones in the '50s shows, with

metal frames and padded plastic seats. Trevor sat down. "What are you going to do to me?" he asked.

"That depends on your story—and whether you tell the truth. If you're lying, I'll know. And I don't think much of liars."

A line from the old song about Santa knowing if you've been bad or good invaded Trevor's mind. *Stupid thought.* He forced it away.

The old man opened the freezer, took out a carton of vanilla ice cream, and filled two bowls. Taking one more scoop, he dropped it into the dog's dish on the floor. The monster lapped it, tail wagging up a storm.

After replacing the ice cream in the freezer, he set the two bowls with spoons on the table. His blue eyes pierced Trevor like lasers. "Eat up. My name's Abner in case you didn't catch it at Buckaroo's. What should I call you?"

Trevor thought about giving a fake name. But he remembered what Abner had said about lying. "My name's Trevor. Trevor Chapman."

"Fine. That's a good start. Now, while you eat your ice cream, you can tell me how you came to be in my barn."

Cooper cursed the silent phone, willing it to ring. It was after eleven, and Trevor hadn't come home or called. Had the boy just lost track of time, or was he in some kind of trouble? Knowing Trevor, neither possibility could be ruled out.

Maybe he should have kept his son at home. But this was Halloween, a night for harmless fun. And so he'd given Trevor a measure of trust and freedom. Had that been a mistake?

Trevor had said he was going trick-or-treating with a friend named Michael. Michael who? Blast it, he should have gotten a last name, or better yet called Michael's parents to make sure the invitation was legit—if Michael was even real.

What kind of father was he?

But the more urgent question was, what should he do now? He couldn't go out and look for the boy. He wouldn't know where to start. And he needed to be here in case Trevor called or came home.

Phone Michael's house—that was the only sensible thing to do. He just needed to find out the kid's last name.

Only one person he knew might be able to tell him that. He felt guilty, bothering Jess at this hour, but the situation was becoming desperate.

He had her number. As he punched it into the phone, he made a mental finger-cross that she would answer, that she wouldn't be annoyed, and that she'd have the answer he needed.

On the second ring, he heard the phone pick up. A drowsy voice—so sexy that it would have set his pulse racing if he hadn't been so worried—murmured, "Hello."

"Jess, it's Cooper. Sorry if I woke you."

Her tone changed instantly, becoming clear and alert. "What is it, Cooper? Is something wrong?"

"I hope not. I'm just trying to track down my son. He said he was going trick-or-treating with some kid named Michael. Now I need to call the kid's house, and I don't know Michael's last name. You're the only one I know who might be able to tell me."

"Michael?" She paused. "Sorry, I'm just trying to think of who that might be. I make it part of my job to recognize every student. But I don't recall a middle school boy named Michael."

The knot in Cooper's chest hardened. He'd trusted his son to tell him the truth, but he should have known better. The boy had clearly lied to him.

"I can imagine how you must feel." She paused. "Sorry, I know that's what a counselor would say. But I really mean it. Is there anything I can do to help?"

"Thanks, but all I can do now is wait by the damned phone and hope that whatever I hear won't be bad news."

"Would you call me when you hear anything—or when Trevor shows up?"

"Yes, if you don't mind my waking you."

"Something tells me I won't be asleep. I'm worried, too."

"Then I'm doubly sorry for bothering you about this. Trevor is probably fine."

"Just call me, whatever the outcome," she said. "Now I'm going to hang up and clear the phone."

The call ended with a click. Cooper knew that he should keep off the phone, but he couldn't rest without making one more call, to the sheriff's dispatcher. If there'd been an accident or an arrest, he needed to know the worst.

The dispatcher was sympathetic. She was probably a parent, too. "The only accident report has been a drunk rolling his car out by Rowdy's Roost," she said. "There've been some complaints about egg throwing. Oh—and earlier there was a call about kids shoplifting a couple of beers at the Crossroads Convenience Store. Evidently the kids got away. That's about it. Pretty quiet for Halloween, but the night isn't over."

Cooper thanked her and hung up the phone. At least nobody was dead or hurt. But the report about those young shoplifters worried him. Had Trevor hooked up with Skip and Cody again?

Maybe he should phone the convenience store and get a description. But the place had probably closed at eleven, and he was not even sure he wanted to know. He could only pace the floor and hope that Trevor wasn't somewhere hiding from the police.

Restless, he switched on the TV. The Movie Channel was

playing a film about teens being stalked by a madman in a mask. Not what Cooper needed right now. He clicked the remote. The TV went blank.

Time crawled. It was almost eleven thirty when the front doorbell rang. Cooper's heart dropped. His hand froze on the doorknob. Was he about to find himself facing a police officer?

He forced himself to open the door. Jess stood on the porch, an oversized trench coat wrapped over her black sweats. Her face was bare of makeup, her hair loose and hastily combed.

"I couldn't sleep," she said, "and since I hadn't heard from you, I thought I might as well come over. Here." She held out a pink bakery box, open to show doughnuts inside. "Will this buy my way in?"

"You never have to buy your way anywhere," he said. "But thanks. Come on in. I'll make us some coffee while we wait."

Chapter 5

Cooper spooned ground coffee into the filter and added water to the reservoir. Jess had followed him into the kitchen. Still wearing her trench coat, she leaned lightly against the edge of the counter, looking soft and muzzy and vulnerable. At any other time, Cooper would have pushed the limits of their friendship to see what might lie beyond. But tonight they were both too worried about Trevor.

"You didn't need to come," he said. "But thank you anyway. I'm glad you're here."

"I guess I feel partly responsible," she said. "If I'd been paying more attention, I might have noticed something at school that could help us now."

"No more responsible than I am for not checking out his story when I let him go tonight."

She covered a little yawn with her hand, looking the way she might look if he were to awaken and find her on the pillow next to his. "Was that the only reason you came tonight—that you felt responsible?" he asked.

She glanced away, the subtle gesture closing a door between them. Had he said the wrong thing? Should he apologize, or would that only make the tension worse?

The awkward silence was broken by the sudden jangle of the phone. Cooper lunged to answer it.

"Dad?" The shaky voice on the line was unmistakably Trevor's. Cooper's knees went slack with relief. Whatever trouble he'd gotten himself into, at least the boy was alive.

But he felt anger, too. Why had his son lied to him? Why hadn't he called or come home sooner?

"Where are you?" he demanded. "Are you all right?"

"I'm okay. I'm with Abner . . ." He sounded scared. "We met him in Buckaroo's, remember? Here, I'll give him the phone."

"Hello, Mr. Chapman." The deep voice jogged Cooper's memory. Jess moved closer to hear him. "Your boy's with me. He's all right, but he'll have some explaining to do when you see him. I'd drive him home, but my night vision isn't the best, so you'll need to come and get him. My place is a bit hard to find at night. If you've got a pen and paper, I'll give you directions."

"Hang on." Cooper reached for the notepad and ballpoint pen he kept on the counter, but Jess stopped him.

"Never mind. I know how to get to Abner's place. I'll go with you."

"You're sure?"

"Even with written directions, it's easy to miss a turn and get lost on those back roads."

"Come on, then, and thanks in advance." After hanging up the phone, he ushered her outside to the Jeep and gave her a hand up. "You're the navigator," he said. "Just buckle up and tell me where to go."

"Take the main road south, out of town, the way you went when you saw that ranch for sale." Jess leaned forward to peer at the slice of road illuminated by the Jeep's headlights. Cooper drove too fast, his mouth set in a grim line. Jess knew she wasn't the one on his mind. He was thinking of his son and pondering how to deal with him. She wouldn't offer advice. At least, not unless he asked for it.

Outside, the moon glimmered through scudding clouds, casting shadows on the ground. The trees along the road, their branches blown bare of leaves, reached skeletal branches toward the sky.

A white-tailed deer bounded into the headlights. Cooper slammed on the brakes, missing the animal by inches as it crossed the road, leaped the bar ditch, and disappeared into the night.

The sudden stop had killed the engine. Cooper took deep breaths, as if trying to calm himself before starting the Jeep again.

"Are you all right?" Jess asked.

"I will be." Cooper put the Jeep in gear and started the engine. "And you?"

"Fine. But I wouldn't be if we'd hit that poor deer."

"Sorry. I didn't mean to scare you."

"It's all right. Nothing happened."

"No, it didn't. But I've got to get a grip on my nerves before I face Trevor, or things could get ugly. Damn it, I wish I knew how to be a better father."

"Kids don't come with instructions," Jess said. "How long have you had Trevor with you?"

"I've had joint custody since the divorce. Until a few months ago, that meant having him summers and holidays. When he was younger, it was fun and easy. We had great times together. But having a full-time teenager is a whole new ball game. I don't want to make him feel like a prisoner, but if I give him any rope, like tonight, he runs away with it. What do you have to say? You're the expert here."

Jess shook her head. "I can spout a lot of theories with

fancy names, but I've never been a parent. That's where you're way ahead of me. But I'd say that Trevor needs something to focus on, something he likes, a hobby, a sport, or even a special friend. Right now, he seems lost. Do you think he misses his mother?"

"In a way. But he's angry with her, too. After all, she chose her new husband over him."

"That would be devastating to any child." Jess peered through the windshield. "Up there, just past those trees, make a right. It's the same road you took to look at that ranch."

"I see it. There's the sign." He swung off the asphalt onto the bumpy dirt road. "Now what?"

"Up ahead, about a hundred yards, you'll see another road that cuts off to the right. Take that and follow the barbed wire fence. At the end of it, you'll see a gate. Abner said it would be open. That's where you turn in."

"For an out-of-towner, you seem to know this place pretty well," Cooper said.

"My job includes some home visits to talk with parents. Abner's children are grown, of course, but I've been out this way enough times to know where he lives."

"I see the gate. And there's a big house down the lane, with a barn behind it. That's the place, right?" Cooper made the turn.

"Yes, that's it. And it looks like Abner's expecting us. The lights are on, and that's him waiting on the front porch."

"I don't see Trevor." Cooper parked the Jeep in the front yard. "My guess is he's probably hiding inside, and I can't say I blame him."

"Do you want me to wait here? I don't want him to think you brought reinforcements."

"No, come on. I want him to know this is serious."

With misgivings, Jess opened the door and climbed to the ground. Abner came down the porch steps to meet them.

"Nice of you to come along, Miss Graver," he said, greeting her before he turned to Cooper. "Your boy's fine. We had a good talk while we were waiting for you. He's promised to tell you everything." He opened the front door. "Come on in."

"Thanks." Cooper took a step toward the porch, then glanced back at Jess, as if asking a silent question.

"I'm staying out of this," she said, seating herself on the top step. "It sounds as if everything's under control. What happens next should be between you and your son, Cooper."

With a nod, Cooper followed Abner into the house and closed the door behind him.

The night breeze was chilly. Jess pulled her trench coat tight around her and watched the moon as it drifted through the clouds. A barn owl, unseen, screeched its hunting call through the darkness. A shaggy, pony-sized dog padded across the porch to settle beside her, its body warm and smelling of the hayfields. As Jess scratched its ears, the dog released a contented sigh.

Inside the house, Cooper would be doing his best to put things right with his son. She'd been wise to stay outside. Trevor didn't trust her, and she was probably in deeper with Cooper than she'd ever meant to be. She'd gone from doing her job to caring for this man who was struggling to be a good father.

"So that's the end of the story?" Cooper demanded. "You fell in with those boys who'd already tried to trick you. You vandalized people's homes with them and helped them steal an illegal drink. Then when things got scary, they rode off and left you. What have you got to say for yourself?"

"I'm sorry." Trevor looked as wretched as a skunk-sprayed hound. "I thought they were my friends. But I was stupid."

"And what now? You lied to your father. You did things that could've gotten you arrested or worse. What will it take to teach you a lesson?"

"I guess you could ground me."

"Yes, I could, and I probably will. And tomorrow morning we're going around to the houses you egged, and you're going to clean their windows. Anything else?"

"Yes, there is something else." The boy looked at the old man, who'd taken a seat with them at the kitchen table. "Abner and I have an idea. You tell him, Abner."

Cooper braced himself for whatever he was about to hear.

Abner cleared his throat. "Like I told you, Mr. Chapman, your boy and I had a good long talk. And we came up with something—some work he'd like to do for me."

"Abner's got a sleigh in the barn," Trevor broke in. "A real sleigh like in Santa Claus pictures—only it isn't finished. It's just been sitting there, covered up by a tarp, for years. But it's amazing. Wait till you see it."

"Trevor wants to help me finish the sleigh," Abner said. "There's a lot of work left to do. He could come by some days after school and on weekends."

"Please, Dad. Abner wouldn't even have to pay me. I could do it instead of being grounded." He gazed at Cooper with hope in his eyes—the first sign of hope Cooper had seen in a long time. "So what do you say?"

"I say that I need to know more about this project and more time to think. How about we start by taking a look at that sleigh? Can you show it to me, Abner?"

"Sure. It's out back in the barn. But there's no light in there. I've got a flashlight but it's not the best. Have you got a good light in your vehicle? That would help."

"It's in the glove box. I'll get it. Oh—and Trevor, Miss Graver is outside. She came along to show me the way here."

Trevor rolled his eyes, as if to say, *Oh, sure, she did.* Ignoring him, Cooper headed out the front door and closed it behind him. He found Jess sitting on the step with the dog.

"I see you found a friend," he said.

"Yes, I did. He doesn't talk, but he's warm, and he likes to have his ears scratched. So how did it go with Trevor?"

"No worse than I'd expected. Come with me to the barn. We're going to see a sleigh."

"A sleigh? You mean like Santa Claus's sleigh?"

"Your guess is as good as mine. Just let me get my flashlight out of the Jeep."

With the high-powered flashlight showing the way, they walked around the house to the ramshackle barn. On the way, Cooper told Jess about Trevor's idea.

"So he wants to work on it?"

"That's what he says. He even seems excited about it."

"But why? If it were something like a motorcycle or a classic car, I'd understand. But a sleigh—it's like this fairy tale thing."

"I know, but I'm willing to go along with anything that gets him interested."

"It's not a bad idea, as long as he stays with it. But you can't just turn him loose. He needs to follow through."

"I agree. But for now we'll just have to take this one step at a time."

They found Abner and Trevor already in the barn. They were lifting a canvas tarpaulin off the object beneath.

"Here it is," Abner said. "Give us some more light, and you can see it better."

With the canvas swept aside, Cooper directed the beam of his flashlight onto the object underneath. He gave a low whistle.

He'd expected to see some kind of oversized sled, or maybe a remodeled wagon with runners. But this was like something out of a Russian fairy tale. It was a real *sleigh*.

The bed, its base and sides cut from a fine, dark wood that

looked like mahogany, was longer than the typical cutter-style sleigh, with a high bench in front for the driver and a more commodious seat for passengers in the rear. But the sleigh, stunning as it was, was far from finished. The wood needed several coats of waterproof varnish. The runners and the hardware for the reins were missing, and the seats lacked upholstery.

"Where's the rest of the sleigh?" Cooper asked.

"I've got everything. It originally came as a kit, and the smaller parts are stored in the cellar. My brother and I bought it decades ago when we lived in Wisconsin. We planned to put it together and make extra money taking folks for sleigh rides around our farm. We'd gotten this far when he was killed in a construction accident. I never had the heart to work on the sleigh after that. But years later, when my wife and I moved to her family's old place in Texas, I knew I couldn't leave it behind. I stored it here in the barn, where it sits to this day. Didn't see much sense in spending time on it. We're lucky if we get one or two storms in a season.

"But if your boy wants to work on it with me, maybe I could at least put it up for sale when we're finished. I've seen sleighs on eBay going for good money."

"Please say you'll let me help, Dad," Trevor said. "I could learn a lot doing something like this."

"What do you say, Abner?" Cooper asked. "After all, you caught this young hooligan hiding in your barn. Do you trust him to work for you?"

Abner nodded slowly. "I'm willing to give him a chance—but only one chance. If he starts slacking, gets in more trouble, or falls behind on his schoolwork, I'll wash my hands of him."

Cooper fixed his son with a stern look. "Do you hear that, Trevor? It means you'll have to finish what you started."

Trevor nodded. "I understand. But I'll need a way to get here. It's too far to walk from town."

"If you're talking about that new bike I promised you on condition that you behave, that's on hold until you earn it. For now, I'll take you and pick you up. So when do we start, Abner?"

"I've got plans for the weekend. But if Trevor can show up early next week, we'll start by getting the barn cleared out and some lights strung in here. Shall we say early next week? I'll let you know for sure. So have we got a deal?"

"Have we, Trevor?"

"You bet!" Grinning, he accepted Abner's handshake.

Cooper had made a commitment, too—and found one more reason to buy the neighboring ranch. He couldn't delay much longer, or the place would be sold, and he'd be out of luck. But he couldn't make an offer until Trevor was on board with the move.

Tomorrow was Saturday. He would take Trevor out here in the daytime, show him the ranch, and make a final decision.

Jess had left her Taurus parked at Cooper's house. She held her tongue on the way there, knowing that Trevor, sitting behind her, would hear and judge anything she said. She wasn't here to comment on his behavior or to give him any ideas about her and his father. Best to say nothing.

Cooper pulled the Jeep into the driveway and handed Trevor his keys. "Go on inside and get ready for bed," he said. "I'll be along in a few minutes. Make sure you brush your teeth."

As the boy disappeared into the house, Jess unlatched her door to get out of the vehicle. "Hang on," Cooper said, opening the driver's door and climbing out. "I'll walk you to your car."

"No need. This is Branding Iron, not Seattle. I'll be perfectly safe."

"But it's Halloween, and there are goblins, even in Branding Iron." He came around the Jeep, opened her door, and held out a hand to help her down.

"Not anymore." She took his hand briefly as she stepped to the ground. "It's after midnight. Halloween is over."

"Why do you have to be so damned contrary, Jess? I just wanted to thank you for coming along tonight."

"All I did was tell you where to turn."

"Wrong. You listened to me when I needed to talk. That meant a lot."

He was standing close to her—so close that if she'd given him a signal, like the slight upward tilt of her head, he might have kissed her. Part of her wanted it to happen. She could almost imagine the feel of those firm, masculine lips pressing hers, the scent of him, the taste of him, his breathing as his arms pulled her close.

"You're becoming important to me, Jess," he said.

At his words the soft emotion that was opening like a flower inside her shrank and hardened. She remembered the flashing cameras and the news stories—written by journalists like Cooper Chapman. She took a step back, away from him. "I need to go," she said. "I need to go now." With that she turned and fled to her car.

Starting the engine, she pulled away from the curb. Cooper had only meant to say that he liked her. But those few innocent words had touched a raw nerve that would never heal. The last time she was important to anyone, she had failed, and because of her failure, people had died. How could anyone live with that? How could any small amount of good she might do in the world make up for the horror of that day?

The next day, after a morning of window washing, Cooper drove his son out to see the place that might—or might not—be their new home.

They had talked about the idea earlier that morning. Trevor, while less than enthusiastic, had at least agreed to look. "I never wanted to be a cowboy," he'd said. "But here in town, I'm nothing but a weirdo with no friends. I might as well check it out."

Cooper felt the pain in his son's words. But at least they wouldn't be going alone. Sam and Grace had planned a lunch and movie date in Cottonwood Springs. They'd left Maggie with Cooper for the day.

She was bubbling with excitement at the prospect of going to the ranch with them. "You'll be so lucky!" she chattered from the back seat of the Jeep. "I always wanted to live on a ranch with horses. Maybe I could come and stay with you sometimes, and you could teach me to ride."

"We haven't even decided to buy it, silly." Trevor had complained about having to babysit, but Cooper knew he didn't really mind. Maggie was such a sunny child, and so wise for her years, that it was impossible not to like her.

"And you said there was a dog!" She ignored Trevor. "Border collies are really smart. Do you get to keep her?"

"We don't know if we're buying the place yet, Maggie," Cooper said. "Give us a chance to think about it before you start making plans."

A few minutes later they drove through the gate. "That's not much of a house," Trevor said.

"It could do with some fixing." Cooper hid his disappointment as he parked the Jeep in the front yard. Until now, he hadn't realized how much he wanted his son to like this place. But the house's appearance didn't have much to offer, and it was even worse inside.

"It's a ranch house. It's not supposed to be fancy." Maggie was out of the Jeep like a shot. "I want to see the horses!"

"All in good time. First, we'll look at the house," Cooper said. "That's the most important thing because it's where we'd be living."

"*If* we decide to live here." Trevor took his time getting out of the Jeep. As his sneakers touched the ground, a black-and-white dog came streaking around the house, barking and wagging its tail to greet the visitors. Trevor shrank away, but Maggie opened her arms. She hugged the dog, squealing with laughter as it licked her face.

Cooper had phoned Clem Porter, the owner, to let him know they were coming. He was waiting on the porch. "What's the dog's name?" Maggie asked him.

"Her name's Glory," he said.

"Like the song!" Maggie began to sing the "Battle Hymn of the Republic." "*Glory, glory, hallelujah!*" The dog danced and wagged as if she understood that Maggie's song was supposed to be about her.

"That's enough, Maggie. We need to talk," Cooper said. "Why don't you stay here and play with Glory while Trevor and I look at the house?"

Maggie picked up a stick and tossed it across the yard. The border collie bounded after it.

Clem Porter's gaze moved from Maggie to Trevor, who stood with his eyes downcast and his hands in his pockets. "So are these two kids the rest of your family?"

"Just Trevor here." Cooper made a quick introduction. "The girl's a cousin who came along for the ride."

"Too bad. It looks like she'd be right at home here. Come on in and see the house, Trevor. Try to picture how it would look all fixed up with new paint and nice furniture."

They walked into the house. Porter had done some work since the last time Cooper had seen it. The tobacco smell was aired out, the trash cleared away, the dishes washed, and the bathroom scrubbed. Still, the place looked shabby at best.

Trevor wandered from room to room. Cooper found himself measuring the minutes of his son's silence. He wanted

Trevor to like the ranch. But if his son was against the move, a selfish decision would be out of the question. He might have his own dreams of a life in the country, but this decision was about Trevor and helping the boy through a difficult time in his young life.

"Which bedroom would be mine if we bought the place?" Trevor asked, then added, "I said *if*."

"Take your pick. You could paint it and decorate it any way you wanted. You can't do that in a rental."

"Even black?" The boy was testing him.

"I wouldn't say no, but you'd have to do the work yourself."

Silent again, Trevor turned around and walked back outside. "Let's go see the horses," he said.

They trailed out to the barn, Maggie and the dog dancing around them. The barn was weathered on the outside, but inside, it was in better condition than Abner's. There was a hayloft, and a rack for saddles, harness, and other tack, with a roomy double box stall for the horses. The grulla and the pinto looked at them with big, soft eyes. They were large animals, not draft size but powerful enough to be impressive.

Clem Porter opened the pinto's stall. Trevor, who'd never been around horses, hung back, as if gathering his courage. But Maggie couldn't wait to pet them. To keep her safe, Cooper lifted her high enough to stroke the pinto's satiny neck. The horse quivered, blowing softly as her little hand touched its sensitive hide. "He's so silky," she murmured. "What are their names?"

"This one's Spot. The other one is Dusty," Porter said.

"Those are funny names. Can I sit on his back?"

Cooper glanced at Porter, who nodded. "He's gentle, but hang onto her," he said. "You don't want her sliding off."

Cooper lifted her higher and settled her gently on the broad back. His hands gripped her tightly beneath the arms so he could snatch her to safety in case the horse made a sudden move, but the big gelding stood calmly while Maggie pretended to ride him, a rapt expression on her face.

Porter chuckled. "I'd say that little lady's got the makings of a real cowgirl," he said as Cooper lifted her safely out of the way. Cooper glanced at his son, knowing the boy wouldn't let himself be shown up by a girl half his size. He stepped forward and, with a shaking hand, reached toward the horse's face.

Cooper held his breath. Not until now had he realized how much he wanted this small ranch and what it represented— freedom, the pride of ownership, the open-space lifestyle, and more.

But he would only buy it if Trevor could be happy here. Otherwise, Cooper resolved, he would walk away and forget he'd ever seen that For Sale sign next to the road.

The horse flinched and snorted when Trevor touched him. Trevor's hand jerked away. "I don't think he likes me," he said.

Cooper's heart sank. But Porter, as if sensing what was at stake, stepped in, put a hand on Trevor's shoulder, and guided him.

"Not like that," he said. "The horse gets nervous when you stand right in front of him. Because his eyes are on the sides of his head, he can't see what you're doing. Stand to the side, like this, where he can see you. That's better. Now stroke his neck with the flat of your hand, like this."

Trevor did as he was directed. As he stroked the horse, the big animal relaxed with a sigh, clearly enjoying his touch.

"Wow, now he likes it," Trevor said. "I've got a lot to learn about horses."

"Anybody can learn," Porter said. "It just takes a little time and patience. Abner Jenkins, my neighbor in the next place over, used to be a great horseman afore he busted a hip. He can't ride anymore, but I reckon he could give you a few pointers."

At the mention of Abner, Trevor's expression brightened. In the silence that followed, Cooper could almost imagine wheels turning in his son's mind.

"Do you think these two horses could pull a sleigh?" Trevor asked.

"A sleigh?" Porter looked puzzled.

"A sleigh?" Maggie's green eyes danced with excitement. "A real, honest-to-goodness sleigh? If we had a sleigh, Santa could ride it in the Christmas parade!"

"Could the horses pull a sleigh?" Trevor pressed his question.

"I reckon so," Porter said. "They've got harnesses and can pull a wagon. A sleigh wouldn't be much different. But you'd need snow for a sleigh. And anyways, where could you get a sleigh around here?"

Trevor grinned. "Abner has a sleigh, and I'm going to help him finish building it. If we lived here, it would be easy for me to get to his place. Right, Dad?"

Emotion welled in Cooper's throat. "We'll need to work out the terms, Mr. Porter," he said. "But I think we just might have ourselves a deal."

Chapter 6

A few nights later, Cooper loaded up on pizza from Buck-aroo's and invited Grace, Sam, Maggie, and Jess to cel-ebrate his purchase of Clem Porter's ranch—as well as Sam's victory in the recent election for mayor.

Now that the papers were signed and recorded, and Clem Porter was packing up for his move to Mexico, Cooper was feeling twinges of buyer's remorse. Everything had hap-pened so fast. What if the ranch turned out to be a bad idea? Or what if he'd taken on more work and responsibility than he could handle?

But a few misgivings were to be expected, Cooper told himself. Besides, apart from his natural doubts, all the signs were good. Even Trevor seemed happy about the coming move. And transferring his lease on the house in town had been no problem. Wynette and Buck had jumped at the chance to take it, with an option to buy the house.

He hadn't been sure that Jess would come. She'd been making herself scarce since their tense parting after Trevor's misadventure on Halloween. Cooper still wasn't sure what he'd said or done. If she didn't like him, why would she have shown up at his house to help him find the boy? But at that last minute next to her car, when he'd told her she was becoming important to him, something had set her off.

Was it that? Or was she just concerned about what Trevor would think if she came to yet another family event?

Taking a chance, he'd left a voice mail on her phone. She'd responded later with a voice mail of her own, saying she'd be happy to come. That had to be a sign of something good.

She arrived ten minutes after Grace's family did. Was that a ploy to avoid being alone with him? Cooper resolved not to dwell on it as he opened the pizza cartons and passed out the iced canned sodas he'd bought.

They sat around the kitchen table, eating on paper plates since most of the dishes were already packed. There were three different kinds of pizza to choose from and plenty of cold sodas. Maggie, an accomplished young cook, had even brought her special chocolate chip cookies for dessert.

"Have you started working on the sleigh yet?" Maggie asked Trevor, probably hoping she'd be asked to come and help.

"Not yet," Trevor said. "Abner needs to get more sandpaper and varnish from the hardware store. The varnish is a special kind. They use it to waterproof boats. It has to be ordered in. We'll need enough for at least three coats, and it has to dry and be sanded in between. It's going to be a lot of work."

His son's enthusiasm made Cooper smile. This was what he'd hoped for—if only it would last. Trevor was capable of losing interest and careening off in some other direction, not always a good one. All he could do was encourage the boy, provide what Trevor needed, and keep his fingers crossed.

Glancing to one side, he caught Jess watching him. Her lips twitched in a self-conscious little smile before she looked away. Cooper cursed silently. What he really wanted was to get the woman in his arms and take things from there. Why did she push him away every time he tried to get close to her?

"Will the sleigh be ready in time for the Christmas parade?" Maggie reached for a second slice of pepperoni pizza. "The parade's supposed to be on December twentieth, the same Saturday as the Cowboy Christmas Ball."

Sam groaned. "Enough about the parade, Maggie. I told you there's no time to put a parade together."

"There'll be time if we start on it soon, and if everybody helps. The high school band can march, the stores can make little floats, and Santa can ride in the sleigh. If there isn't any snow, we can put the sleigh on a hay wagon. We've even got horses to pull it, haven't we, Uncle Cooper?"

Cooper chuckled. "Leave me out of this, Maggie. The parade is up to your dad."

Sam sighed. "I know you want a parade, Maggie. But right now, we don't even have a Santa for the Christmas ball."

"What?" Maggie's jaw dropped. "What about Archie McNab? He's always done it, except for last year when he had that hip operation."

"Archie and his wife moved away last month. They left us his old Santa suit, but we don't have anybody to wear it."

"Well, you wore it last year. You could do it again."

"That's enough, Maggie. I said I'd only play Santa one time. I'm the mayor now. I've got other things to do. Christmas in Branding Iron will be just fine without a parade this year."

"But what about the Christmas ball? We'll need a Santa for the little kids."

"Well, maybe somebody will volunteer. You can be in charge of asking around. How's that?"

Maggie scowled at him over her can of root beer. "I love

you, Daddy. But you were a lot more fun before you got to be mayor."

"I love you, too, Maggie," Sam said. "But some things are what they are. You'll just have to accept that."

"No, I don't." Maggie spoke in a low voice, maybe to herself. But Cooper, seated next to her, heard her words. And so, evidently, did Jess. She gave the little girl a conspiratorial smile.

"Maggie," she said, "if you ever run for public office, like mayor, or even president, I promise you'll have my vote."

"And mine," Cooper said.

Sam reached for the last slice of supreme combo pizza. "So, Cooper, do you plan to do all the work on that house yourself?" he asked, changing the subject.

"Most of it, with some help from Trevor. He's going to learn a lot about remodeling—when he isn't in school or helping Abner with the sleigh. But it's going to take time, and I've got to keep up on my writing assignments. We may have to rough it for a while."

"And how about you, Trevor? Are you going to learn to ride those horses?"

"Maybe next spring after they're used to me. I'm not in a hurry."

"And Maggie says there's a dog, a border collie," Grace said. "Are you going to keep her?"

"I guess," Trevor said. "I've never had a dog, but she seems pretty smart. Maybe I can teach her to do tricks."

"If you need extra muscle to move your things, Cooper, I'll be right there," Sam said. "So when are you actually moving?"

"Our rent's paid here until the fifteenth. But we're hoping to get settled before the weather turns—and I know that Buck is eager to get this place fixed up for his bride. Right now, we're just waiting for Clem Porter to clear out and hoping he won't leave too much of a mess for us."

"The mother of one of my students cleans houses for extra money," Grace said. "With the holidays coming up, I'm sure she'd be glad for the work."

"That would be great," Cooper said. "She could clean the ranch house and then this house before Buck takes over."

"I'll give you her phone number and mention that I talked with you," Grace said. "Her name's Ruth McCoy."

"Thanks." Cooper passed around the last box of pizza. Things were falling into place. Even after the woman's name registered, and he realized who she must be, he refused to worry. Everything was going to be fine.

Grace, Sam, and Maggie had left, and Trevor was in Cooper's office, doing his homework. Jess would have left, too, but it seemed rude to leave her host alone to clean up. Without asking, she began to clear the table, stuffing the paper plates in the waste can and stacking the pizza boxes to be carried outside to the trash.

Cooper gave her a melting smile. "You don't need to help, but thanks anyway."

"It's an easy job—the least I could do after you were nice enough to invite me here."

"I always like having you around. But this time I confess that I had an ulterior motive."

"Oh?" Her defenses sprang to full alert.

"I've been wanting to talk to you." His words triggered a tick in her pulse. If he was going to tell her she was becoming important again, and maybe ask her out, or pry into her past, it was time to make a fast exit.

"About what?" she asked.

"It's just that I haven't asked you how Trevor is doing at school lately. Those two boys aren't bullying him, are they?"

Relief, tinged with disappointment, washed through her.

This was a safe subject. But had she really wanted to hear something else? Did she even know her own mind?

"Not that I know of," she replied. "In fact, I haven't seen those boys with Trevor at all. Maybe they're afraid he might go to the police if they bother him."

"So he's alone again?"

"It appears so. The teachers say he's no trouble. He sits in the back of the room and doesn't talk much—although he does answer questions and hands in his homework on time."

"What about the lunchroom?"

"I've checked when I was there, but I've never seen him. I think he's hiding out, maybe running over to that little five-and-dime across the street to buy snacks with his lunch money. I can't say I blame him. The lunchroom is where the pecking order gets set up, and you know how mean kids that age can be."

Cooper shook his head. "Actually, I don't. I was a big, confident kid, an athlete, and popular. I was never bullied or left to sit alone. That's just one reason I have a hard time relating to Trevor." His blue eyes, flecked with silver, studied her face. "What was it like for you?"

"I was quiet—I guess you'd call me a nerd. I didn't have many friends, but I didn't care. I spent most of my time with my nose in a book. So yes, I can relate to your son."

"Thanks for that." They were standing by the kitchen table, his big body looming over her. "I'd like to know more about you—a lot more. But I know better than to push. You're a very private person, Jess, and I'm learning to respect that. But I hope it doesn't mean we can't be friends."

Friends? Panic fluttered like a trapped insect against her ribs. First friends. Then what? When would the questions start? What would happen if she began to trust him—to trust a *journalist*? And how long could she hold out against his charm before he broke down the barriers that protected her and she told him everything?

It was time to make a fast escape.

She buttoned her wool cardigan against the chill and gathered up the stack of pizza boxes. "I'll just drop these in the trash can on my way out," she said.

"No, it's dark outside. Give me those. I'll take them and then walk you to your car."

"As I keep telling you, this is Branding Iron, not Seattle. I'll be fine."

She took a step toward the door. Moving into her path to take the boxes, he bumped her shoulder. The boxes fell out of her arms and scattered across the kitchen floor.

Reflexively, she dropped to her knees. "Sorry, I'll get them," she muttered.

"No, here—" He crouched beside her. When he reached for the same box as she did, their hands collided. Brief as it was, the contact of his skin with hers sent a sensual jolt through her body.

Had he felt it, too? One look into the blue eyes that locked with hers answered that question.

Her breath stopped as his free hand brushed her cheek. Jess knew she should draw back, but she found herself craving his touch, wanting more.

"Jess—" His lips formed her name, but the sound was blocked by a shout from the office down the hall.

"Hey, Dad, I can't get the printer to work. What's wrong with it?"

"I'll be right there, Trevor." He gathered the pizza boxes and laid them on the counter, then reached down to give Jess a hand up. His palm was cool and smooth, sending subtle quivers up her arm as he pulled her to her feet. For a beat too long, his clasp lingered. Feeling a mild surge of panic, she jerked away.

"I need to go," she said.

"Thanks for coming. I'll take the boxes out. Leave them. That's an order."

Jess hurried down the sidewalk to her car. The night breeze was cold through her sweater. But her face felt warm, almost hot. What might have happened if Trevor hadn't needed help?

She'd told herself that she was in control of her own emotions. But her sheer physical response to his touch had struck like a lightning bolt, leaving her helpless and confused.

As she drove home, dry leaves blowing against the windshield, she forced her thoughts away from what had just happened. Earlier, she'd been considering a vacation—something she needed more than ever. If she was to get away for the Christmas holidays, she would need to start lining up flight and hotel reservations. Tonight she would get on her computer and check for available destinations—Hawaii, maybe, or Costa Rica. The thought of lapping waves on tropical sands might even be enough to take her mind off Cooper.

She rounded the last corner and pulled her car up the driveway of the house with the giant dead cottonwood in the front yard. The tree's skeletal limbs, like bone-white fingers against the dark sky, swayed lightly in the wind.

The tree had been long dead when she bought the house. She'd checked on the cost of cutting it down and hauling away the mountain of wood, but the lowest bid had been more than a thousand dollars—money she still couldn't spare. So there it stood, looming like Godzilla over her small house.

As she climbed out of her car, she noticed the tan SUV with the sheriff's logo on the door parked alongside the curb. She recognized it as the vehicle Buck drove when he was working. But he didn't usually stop by to see Wynette when he was on duty. Was something wrong—some kind of emergency?

The front door was unlocked. Jess walked into the house to find Buck and Wynette together on the sofa, holding hands. Apart from the worried looks on their faces, everything appeared to be all right.

Seeing the couple together was always a pleasure—both of them blond and blue-eyed, so much alike that they could have been brother and sister. They would no doubt have beautiful children. And if the way they looked at each other was any indication, those children wouldn't be long in coming.

But tonight something was off. Buck's expression looked frayed, while Wynette appeared to be consoling him.

"Is everything all right?" Jess asked.

Buck answered with a ragged sigh. "I should probably say yes. But I'm not that good at walking away from my job after I've done what I can.

"Tonight I got a domestic call from the McCoy place, out past town. Ed was drinking, and Ruth was pretty badly beaten up—black eye, bloodied nose, and a dislocated shoulder. I called the paramedics for Ruth, cuffed Ed, and took him to jail. If it's like every other time, he'll sit there until Ruth comes in tomorrow, declines to press charges, and takes him home until the next time—if he doesn't kill her or send her to the ER first." Buck shook his head. "It just gets to me how folks who loved each other enough to get married could end up like that."

"Doesn't Ed have a job?" Jess asked. "How can he work without getting fired when these things happen?"

"Ed works in construction. His cousin Cecil is his boss, and evidently the two are close. When Ed gets out of jail, Cecil will put him right back to work."

"What about the children?" Jess knew the family had two little girls and an older boy by a different father—that boy would be Skip McCoy.

"The girls are all right," Buck said. "The boy's about fourteen—he said he'd take care of them till their mother gets home. He seems like a responsible kid, but he's got a lot on his shoulders. When he gets big enough to defend his mother against Ed, anything could happen."

"What about Social Services? Could they help?" Jess asked.

"I suggested that to Ruth. But she won't hear of it. She's scared they might take her kids. What she needs to do is have the bastard put away and file for divorce, then get some help. But that won't happen. The same thing was going on when Sam was sheriff. It never seems to change."

And it wouldn't, Jess thought—not until Ed McCoy did something even worse. She'd seen similar things in the past. And she didn't want to recall how one situation had ended. The memory would fuel her nightmares for the rest of her life.

Two weeks later

The yellow school bus paused outside the gate long enough to let Trevor off, then moved on down the narrow dirt road. From the porch, Cooper watched his son trudge up the long driveway, his body leaning into the wind, his school pack straining his thin shoulders.

Was Trevor happy here on the ranch—or at least happier than he would have been living in town? It appeared so. But he was still friendless at school. Cooper's occasional check-ins with Jess and with Trevor's teachers confirmed that the boy was a confirmed loner, dressing in black, his hair barely trimmed to regulation length for school. His grades were decent, but for a lonely boy, grades were no substitute for friends.

The dog came around the house. Catching Trevor's scent, she was off like a ball of black-and-white fire, running to greet her new favorite person. Cooper had to smile as Trevor stopped to pet and hug her. For a boy who hadn't been around animals, he'd bonded quickly with Glory as well as the horses. He hadn't asked to ride the big, gentle beasts, but he petted and talked to them when he brought their hay and water in the morning. It was a beginning.

"Hi, Dad." Trevor mounted the porch steps with Glory at his heels. A fresh bruise darkened his left cheekbone.

"What happened to your face?" Cooper asked.

He shrugged. "Nothing much. We played dodgeball in phys ed and I caught a hard one. Can I go over to Abner's now? I did my homework in class."

"Fine. But we've been invited to Grace and Sam's for spaghetti tonight. They'll be sitting down at six thirty, so you'll need to be home by six to clean up. Put on those old coveralls Abner lent you so you don't get varnish on your clothes."

"Right." Trevor was off to his room. Cooper wondered about the bruise—he didn't buy the dodgeball story. If Jess showed up tonight, maybe he could take her aside and ask her about it. Not that he was likely to see her. She'd been making herself scarce since the night of the pizza party.

"'Bye, Dad." Trevor was out the door, headed for Abner's place, an easy walk from here. Cooper called the dog to him so she wouldn't follow. "Watch the time," he called out. "Remember you need to be back here by six."

With his son gone, Cooper went back into the house to spend what he hoped would be a couple of productive hours working on the profile piece he was doing for *Sports Illustrated*, based on a phone interview with a retired NBA great.

The house was looking better, he thought. With Trevor's help and some muscle from Sam, he'd managed to paint most of the walls and haul away the worn-out carpets to expose the hardwood underneath. Everywhere he looked, there was work to be done. But right now he needed to earn a living.

Sitting at the computer, he opened up his notes and the introduction he'd started and tried to focus on his work. But his thoughts kept wandering to Jess and the elusive secrets she kept hidden behind the wall she'd built against the world.

Where had he seen that haunting face before? Even her name had a familiar ring to it.

Bringing up a search engine, he entered her first and last names. The results yielded several possibilities—a romance author—not her—and three obituaries for elderly women. There was nothing here that could be of any help.

He tried another search, adding the few things he knew about her. She had a degree in psychology, and she'd mentioned she was from Chicago, which might or might not be true. Either way, nothing of use came up. Cooper was about to give up and get back to work when another idea struck him—a good one this time.

Fingers flying, he typed a new query in the search window: *Texas Education Agency.* When the home page came up, he found the tab marked *Personnel Directory,* clicked on it, and scrolled down the long list.

Bingo. There was her name, with a tiny, blurred photo next to it confirming her identity. Cooper's pulse kicked up a notch as he began to read.

> *Jessica Marie Graver, Youth Guidance*
> *Counselor, Branding Iron School District. B.A.*
> *University of Chicago, 1982. M.A. pending.*
> *Employment history: U.S. Federal Bureau of*
> *Investigation, 1983-1994.*

Cooper's mouth went dry as he re-read the entry. Trevor had said that Jess had *cop* written all over her. Cooper had dismissed his son's words as blowing air. But the boy's instincts had been right on. That Jess had been a cop was enough of a surprise. But *FBI*? For eleven years?

This couldn't be real.

"Dad, I'm home. I'll be ready in a minute." Trevor's voice carried down the hall from the living room. Cooper shut down his computer. If Jess had wanted people to know about her past, she would have said something. For now, until he knew more, he would keep her secret. But he wouldn't be satisfied until he'd learned the whole truth.

When Cooper drove up to Grace's house and parked at the curb, the first thing he noticed was Jess's silver-gray Taurus parked across the street.

She was here. But this was no time to put her on alert about what he knew. The full story would have to come from her, and that wouldn't happen until she learned to trust him.

He walked into the house with Trevor, carrying the double-chocolate-chip ice cream he'd brought for dessert. Grace and Jess were in the kitchen. He could hear the low, muffled murmur of their voices.

Maggie had welcomed them at the door. "Put this in the freezer, please, Maggie," Cooper said to her.

"Sure. We don't want it to melt." Her green eyes sparkled as she took the carton and danced off to the kitchen with it. Cooper knew that look. His niece was cooking up some kind of surprise.

Sam was watching a college basketball game on TV. Trevor joined him. After a few minutes, so did Cooper, although it was an effort to concentrate on the game. Anytime now, Jess would come out of that kitchen. How would he look at her now? What would he say to her?

How would he keep her from sensing that something had changed between them?

Did Grace know about her friend's past? The question rose in his mind as they took their seats around the table. Grace had lived with Jess for nearly a year before her marriage. Surely the two of them would have shared some secrets.

But what if Grace didn't know? For now it would be safer not to alert anyone to his discovery.

They bowed their heads over the blessing and passed around dishes of steaming pasta and meat sauce, crisp green salad, and buttery garlic bread.

Cooper stole glances at Jess, who was seated across from him, next to Maggie. She looked beautiful tonight, in a jade-green cashmere sweater that matched the polished stones in her earlobes.

Jessica Graver, former FBI agent. He could still scarcely believe what he'd read. What had she done in those years with the bureau? Why had she left what had to be a well-paid position for a job with a small, poor school district in the middle of nowhere? Was she in danger? Was this something like witness protection? The urge to corner her and demand answers was driving him crazy. But unless Jess chose to offer information, her past was none of his business.

By now the plates were empty. Once they were cleared away, it was time for ice cream, served in pretty glass bowls with sturdy stems.

As spoons were digging in for the first bite, Maggie stood up and clapped her hands for attention. "Listen, everyone," she said. "I have an announcement to make."

Her parents exchanged puzzled glances as she lifted a manila folder from the seat of a chair. "This is for the mayor of Branding Iron, who just happens to be my dad," she said, opening the folder to show a sheaf of papers inside—lined pages containing what looked like signatures.

"Mister Mayor," she continued, sounding very grown-up, "my friends and I collected more than three hundred names—school kids, parents, and businesspeople—all in favor of having a Christmas parade this year. To get things started, on the last page is a list of people who've signed up to help."

She thrust the folder at her father. "I'm giving you this petition to show the town council. We want our parade!"

In the hush that followed, Cooper surveyed the faces around the table—Sam looking floored, Grace showing pride in her daughter, Jess mildly amused, and Trevor amazed.

Sam recovered his voice. "Well, Maggie, if the council approves, you've got yourself a parade. But it's going to take a lot of work, and we still don't have a Santa Claus. I'm putting you in charge. So get busy."

Chapter 7

"**I**'ll walk you to your car, Jess."

Cooper's offer no longer caught Jess by surprise. Knowing better than to argue, she gave him a shrug. "Why not? I'll be fine, but it's easier than trying to talk you out of escorting me."

"Hey," he joked. "You never know when some bogeyman is going to jump out of the shrubbery and grab you. Better safe than sorry."

"If it happens, you can say, 'I told you so'—before I deck him with my unarmed combat training."

Had she said the wrong thing? The startled expression that flashed across his face was swiftly replaced with a smile. But Jess couldn't help wondering what he'd read into her accidental slip of the tongue. She would have to watch herself around him, or the next thing she knew, he would be firing questions at her like the journalist he was.

He lifted her trench coat off the rack and held it for her. "Good night, Grace," she called back toward the kitchen. "Loved the spaghetti. Next get-together is on me."

The reply from the kitchen was muffled by the sound of

the TV sports commentator doing the game wrap-up. "I'll be going home soon, too," Cooper said. "But I won't be able to drag Trevor away from the TV till the post-game show's over."

She buttoned her coat against the wind as they stepped out onto the porch. If Cooper was cold in his woolen shirt and vest, he didn't complain. "Wasn't Maggie something tonight?" she said, making conversation as he guided her past the crack on the sidewalk. "I can't believe she's only seven. That girl's a natural politician. And it looks like we've got ourselves a Christmas parade. Do you plan to help out?"

"Maybe with the horses and sleigh. How about you?"

"Not me," she said. "I've got plans that involve sun, lapping waves, and sparkling sands." They had reached her car. Next door, the lights were on. Wynette's car was parked in the driveway behind Buck's pickup. "Of course, I'll have to work my vacation around Wynette's wedding," Jess said. "I wouldn't miss that for anything. At least, with her big family close by, I won't have to worry about being a bridesmaid."

He studied the western sky, where sooty clouds, blown by the wind, were rolling over the horizon. "You'll be alone after she leaves," he said. "If you need help with anything, or just want company, don't hesitate to call me. No strings attached. I mean it."

"You mean if I hear a noise under my bed and think it might be that bogeyman you mentioned?"

He shook his head and opened her car door. "Get going, you stubborn lady. There's a big storm moving in. You need to be safely home before it hits."

As Jess drove away, she could see him in her rearview mirror, standing on the dimly lit curb, watching her go. At least he hadn't asked her out for coffee this time. That should've come as a relief. So why did she feel let down?

She'd taken extra pains with her hair, makeup, and clothes

this evening. Was it Cooper she'd meant to impress? But who else?

Idiot! She gave herself a mental slap. The farther she stayed from Cooper Chapman, journalist, the safer her hard-won privacy would be. She knew the man was trouble. So why did her pulse do a little polka step when she was with him?

But that was only a natural reaction to Cooper's masculinity, she told herself. It was hormones, nothing more. And she couldn't let those hormones control her actions.

By the time she made it across town to her home, the wind had risen to a howling gale. The clouds had moved in, roiling across the sky. Guided by the porch light she'd left on, she parked in the driveway and opened the car door. The wind yanked the door out of her hand, almost snapping it off the hinges before she wrestled it closed. Gripping her purse, she staggered to the house. On the porch, she unlocked the door, stumbled inside, and locked it behind her.

There'd been no tornado warnings—Jess had learned to check the weather each day. But this storm was a wild one. Thank goodness she was safe at home and not on the road.

Wynette would still be at the new place with Buck. Earlier, she'd said something about painting the kitchen cabinets. She'd probably stay put until the storm passed, or most likely, all night.

The hour was still early, but she was cold and tired. Bed sounded like a great idea. After changing into her flannel pajamas, she checked the windows and doors, then crawled beneath the covers. Wind howled around the house, sounding like a pack of hungry wolves. Hail battered the windowpanes.

Jess's bed was comfortable. The down quilt bundled her like a warm cocoon. But in the dark, with the storm outside, the awareness of how alone she was triggered a melancholy mood. A night like this was made for snuggling—safe in the arms of someone who loved her. But that idea was nothing but an idle fantasy.

She'd had a few casual relationships in college, but once she'd joined the FBI, she'd been totally involved in her work—as well as being frequently on the move. And since leaving the bureau, even with Grace trying to push her into Cooper's arms, she was too broken for romance. But tonight, the thought of taking refuge against that big, strong body triggered an ache inside her.

Don't be a fool. Go to sleep.

She closed her eyes and tried to picture herself on a tropical beach with the waves lapping at her feet. Lapping . . . lapping . . .

At last, with the wind wailing outside, she sank into slumber.

By the time Cooper and Trevor drove through the ranch gate and up to the house, the wind was whipping the tall Lombardy poplars and battering the windshield with hail and debris. They found Glory, who usually spent her nights in the barn, huddled on the porch, damp and shivering. "She must've been wondering why her people hadn't shown up," Trevor said.

"Take her inside and get her warm," Cooper told his son. "She can stay in the house if you want her to. I'll go and check on the horses."

Cooper found his flashlight in the glove box. Fighting against the wind, he made it to the barn. The barn door had come unlatched and was banging in the wind. The horses were in their stalls, restless and snorting but safe.

Cooper calmed the animals, made sure they had food and water and that the door was securely latched. Then, giving himself a future reminder to check on them before leaving the ranch again, he staggered back to the house.

The light was on in the living room. Trevor had lit the wood in the fireplace and was rubbing the dog dry with a towel. Glory was enjoying the attention. Her eyes were closed, her feathery tail thumping on the hardwood floor.

"Do you think Abner's all right?" Trevor asked.

"I imagine he is. But if you're worried, you've got his phone number. You could try calling him."

"Good idea." Leaving the dog, he crossed the room to the landline phone mounted on the wall next to the kitchen. Lifting the receiver, he put it to his ear and frowned. "Something's wrong. The phone's gone dead."

Cooper took the receiver and listened. "The line must be down. Probably the wind. At least we've got pow—"

The house went dark. He bit back a curse. "Well, there we go. We'll just have to wait until it's fixed." He turned on the flashlight he'd carried in from the Jeep and gave it to Trevor. "Here, you can use this to get ready for bed. I'll come in and get it later. Let's hope the batteries last."

"What about Abner?"

"Any man who's lived here for as long as he has will know what to do in a storm. He'll be all right. We can check on him in the morning."

Trevor's flashlight beam, with the dog following, vanished down the hall. Watching him go, Cooper swallowed the tightness in his throat. Underneath the layer of teenage rebellion, his boy was a decent, caring person. His concern for Abner was a sign of that. As a father, Cooper could only hope to protect and guide his son through the challenging years ahead.

Fifteen minutes later, when Cooper came to get the flashlight, he found Trevor asleep with Glory curled next to his legs. For a moment, he stood looking down at them. Then he walked softly out of the room.

* * *

The crash that awakened Jess was like a bomb going off. First there was an ear-splitting boom, then the sound of splintering and cracking above her head. As the ceiling began to sag, she bolted out of bed and raced for the front door, grabbing her coat on the way out. Was it an earthquake? A tornado, or some kind of wreckage from the air, crashing into the house?

Only as she cleared the porch, the ground icy beneath her bare feet, did she see what had happened. The wind had broken off a huge limb from the dead cottonwood in the yard. The limb had crashed into the roof, right above her bedroom. A shudder passed through Jess's body. With a heavier limb or a different angle, she could have been crushed.

As the shock wore off, she assessed her situation. Could she go back inside—certainly not to stay but to get what she needed? What if the limb were to shift or the ceiling collapse? What if the tree itself were to topple in the wind?

Her car, parked in the driveway, was all right so far. If she could move it out of the way, it would provide warmth and shelter. But the keys were in her purse, in the bedroom. She also needed shoes and some clothes to put on.

The entire street was dark. A power line must've gone down somewhere, and probably phone lines as well. So there was no way to call for help.

The fallen limb appeared stable, although there was no way to tell for certain. She would hurry into the house, grab the basic things she needed, and drive to a safe place. That was plan enough for a start. There would be time in the morning to call the insurance company and decide whether it would be safe to rescue the things inside.

Clutching her coat around her, she hurried inside and down the hall. The house was mostly dark, but she knew her way. Wynette's bedroom, at the far end, appeared to be untouched, but as Jess entered her own room, she could hear what sounded like bits of plaster falling onto the quilt. Her purse and the clothes she'd worn last night were on a chair, her shoes on the floor nearby. She grabbed everything and rushed out of the room just as a hunk of loose plaster crashed onto the bed. Heart pounding, she fled back to the living room, dressed, and after locking the door behind her, made a fast escape to her car. The dashboard clock read 2:08 a.m.

Safe for the moment, she drove toward the main part of town, hoping to find a place offering shelter and a phone. But the power appeared to be out everywhere. A police cruiser passed her going the opposite direction, lights flashing, siren blaring. Someone was in trouble. No help for her.

So what now? She had less than a quarter tank of gas in her car and couldn't fill the tank while the power was out. She couldn't just keep driving to keep warm, and she didn't relish spending the night in a cold parked car, especially with no bathroom facilities nearby.

She could go to Grace and Sam's or join Buck and Wynette. But their power was out, too. She'd be disturbing them for nothing. Cooper, however, lived outside of town. There was a chance his place still had power along with a working phone and computer to report the damage. He'd urged her to contact him any time she needed help. Well, she needed help now.

Praying there would be no trees down, she headed south on the road to his ranch.

She spotted the turnoff, where the For Sale sign had hung. However, as she drove along the bumpy dirt road, there were no lights anywhere. It appeared that the power was out here, too. But if she were to turn around and head back to town, she could run out of gas on the way. She was out of choices.

As she passed the ranch gate and swung the headlights toward the house, she saw the flicker of a light. Cooper stood in the open doorway holding a flashlight. As he recognized her car, he came sprinting across the yard. He was fully dressed. Maybe he'd stayed up to keep an eye on things at the ranch.

As he came up to the car, she lowered her side window. "Jess? Are you all right?" he asked.

"I'm all right, but my house isn't." She told him what had happened.

"Good Lord, you could've been killed!" He opened the door and lent his hand as she braced herself against the wind. Swaying and stumbling, they made it to the porch.

"Sorry about the power," he said. "The phone lines are down, too. We're living like pioneers out here."

"It's the same all over town. I was hoping your place would have light. But either way, I'm afraid you're stuck with me. My car is almost out of gas."

His laughter was deep and mellow. "Well, then, I'd say this is my lucky night. Come on in."

He opened the door. She was met with a rush of cheery warmth and soft amber light from the smoldering fireplace.

"Here. Take the chill off while I build up the fire." Cooper tossed her a soft woolen blanket before he added another log and a few more sticks of kindling. Flames caught the dry wood, which soon became a crackling blaze. Curled on the sofa, Jess snuggled into the blanket, basking in the warmth of the fire.

"How are you doing now?" Cooper asked.

"Heavenly. Thank you."

"Then how about some hot coffee? The electric machine is out but I can make it cowboy-style on the gas stove." He picked up a battered and burned metal coffeepot. "This came with the house. When I worked on a ranch one summer, the cook made coffee in a pot like this. It just needs to boil for a while." He measured the coffee and water and set the pot on the gas flame.

"No filter?" she commented from the sofa.

"This is cowboy coffee. Filters are for sissies." He settled himself next to her on the sofa—close enough to talk but not close enough to invade her private space.

"I'm sorry about your house," he said. "That old tree should have been taken out a long time ago. How bad is the damage?"

"If it was a car, it would be totaled. I'll have to see it in the daylight to be sure, but it looks like the roof will have to be rebuilt, and at least the ceiling in my room. If we get rain or snow in the night, there could be water damage, too. Thank heaven I've got insurance. But all that's going to take time, especially if we have a bad winter. Meanwhile, the place won't be fit to live in."

"I suppose Wynette can just move into the new house early. But what about you?"

Jess sighed, overwhelmed by the way her life had turned upside-down. "I'll look for a rental. That'll be my next priority after I call the insurance company."

The pot on the stove was boiling fiercely. Cooper rose, set out two thick stoneware cups, and filled each one using a wire strainer to keep out the grounds. "Out on the range they didn't bother to strain the coffee—or if they did, they poured it through a bandana. Do you like it with cream and sugar? I forgot to ask. And I think we've got some Oreos in the cupboard if you're hungry."

"Just a dab of milk, thanks. And I'll pass on the Oreos."

He handed her the cup. The coffee was bracingly strong, with an earthy taste that she hadn't expected. But it wasn't bad, and it did bring her back to life.

He stood at the end of the sofa, sipping from his cup. "Why not stay here with us? We've got a spare bedroom."

Jess would have choked on her coffee if she hadn't stopped herself. "You're joking."

"Think about it. Finding a new place might take time—along with the hassle of filling out an application and paying a deposit—and more hassle when your house is ready and you move out. I know Grace and Sam would take you, but they only have three bedrooms, and one of those is Sam's office. Wynette would probably take you, too. But do you really want to put a wet blanket on her and Buck's privacy? We've got four bedrooms. I wouldn't charge you, but if you wanted to bring home a few groceries and help out around the place, that would be fine."

Jess's head was swimming. So many decisions to make. "But what would people say? The gossips could claim that we were shacking up."

"Not with Trevor here. He'll make a fine chaperone."

"I don't think your son even likes me, Cooper." She set her cup on the coffee table, her hand unsteady.

"He'll learn. I, for one, happen to like you a lot. But I would promise to be a perfect gentleman. Think about it. You can let me know in the morning."

Jess scrambled for a reply. She couldn't just move in with Cooper and put down roots. But she did need shelter until she could find something suitable. "That won't be necessary," she said. "I'll start looking for a rental tomorrow. Until I find one, I hope you won't mind my camping here—on a temporary basis."

"Whatever works for you. The invitation stands. Now, what do you say we get some rest before the sun comes up."

"Good idea," she said. "I'll take this comfy sofa."

"I was thinking of taking that spot myself and offering you my bed. If Trevor wakes up early and sees you, that might give you both a start. But if he sees me first, I'll have a chance to explain. Either way, with the storm outside, I don't plan on sleeping much."

He was making sense. And even with the coffee in her system, Jess could feel the weight of exhaustion. "Take the blanket," he said. "First door on your left. Bathroom's across the hall. Take the flashlight. I'll be fine."

Cooper's room was plain and neat, the bed made up and unslept in. Cooper must have planned to be up all night, keeping an eye on his property during the storm. That would explain his being dressed when she'd arrived.

Leaving her shoes next to the bed, Jess wrapped herself in the blanket and lay down on the coverlet. She hadn't expected to sleep, but as the night's fear and tension fell away, she began to relax. She was safe and warm, with a roof over her head and a man nearby who would protect her. Little by little, she eased into sleep.

By the time the darkness began to fade, the storm had passed. Not long after first light, the power came back on. Cooper, who had fallen asleep on the sofa, was awakened by the blare of the radio from Trevor's room. The sound stopped as abruptly as it had begun, probably because Trevor had punched the power button and gone back to sleep. Since it was Saturday, he no doubt figured he was entitled.

As Cooper rubbed the sleep from his eyes, Glory came down the hall and walked to the front door.

Cooper pushed to his feet and crossed the room to let her out. Only then did he remember Jess. Had the radio awakened her? Was she even here, or had he dreamed the whole crazy episode of her showing up?

A glance out of the front window confirmed that Jess's Taurus was parked in the yard.

At least, now that the power was on, he could use the coffeemaker. He brewed two cups and carried one down the hall on the chance that Jess was awake and unsure whether to show herself.

The bedroom door was closed. He rapped lightly and heard her muffled response. "Was that a 'come in'?" he asked.

She opened the door, dressed in her rumpled slacks and

green sweater, her tousled hair framing her face. Her sleepy eyes and damp, swollen lips gave her a meltingly sexy look. But there wasn't much he could do about that.

"Hi." He handed her the steaming cup. "Did you manage to get some rest?"

"Enough." She took a sip. "Thanks. This is better than that cowboy brew you gave me last night."

"I can improve on that. Come on in the kitchen, and I'll rustle you up some toast and eggs."

She hesitated. "What about Trevor?"

"He's still asleep. We'll have to wing it."

"Whatever." She handed him the empty cup. "Don't bother with the eggs. I'll need a minute in your bathroom. Then I want to go into town, look at the damage to my house, and maybe grab a few things I need. Then I should get in touch with the insurance company if they're open on Saturday." Her breath caught. "Oh—and Wynette. She'll be in for a shock. But at least her things should be safe to move."

"Understood. But I'm going with you. You're not going into that house alone."

She frowned. "All right. But I wish you'd get over the notion that it's your duty to protect me. I can take care of myself."

Cooper chose to ignore her this time—even though, going on what he knew about her, she was probably right. "Go ahead and wash up," he said. "I'll let Trevor know where we're going and meet you outside. We'll take my Jeep. It's got plenty of gas in the tank."

In the bathroom, Jess splashed her face, rinsed her mouth, and finger-combed her hair. That would have to do for now. With luck she'd be able to get her toiletries out of her house. Or, if that failed, she had credit cards. She could always buy what she needed.

With winter coming, replacing her roof and repairing the ceilings could take until spring. Meanwhile, she might or might not be able to live in the house. But at least no one had been hurt when the limb fell.

Outside, the morning was clear but cold. Cooper was waiting for her by his Jeep. He could be right about her needing somebody with her. If she went into the damaged house alone, she could get injured or trapped, and no one would be there to help her.

But why did he have to be so high-handed about it? At least the man could've asked her if she wanted him along. She was getting tired of his treating her like a helpless female. The next time he did it, she'd be sorely tempted to tell him off.

"Ready?" He held the door for her.

"Did you talk to Trevor?"

"I did. He was half asleep. But at least he should be aware that you're around. He said something about going to Abner's to work on the sleigh, so that should keep him out of trouble."

"Let's go." She fastened her seat belt. "I'm not looking forward to seeing my house, but we might as well get it over with."

"Do you want to tell Wynette first?" he asked her as they drove onto the paved highway.

"It's early yet, and she works the late shift at the bakery today. Let's go to the house first. If I've seen it, I can tell her what to expect."

As they drove into town, Jess could see other damage from the wind. Several big trees had toppled, including one of the eighty-year-old spruces in the town park. Power and phone crews were working on the lines.

"Do you think Sam and Grace's house is all right—and Buck's next door?" she asked.

"Let's hope so. At least they don't have any big trees close by. But Sam must've had a busy night. Getting the crews here early would've been part of his job."

Every other street seemed to be blocked by fallen debris and work crews, but eventually they found their way to Jess's house. The sight that met her eyes made her gasp. "Oh . . . oh, no!"

The limb lay across the smashed roof, as it had when she'd last been here. But there was even more damage now. Sometime after she'd left, the entire tree had toppled. The trunk lay across the lawn, with the limbs resting on the solid cinder block wall that separated her property from her neighbors'. The neighbors' yard was littered with broken twigs and branches, but at least their house had been spared.

"Where is everybody?" Jess looked up and down the street. "No one's working here."

"This is private property," Cooper said. "You'll need to get in touch with your insurance company to arrange the work. I've got a new digital camera in my glove box. They'll want some photos of this."

"Thanks. I'll look around for the best way inside." Jess opened the door of the Jeep and climbed out.

"Hang on," he said. "Don't go anywhere without me. It isn't safe."

He was doing it again—treating her like a child!

Mildly annoyed, Jess ignored his warning and strode toward the house. She needed a few things from her room and from the bathroom. And she didn't need Cooper bossing her.

A heavy limb, still attached to the trunk, lay across the front porch, partially blocking the door. But it appeared that if she could squeeze around it, she should be able to unlock the door, push it inward, and get into the house. Jess had left her purse in the car, putting her housekey in her pocket.

She'd also stuffed a folded plastic garbage bag in her jacket to hold whatever she could salvage. After squeezing under the limb, she used her key to unlock the door, pushed it open, and stepped into the house.

The living room had an ugly crack across the ceiling and a sprinkle of plaster dust on the dark rug but was otherwise intact. So was the kitchen, except for a vent fan hanging loose by its wires. The serious damage was to her bedroom, the bathroom, and the hallway, where the huge limb had struck. Looking past it, she could look into the open door of the room at the end of the hall—Wynette's room, which appeared undisturbed. Good news, at least, for her friend.

But enough looking. She needed to go into the rooms, grab what she needed, and get out. Pocketing the key and opening the plastic bag, she ventured into the bathroom. Here, most of the ceiling had fallen to the floor. But the medicine cabinet above the basin, which held her toothbrush and comb, her makeup, and other needs, was all right. She scooped everything into the bag and crossed the hall to her bedroom to get some clothes and shoes. The bed was covered with chunks of fallen plaster. She could see the end of a branch poking through a hole in the ceiling. But nothing more was happening. She would be all right.

She was pulling underthings out of a dresser drawer when she heard an ominous groan overhead and the sound of something shifting. She froze, ready to flee to safety, but when she heard nothing more, she moved to the closet. She was rummaging for a second pair of shoes when she heard the groan again, like the sound of timbers shifting overhead.

"Jess! Get out!"

In the next instant, Cooper had seized her, hooking her waist with his powerful arm, dragging her roughly out of the room and along the hallway into the living room. Glancing up at the ceiling, she could see the crack getting wider. Saucer-sized chunks of plaster were crashing to the floor.

The front door was open, as she'd left it, but the exit was blocked by the heavy limb that had fallen across the porch. There was no time to get safely past it. Cooper pulled her into the sturdy frame of the door, protecting her with his body as the ceiling broke. Hunks of plaster came crashing to the floor.

They stood in the doorway, his arms around her, his back to the room. As the plaster dust settled around them, he glared down at her. "Damn it!" His voice shook. "You could have been killed! Why didn't you listen and wait for me?"

Jess's anger surged, drowning fear and gratitude. "Because everything you tell me sounds like an order—and I'm tired of being treated like a child. Why do you always—"

"Be quiet, Jess."

He kissed her.

Chapter 8

Cooper's kiss went through Jess like black coffee laced with moonshine—strong, hot, and bittersweet. Caught by surprise, she went rigid, then slowly melted against him. Deep in her body, arousal woke and stirred, firing her pulse and sending desire coursing through her veins.

This is wrong. It shouldn't be happening. Caution blared the warning in her head. She knew she should pay attention, but his firm, seeking mouth on hers felt so good . . . so good . . .

Only when she felt the probing flick of his tongue did she jerk herself back to reality. Her hands pushed against his chest, breaking the kiss and opening space between them. Breathless, she struggled to find her voice.

"Stop! We can't do this!"

"At least not while your house is falling down around us."

"You're not hearing me. I mean not anywhere, anytime. We can't do this."

His expression hardened as his arms dropped away. "We can talk later. Right now, what we need is to get out of here."

Crouching, he ducked under the limb and reached back to help her.

"My things—" The bag of possessions she'd salvaged had been in the bedroom when he'd grabbed her. She made a move to go back inside.

"Don't be a dunce. They're buried. You can have the workmen find them."

"You're doing it again—treating me like a child!" She squeezed past the limb on her own and stood facing him on the porch. Both of them were covered with plaster dust. "Besides, what about Wynette? Her wedding dress is in there, in her closet."

"That end of the house looks all right. Buck can help her clear it out. Come on, let's dust ourselves off and go find them."

He lent her his handkerchief to brush the worst of the chalky dust from her hair and clothes and from his back, which had taken the worst of it when the ceiling collapsed. Neither of them spoke about what had just happened. It was too new, too raw—and, as Jess knew, it couldn't be allowed to continue.

They found Buck and Wynette at their new home. Wynette was horrified when she heard the news. "Heavens, Jess, you could have died when that limb fell. And then you went back into the house. I can't believe you were crazy enough to do that."

Wynette was worried about her wedding gown. But after Buck offered to go in by the room's safer back window and retrieve the treasured gown, her laptop, some clothes, and anything else she might need, she managed to calm down.

"At least I can move in here early," she said. "But what about you, Jess? You'd be welcome to stay with us, except that . . ." She gave Buck a sidelong glance. "We only have one bed and not even a couch yet."

"Don't worry about it. I'll figure something out." After that kiss, Jess certainly wouldn't commit to moving in with Cooper. Not even with Trevor in the house. There was always a motel. She could use her planned vacation money to pay for it. But the nearest one was in Cottonwood Springs, an hour away. She would have to commute for work and to check on her house.

Blast!

Leaving Wynette and Buck, they headed back to the ranch. This would be their best chance to talk privately and for Jess to say what needed to be said.

She cleared her throat. "You know that after what happened, I can't stay with you."

At least he didn't need to ask what she meant. "I didn't plan for that kiss to happen. But it did, and I enjoyed it. I had the impression that you enjoyed it, too. Can you honestly deny that?"

She didn't reply.

"This is no time for evasions, Jess."

She exhaled. "All right. It didn't exactly leave me cold. But that's part of the reason I can't stay. I have my life ordered the way I want it—no strings, no relationships, just me doing things my way."

"And I'm threatening to change that? Change can be good. But if that's not what you want, I can promise not to lay a lustful hand on you."

"Fine. But there's also Trevor. I know you moved here to give him a new start. He needs his father. And if I stay, he'll resent me even more than he already does."

"He doesn't know you. Give him a chance."

Again, Jess didn't answer him. He was hacking away at her defenses with a battle-ax.

"Let's say you leave today. What will you do?" he asked.

"I'll check the notices in the post office and library.

Maybe somebody needs a roommate, or would be willing to rent out a room in their basement. I could even put up a notice of my own."

"And while you're looking, you could sleep in your car, or on a bench in the park. Give yourself a break, Jess. And don't insult me by saying you're afraid of what might happen here. I'm capable of controlling myself—at least as capable as you are."

Those last words stung as she remembered her flaming hot response to his kiss. "All right," she said. "But I mean to move out from under your roof as soon as I can find a place. And meanwhile, I'll expect to earn my keep by working. No charity. Are we square?"

"Square." He gave her a nod, then swung the Jeep through the ranch gate and stopped next to her car.

"One more thing, Cooper," she said, as he opened the driver's side door.

"What's that?" Suspicion flashed across his face.

"Nothing. I just wanted to say thank you. I mean it."

Forty-five minutes later, Cooper stood on the porch and watched her drive away. She'd used his phone to call her insurance agency. The agent had promised to have an investigator at the house within twenty-four hours. After emailing him Cooper's photos, she'd cleaned herself up as best she could, eaten a quick peanut butter sandwich, and set out on a shopping expedition to the mall in Cottonwood Springs. "Don't wait supper for me," she'd said as she strode out the door. "I've got a long list of things to buy."

"Just don't forget to put gas in your car. You should be able to make it to that station on the main highway."

"I won't forget, Cooper. Remember, I'm a big girl. I've been taking care of myself for a long time, so stop acting like you're my father."

"Got it. I'll do my best." Reminding himself that she was a former FBI agent should help, Cooper told himself.

He'd wished her luck and waved her off as she climbed in her car and pulled away. Independence was riveted into Jess's nature. He was getting used to that. But he wouldn't mind having her lean on him once in a while.

Still struggling against the memory of that searing kiss, Cooper went back into the house. Trevor had been gone when he and Jess had returned from town. A box of Cap'n Crunch and an empty cereal bowl on the counter gave evidence that he'd eaten breakfast and gone to Abner's place.

Glory had followed Cooper into the kitchen. She nosed his hand, wanting to be petted. He scratched her ears. "Looks like it's just you and me for the next few hours," he muttered. "Let's hope I can use the time to get some writing done."

But writing wasn't in the cards today. He'd no sooner seated himself at his computer than he realized he needed to get the spare room ready for Jess. Right now it was little more than storage space for boxed books and other odds and ends. Clem Porter had left furniture in the house. Most of it was junk, which Cooper had paid to have hauled away. But he'd kept a few good pieces, like the cherrywood bedroom set—a full-sized bed frame and matching mirrored dresser— that he'd stored in the spare room. By a stroke of luck, the mattress was in its original plastic wrapper, which had kept it clean underneath. Cooper had plenty of spare bedding, also boxed and stored. All he needed to do was clear out the boxes, set up the dresser and bed, and find some extra sheets and blankets, which he had somewhere. Items like curtains and rugs could wait. If Jess found another place to stay, she might only be here a day or two.

Do I want her to stay—with all the complications that her being here would involve?

Maybe, for now, that question was best left unanswered.

Cooper had the room set up and was rummaging through boxes for a spare mattress pad when he heard a knock at the door and a welcoming *woof* from Glory—a signal that the visitor was someone the dog knew.

But the man standing on the porch, a rangy Clint Eastwood type dressed in worn but well-made work clothes, was a stranger to Cooper.

"Is there something I can do for you?" Cooper had lived in the city too long to trust every person who came to his door.

The stranger smiled. He had startling blue eyes in a face burnished by sun and wind. "I take it you're Cooper Chapman. I'm Judd Rankin, one of your neighbors. You can call me Judd." He extended a hand, which Cooper accepted. His grip was strong, his palm callused and leathery.

"Is something wrong?" Cooper asked.

"Not at all. I was talking to Clem Porter before he left, and he mentioned that you might be interested in leasing out your pastureland. I've got cows that need some fresh winter forage." He paused. "Clem said you are new to ranching. But no worries there. I'd do all the work—water them, put out salt and hay if they need it, maybe put up some temporary shelter. I'd pay you by the month—at the going rate. Would that suit you?"

"It might. But I'd like some time to think it over."

"Fine. But let me know soon. I need to move the cows before winter sets in. And I'd buy that dog from you if she's for sale. I've seen her work cattle. She's a born herder."

"Selling Glory would break my son's heart. I could never do that. But if you end up with your cows here, I don't see any harm in your putting her to work. She'd probably enjoy that." Cooper stepped back from the door. "Come on in. Since we're neighbors, we ought to get acquainted."

"Thanks, though I can't stay long."

Cooper pulled out a chair from the kitchen table. "Have a

seat. I can offer you some coffee or a Coke. You'd probably rather have a beer, but with a teenage boy in the house, I don't keep it around."

"Coke's fine. Drinking got me into a mess of trouble years ago. After that, I quit. Haven't touched a drop since."

Cooper knew better than to ask his neighbor for details. "Have you got a family?"

Judd shook his head. "My wife left me early on. I got divorce papers in the mail—signed them and sent them back. Never did find out what became of her. I inherited the ranch when my folks died, and it's been a good thing for me—given me roots."

He swigged the last of the Coke Cooper had given him, reached into his denim jacket, and drew out a folded paper. "I filled out this standard lease agreement for your pasture. Look it over. If it seems fair, and you want to go ahead, sign it. I'll pick it up tomorrow and give you the first month's rent. If you'd rather not, let me know. No hard feelings. All right?"

"Fine. And thanks for giving me time."

Cooper watched Judd Rankin drive away in his heavy-duty black Chevy pickup. Interesting man. Cooper was inclined to trust him. But life had taught him to be cautious. Maybe he'd show the lease agreement to Abner and ask him what he knew about Rankin. Also, it wouldn't hurt to check on Trevor.

Abner's place was an easy walk from here. Tucking the paper into his jacket, he whistled for Glory, closed the house, and set out along the narrow lane.

When Abner's barn came into sight, Glory raced ahead of him. Minutes later, Cooper arrived to find Abner and Trevor in the barn with a large assortment of brass pieces, screws, and bolts laid out on a canvas tarpaulin. With the dog licking his face, Trevor looked happier than Cooper had seen him in a long time.

Easing Glory away from him, Trevor gestured toward the brass parts. "It's like a puzzle, Dad. These pieces came in the kit for the sleigh, but Abner says the instructions were lost. So we have to figure out where everything goes."

Abner, observing and commenting from a plastic lawn chair, beamed and nodded. "He's doing a good job—found more matches than I ever could. How's it going, Cooper? I hear Miss Graver had a limb fall on her house."

"The whole tree's in the yard now," Cooper said. "She'll be staying with us until she finds a place to rent. She's got insurance, but repairing that house is going to take time."

"At least nobody was hurt." Abner picked up an odd-shaped length of brass and studied it, frowning. "I think this might go along the back of the sleigh, Trevor," he said. "Here, see if it's the right shape. Then all we'll need to do is find the bolts."

"There's about a hundred of those," Trevor said, taking the brass. "Something ought to fit. Oh, Dad, I just remembered something. Maggie and Aunt Grace came by. There's a meeting of the parade committee on Monday night at the library. You're invited to go if you want to."

"Invited? Was it a threat?"

"No, but since we'll probably need our horses for the sleigh, they might want you there."

One more item to remember. Cooper sighed. "I'll think about it. Meanwhile, Abner, I've got something to ask you. I met a neighbor who wants to lease my pasture. Judd Rankin. Do you know him?"

"Judd? Sure I do. His family goes way back in these parts. I knew his folks before they passed on and he came home to take over the ranch. Nice fellow, though pretty much a loner. He owns those Black Angus cows that you pass when you turn off the main road."

"This is the contract he offered me." Cooper drew the

paper out of his jacket, unfolded it, and handed it to the older man. "Take a look and tell me if you think it's fair."

Abner adjusted his glasses and scanned the page. "Looks fine to me. Pretty standard terms, and the price seems fair. I don't see a problem with it." He returned the contract to Cooper. "Judd plays his cards pretty close to his vest, but when it comes to business, you can trust him to keep his word." Abner yawned and pushed to his feet. "Trevor, you've done a good job today. But I feel a nap coming on. You run along with your dad. Tomorrow's Sunday, but you can come back if you're not busy with other things—and if it's all right with your dad."

"We'll see about that. Come on, Trevor."

They walked back down the lane, the dog trotting alongside them. Cooper thought of asking the boy whether he was happy, how he was doing in school, or whether he'd found any new friends. But if he knew Trevor, that would only shut him down. Better to keep the easy peace that had settled between them as the late afternoon light faded across the November fields.

"Dad," Trevor said, "can I ask you something?"

"Ask away."

"Is Miss Graver your girlfriend?"

Cooper's throat jerked as the memory of that kiss flashed through his mind. But it was already past history. "No," he said. "I don't think Miss Graver wants to be anybody's girlfriend. Certainly not mine."

"So why are you letting her move in with us? Couldn't she stay with somebody else, like Aunt Grace or Wynette? They're her friends."

"Your aunt doesn't have room. And Wynette's place is still being worked on, so I invited Jess to stay with us. I had to talk her into it—she didn't want to impose. And as soon as she finds a place of her own, she'll be moving out. So don't worry about it, all right?"

The two of them had walked a few minutes in silence when Cooper decided to tackle the issue head-on. "Jess is a nice person. But I get the impression you still don't like her. Can you explain why?"

Trevor looked down, scuffing his sneakers in the gravel. "I told you before, there's something fake about her. She acts friendly, but you can't tell what she's thinking. It's like Abner would say, you can tell she isn't putting all her cards on the table."

"Give her a chance, Trevor. You barely know her."

"Oh, I'll be nice and polite. You won't have to worry about that. But that doesn't mean I have to trust her."

"Understood. Thanks for being honest with me."

"So can I count on you to be honest, too?" Trevor asked. "Will you let me know if things start to get serious between you and Miss Graver?"

"Sure, I'll let you know. You can count on it—not that anything's going to happen. Jess and I are just friends, and barely that."

But was he being honest now? The memory of that torrid kiss had already made lies of his words.

Cooper could see the house in the distance. There was no sign of Jess's car. But she'd said she might be late. He would make some grilled cheese sandwiches and tomato soup for supper, then work on his unfinished magazine article while Trevor watched TV.

They were approaching the gate when the full implication of what Trevor had said came crashing in on him.

The boy wasn't worried about Jess because of her secrets or because, as he claimed, she was "fake." His reservations were based on something deeper and darker.

Trevor's mother had remarried and chosen her new husband over her son.

Trevor feared that he would lose his father the same way.

* * *

The next day was Sunday. Jess took over the kitchen and made her grandmother's pot roast—the one recipe she remembered by heart. She'd also bought a loaf of French bread and a blueberry pie from the bakery yesterday on her way out of town. Wynette, working behind the counter, had mentioned that her wedding dress was safe and Buck had rescued enough of her clothes to last for a few days, until the limb could be removed and the house could be stabilized.

"Could you let me know if you hear of any rentals?" Jess had asked her friend. "I'm staying with Cooper and his son, and I don't want to wear out my welcome. I need another place as soon as possible."

"You bet. I'll post a notice on the wall. But with such a handsome, sexy housemate, why be in a hurry to leave?"

Jess had sighed. "Let's just say there's some tension involved. Trevor's not happy to have me around. And as for the handsome, sexy housemate . . . Well, never mind."

"Got it." Wynette had grinned. "I'll let you know if I hear of a place for rent."

As she worked in the kitchen, Jess's thoughts went back over yesterday's events. After returning to the ranch with Cooper, she'd spent the rest of the day shopping for clothes and other necessities in Cottonwood Springs. She'd eaten a stuffed croissant in the mall, picked up supplies for Sunday dinner at a big-box supermarket, and made it back to the ranch about nine thirty. Staggering into the house under a load of bags and boxes, she'd found Cooper working in his office and Trevor watching TV.

"Welcome back." Cooper had stuck his head out of his office door. "Is that the whole load or is there more to bring in?"

"One more trip should get everything."

"Fine. Your room's the third door down the hall. Trevor, get up and give the lady a hand. Come on, move it."

Jess had never heard him sound so brusque. Had something gone wrong? Maybe she'd have a chance to ask him later.

The bedroom had been a lovely surprise. She'd expected, maybe, a camp cot and a sleeping bag for her first night here. Instead, Cooper had set up a comfortable bed, a dresser with drawers for her things, and a chair. The fact that he'd taken the time, when he had his own work to do, made her feel even more grateful.

She'd dropped her packages on the bed and directed Trevor to do the same with the remaining ones he'd brought from the car. He'd responded to her thanks with a murmur and returned to his TV program.

The groceries she'd bought earlier had stayed cold in the trunk. She'd carried them to the kitchen and put them away. After that, before going back to her room to unpack her other purchases, she'd wanted to thank Cooper for the work he'd done.

His office door had stood ajar. She'd rapped lightly, then when she heard his voice, stepped inside.

He was working at his computer, his desk piled with notes, books, and magazines. As Jess walked in, he'd swiveled his chair in her direction. "Hi." His voice had sounded cool, or maybe just strained. "Is there something I can do for you, Jess?"

"Not now. I just came in to thank you for setting up the bedroom. That was going the extra mile."

"No trouble at all. I figured you'd be too tired to do it yourself."

"But you were busy, and you still took time. I appreciate that." When he didn't respond, she'd continued. "I can see you're busy now, so I'll leave you to get back to work. I won't be underfoot long, Cooper. Something's bound to turn up soon."

If she'd expected him to assure her that she was welcome, she'd been disappointed. Earlier in the day, he'd invited her to stay, even talked her into it. Had he changed his mind? Was it something she'd said or done?

The same questions nagged at her as she put the finishing touches on Sunday dinner. At first she thought she might be imagining the change in Cooper. But no, the man who'd kissed her so deliciously yesterday was definitely avoiding her, especially when Trevor was around. As a psychologist, she prided herself on her ability to read people. But when it came to those involved in her personal life, she was as clueless as the next bewildered woman.

They'd invited Abner to come and share the meal this afternoon. That should ease the tension around the table. But if Cooper continued to send his silent messages, she would need to find another temporary refuge, even if it meant taking a motel room in Cottonwood Springs.

Cooper finished his second helping of pot roast and fresh buttered biscuits. Jess had gone all out to prepare a tasty meal—and the food was wonderful. But now, as he studied her from across the table, he could see anxiety written on her beautiful face. Knowing that he was the cause was its own kind of hell. Every time he looked at her, the urge to hold her in his arms made him want to curse. But his choice had been made clear—Jess or his son. And there could be no doubt about which way to go.

The worst of it was, he was just beginning to realize how much he cared for her.

Abner soaked up the gravy on his plate with the last hunk of biscuit. "My, but that was the best meal I've had in a racoon's age. I've been eating my own cooking for so long, I'd forgot what good food tastes like."

Jess smiled. "There's plenty left over. I'll give you some to take home and warm up. Now how about some blueberry pie for dessert? I didn't bake it myself, but nothing beats the pie from Stella's Bakery."

"I've saved just enough room," Abner said. "How about the rest of you? Pie for all?"

Cooper and Trevor nodded. Jess got up from the table, carried the empty plates to the sink, and was about to slice the pie when a sound like the rumble of oncoming thunder rattled the windowpanes.

"They're coming!" Trevor jumped out of his chair and raced outside. Jess flashed Cooper a startled look. Only then did Cooper realize that he hadn't told her about the contract with Judd Rankin for the lease of the pastures. Cooper had signed the papers yesterday and dropped them off at Judd's impressive rambling ranch house. Now the cows were here.

"It's all right, Jess. The pie can wait," he told her.

Abner had already headed outside behind Trevor. Cooper stepped out onto the porch to see a herd of fifty Black Angus cows thundering up the lane. Driving them were two men on horseback. One was a young stranger, probably a hired hand. The other, mounted on a fine palomino, was Judd Rankin.

Cooper had left the pasture gate open. As the lead animals came into the yard, Judd turned them aside, through the gate. The others began to follow them, with Glory doing her job, barking and darting, keeping them in line.

"Wow!" Trevor stood beside his father. "This looks like something out of a western movie."

"Except that the cows are Angus instead of longhorns or Herefords." Jess had joined them on the porch.

"But those guys are real cowboys!" Trevor said. "Not like those fake guys at school. Look, they've got ropes and everything. This is cool!"

Getting all the cows through the gate and into the pasture took no more than ten or fifteen minutes. The hired cowboy closed the gate and began filling the water trough from a hose attached to a pump outside the fence.

Judd rode up to the porch. In the saddle he looked as impressive as John Wayne. "Sorry about the racket," he said to Trevor. "They'll spread out and settle down to graze before long. After that you'll barely notice they're around. Let me know if there's any problem."

"I'll be sure and do that," Cooper said.

Judd's gaze fell on Jess, who stood looking up at him. His hand went to the brim of his Stetson. "Ma'am," he drawled, tipping his hat. Then he turned and rode off.

It was like a scene from a damned movie, and Jess was looking after him as if he was some kind of hero riding off into the sunset.

Cooper tore his gaze away from her. Heaven help him, could he be *jealous*?

Chapter 9

Late November

Thanksgiving had come and gone. The yellow fields were silvered with frost, the trees stark and bare. Now, when Trevor went outside to feed the horses in the morning, he could see the white clouds of his breath.

On Main Street, the Christmas lights were going up. The hardware store had opened a Christmas tree lot—a first for the town. Folks were excited about that. Now, instead of driving halfway to Cottonwood Springs, they could buy their trees right here in Branding Iron.

Trevor didn't much care whether his dad bought a tree or not. They didn't have any decorations, and he was still homesick for Seattle.

Miss Jessica Graver was still sharing the ranch house with Trevor and his dad. She'd found a basement apartment to rent, but it wouldn't come vacant until after Christmas, and there was nothing else available. The repairs on her house wouldn't be finished until spring, so for now, she had nowhere else to go.

Having her around wasn't that bad. She was quiet and didn't bother Trevor much or try to be his buddy. And she was a great cook. But something was going on between her and his dad—a tension that he couldn't quite figure out. It was as if they liked each other, but neither of them wanted to show it. Being around them was like watching a bad movie where you keep waiting for something to happen and it never does—just polite dialog that doesn't mean anything or go anywhere.

School sucked, too. Trevor was becoming sure that he'd never fit in. Once the bullies discovered he didn't react to their taunts, they'd moved on to more entertaining targets. Still, wandering the halls alone, trying to make himself invisible, was getting old.

At least he had Abner and the sleigh. He didn't fully understand his attraction to the wise old man and the beautiful object they were building. He only knew that when he was working on the sleigh and listening to Abner's stories, he felt almost happy.

Today, the Saturday after Thanksgiving, he planned to spend most of the day in the old barn. He was bringing along a pan of Miss Graver's lasagna to share with Abner for lunch. Maggie, who showed up now and then, would be coming later. Trevor didn't mind her joining them. For a little girl, she was all right. She knew how to be helpful without getting in the way, and she brought updates on the progress of the parade committee—of which she was an honorary member.

Today she arrived after lunch, dropped off by Trevor's Aunt Grace, who was on her way to visit her brother. She skipped into the barn, pausing to hug Butch, who was dozing in the straw.

"So what's the latest on the parade?" Trevor asked her.

"It's going to be great! The Branding Iron High School band is planning to march—and now the band from Cottonwood Springs is coming, too. Some of the stores are making floats, and Tex Morgan, the TV star, has promised to come—he grew up here in Branding Iron. Everybody's excited about the sleigh, except . . ." Her voice trailed off.

"Except what?" Abner asked her.

"Except we still haven't got a Santa Claus. I don't know what we're going to do about that."

"What about your dad? Didn't he do it last year?"

"Yes. But he's the mayor now. He can't be Santa, too." She sighed. "I've been talking to kids at school. They want a Santa they can believe in—not like those grumpy fake ones at the mall. Somebody who's kind and jolly and loves kids—somebody like the real Santa would be."

"I didn't think you believed, Maggie," Trevor said.

"I don't—heck, last year it was my dad, and he can be a real grump. But a lot of kids still believe. We don't want to let them down."

Abner cleared his throat. "Well, talking about Santa isn't going to get this sleigh finished in time for the parade. Come on, let's get to work."

Cooper had just finished proofreading the article he'd written when he heard a vehicle drive up outside. Could it be Jess? She'd left on a shopping expedition with Wynette that morning and had been gone all day. With Trevor at Abner's place, the house seemed almost too quiet.

He was about to send the article off when he heard a rap on the front door. Jess wouldn't knock. He got up and strode to answer it. He found his sister standing on the front porch.

"This is a nice surprise," he said. "Come on in."

"I won't be staying long," Grace said, giving him a quick hug. "I just came out to drop Maggie off at Abner's. She's quite taken with that sleigh. Did I interrupt your work?"

"Nope. I was at a good stopping place. Come on in the

kitchen. I can make you some instant hot chocolate, with or without marshmallows."

"Thanks, but don't bother. I'm on the run." She glanced around. "Is Jess here?"

"She's bridal shopping with Wynette today, so I've got the place to myself. Have a chair."

Grace took the rocker by the fireplace, perching on the edge like a bird paused in flight. "So how have things been with her here? I was hoping . . . You know."

"I know what you were hoping." Cooper sat facing her. "But nothing's going to happen. Jess is a great woman, but the timing's all wrong. Right now, I need to focus a hundred percent on being a father."

"So let me guess," Grace said. "This is about Trevor. You don't want him to see her as a threat, so you're keeping your distance. Right?"

"Right. After what his mother did to him, he's still hurting—and he's scared it might happen again. I can't let him think I might abandon him for some woman."

"But I know Jess. She loves kids. That's why she works with them. She would never ask you to give up your son."

"I know that. The trouble is, Trevor doesn't. And Jess doesn't care to get involved either. She has issues of her own. You lived with her for almost a year. Did she ever tell you that she used to work for the FBI?"

"What?" Grace's eyebrows shot up behind her John Lennon glasses. "No, she never mentioned her past. But I had an incident last year with my principal, who was threatening my career if I didn't sleep with him. Jess lent me this tiny cassette recorder and told me exactly how to use it. I got his threats on tape, and he never bothered me again. I wondered back then how she knew what to do. But I never asked her, and she never told me. So how did you find out?"

"I did some checking online. But that was about all I learned."

"You know how Jess would hate it if she knew. She's such a private person."

"I know. And part of me feels like a jerk. But I want to understand her, Grace. I want to know why she left the FBI and why she'd take a job in a nowhere place like Branding Iron. And, damn it, I want to know why I had that flash of déjà vu the first time I saw her."

"Actually, brother, most of that is none of your business."

"Not even if I care about her?"

"Do you care? Or is that just your journalist's curiosity talking?" Grace stood. "You need to do some soul-searching before you dig any deeper. Jess is one of the finest people I know. If you do anything to hurt her, you'll answer to me."

She touched his shoulder to show she wasn't really angry, then walked out the door. A moment later, Cooper heard the sound of her car starting. He walked back to his office and sat down at his desk, but he found it impossible to focus on his work. Grace was right. He needed to question his own motives before he dug any deeper into Jess's history. If he cared for her and wanted to protect her—and he did—it might be best to back off and let her keep her secrets.

But what if he loved her? What if he wanted more than that single searing kiss? What if, in spite of everything, he wanted forever?

Would that justify probing into her past?

Now that most of the brass fittings were attached to the sleigh, it was time to work on the seats. There were two of these—a bench in front for the driver, and a larger seat, shaped like an armchair, with a curved back, to fit inside the bed of the sleigh. Before they could be installed, the quilted upholstery, which had come in a box as part of the kit, would have to be fitted and tacked into place. The runners had been left for last, simply because it was easier to work on the sleigh bed without them.

The cotton velveteen fabric, once bright red, had faded to a deep rose color. It had come all in one large piece, with a paper pattern that had to be pinned into place for cutting. This was going to be a real challenge because there was only enough cloth to be cut once—no mistakes allowed. Once it was cut, it would be backed with a layer of cotton batting and fastened to the seat frame with decorative brass tacks.

"This is going to be hard!" Maggie said as she helped Trevor spread the cloth on the flatbed of the hay wagon.

"But if we do it right, it'll look good," Trevor said. "Once it's pinned, we can hold it in place while Abner does the cutting."

They were so intent on their work that, at first, they didn't notice when the door creaked open and someone walked into the barn. Trevor glanced around to see a tall boy standing nearby. It was Skip McCoy, who'd pretended to be his friend, gotten him into trouble, then ridden off on his bike and left him in Abner's barn.

Trevor was tempted to ignore Skip, or to put him in his place with a cutting remark. But then he saw the two little girls with him. They appeared to be about three and four years old, their blond hair mussed and their play clothes rumpled. Their faces were tear-streaked, their eyes swollen from crying.

It was Abner who spoke first. "I know you," he said. "You're Ed and Ruth's boy. And these must be your little sisters. Is there something we can do for you?"

Strain showed in Skip's face. "Could we just stay here for a while? My stepdad's drinking, and my mom told me to take the girls and go somewhere. But it's cold, and we don't have anywhere to go except here."

"Sure, it's fine." Abner had been sitting but he pushed to his feet. "Can I get you something to eat?"

"Thanks, but we're all right," Skip said. "We just needed to get out of the cold for a while." None of them, Trevor noticed, were wearing coats.

Skip sat down on a hay bale. The little girls clung to his side. "I'm worried about my mom," he said. "Ed gets mean when he's drinking, and he's hurt her before, but she won't leave him. I'm not big enough to protect her now, but I've been working out. I want to get strong enough to fight him, and then he'll never hurt her again."

"Do you want me to call the sheriff?" Abner asked.

"It won't make any difference. The sheriff will take Ed to jail, and the next day, Mom will go and get him out. Then he'll be nice to us until he starts drinking again."

"Well, you can come here anytime," Abner said. "You can even help us work on this sleigh. I believe you know Trevor, here. And this young lady is Miss Maggie."

"Hi." Maggie gave the little girls a friendly grin. "Can you tell me your names?"

The older girl squirmed shyly. "I'm Janeen. And my sister is Tammy." Her gaze swung to Butch, who'd raised his shaggy head. "Is that your big dog over there? Can we pet him?"

"He's Abner's dog," Maggie said. "Is it all right for them to pet him, Abner?"

"Sure. Scratch his ears. He likes that."

The two girls walked cautiously toward the dog. Janeen held out her fist. Butch sniffed it and thumped his tail. Little hands reached out to stroke and pat. Moments later, the sisters were giggling as the dog tried to lick the salty tear trails from their faces.

"I brought some homemade cookies today," Maggie said. "They're in the kitchen. I'll go and get you some." She slipped out of the barn door and raced off toward the house.

Unsure of what to say, Trevor had worked in silence, smoothing out the fabric and experimenting with the layout of the pattern. Until now, he hadn't known about Skip's family situation. He felt sorry for his former so-called friend. But that didn't excuse the way Skip and Cody had treated him. That had hurt. It had hurt a lot.

He became aware that Skip was standing behind him, as if waiting for him to speak. "So where's your friend Cody today?" Trevor asked without looking up from his work.

"He moved," Skip said. "His mother found a new man who hitched up her trailer behind his pickup and hauled it away. Cody went with them. I don't even know where."

"Well," Trevor said, "if you're looking for a new friend, it'll have to be somebody stupider than I am. I've learned my lesson—and you two were my teachers."

Skip didn't respond, but Trevor could hear him breathing. Trevor kept on working. Part of him wanted to turn around, but he was half afraid he might find the older boy in tears. What would he do then?

Surely, he reasoned, Skip couldn't take all the blame for the way he was. How would it feel to watch your stepfather beat up your mother time after time, and be helpless to do anything about it? Maybe the only way to ease the hurt would be to hurt somebody else.

Like him.

"I'm sorry, Trevor," Skip said in a low voice that the others wouldn't hear. "Cody and I were just having fun, but we were jerks. We got you in trouble. Then we ran off and left you to face the consequences. If you hate me, I don't blame you."

Trevor didn't answer. He didn't hate Skip, but he'd been so desperate for friends that the hurt had gone deep.

"I heard what your dad did," Skip said. "How he took you around to the houses we egged and made you apologize and wash all the windows. Do you know that I'd give anything for a dad like that? My real dad would have done that, too. But he died when I was eight—he was working in a gas station and got shot by a robber. My mom was so lost that she married the first man who said nice things to her. I've begged her to take the girls and leave him. But she never will." He cleared his throat. "I don't know why I'm telling you all this. It probably won't make any difference."

But it had made a difference. Trevor felt something stir, like a knot loosening inside his chest. Skip deserved a second chance—and Trevor could use a friend. The problem was knowing what to say next.

Maggie had come back with the cookies and was passing them around. Abner was talking to the little girls. He had just said something that made them laugh.

Trevor glanced around at Skip. "Hold that side of the cloth down while I measure it," he said. "It has to be cut just right."

After emailing a pitch for a new article, Cooper took a break and walked out onto the porch for some air. In the pasture beyond the yard, the Black Angus cows were grazing on the rich, yellow winter grass. The breeze carried their musky aroma to Cooper's nostrils. The earthy scent brought back memories of the summer he'd spent on his friend's ranch.

Judd had mentioned that these cows had been bred and were due to drop their calves in the spring. Their bellies already showed signs of rounding, but the excitement of calving wouldn't happen here. For that, they'd be herded back to Judd's place, where they could be watched and tended.

Cooper had seen little of his mysterious neighbor. The hired man did most of the watering and feeding. Judd showed up every few days, usually in his pickup, to check the herd. He didn't engage in small talk—just a nod and a "Howdy" if Cooper happened to be outside.

Jess was rarely here when Judd came by. Cooper had chided himself for the jealousy that had surged when the two first met. Jess was her own woman. She could like or dislike whom she pleased. He had no claim on her, and her past was none of his business.

Still, his conversation with Grace today had reawakened his curiosity and roused it to a fever pitch. This afternoon, while he was alone, it wouldn't be a bad idea to do more checking.

He would never confront Jess or question her. All he wanted was to understand her.

Dismissing the guilt that nagged at him, he sat down at the computer and brought up a search. If he'd seen her lovely face before, it could have been in a news article. Back in Seattle the paper he read most frequently was the *Seattle Times*. He would start there.

Acting on a hunch, he opened the paper's archives. Maybe if he did a search for FBI and Jessica Graver, he'd get lucky.

He'd typed the parameters in the blank window and was about to click on the search button when he heard a cry from the direction of the front porch. The voice sounded like Jessica's.

Swiveling his chair away from the desk, he jumped up and raced through the living room. The front door was closed. He flung it open to find Jess sprawled on the front steps. The two paper bags of groceries she'd been carrying had split open on impact, scattering her purchases all over the porch.

"Jess, are you all right?" He made his way through the cans and produce to crouch by her side. "Don't move until we know you're okay."

"I'm fine. Nothing feels broken." She winced as she sat up, worked her legs under her, and stood.

"What happened?"

"When Wynette got tired early, I decided to do a week's grocery shopping on the way home. I couldn't see past the bags, and I tripped over the second step—just being clumsy. Now look at the mess I've made."

Groceries lay in all directions—fruits and vegetables, cans, cartons of milk, a jar of spaghetti sauce that was cracked, and other odds and ends. All of it would need to be picked up and taken inside.

"I'll help you." Cooper began gathering the scattered items.

"We'll need something to put them in." She rushed into the house.

Only then did Cooper remember leaving the search up on his computer screen. If Jess were to see it, she'd be livid. "Wait, I'll go—" he called after her. But she was already beyond hearing.

Jess rummaged through the kitchen for spare paper bags. She found none. But she did remember seeing an empty cardboard box in Cooper's office. He'd left it there after unpacking some books. It should be big enough to hold everything.

The office door was open. She could see the empty box in one corner. Perfect. She hurried inside, picked it up, and turned around. That was when she noticed her name typed into the search bar at the top of the computer screen—along with the letters *F B I*.

By the time Jess came back outside, carrying the box, Cooper was braced for hellfire. One look at her face and he knew what had happened.

"What you saw, Jess—it's not what you think." It was a lame response. She had him dead to rights.

"Then what is it?" She flung the box at him, her dark eyes flashing fury. "You've been checking me out—probably wanting to see if there's any good story material in my background. Why didn't you at least have the decency to ask me?"

She picked up a can of tomato sauce, her hand going back as if she meant to fling it at his head. Then she lowered her arm and dropped the can into the box. "You are a sneaking, conniving jerk, Cooper Chapman. Right now, I'm wishing I'd never met you." She picked up a ripe tomato. "So, do you have anything to say for yourself?"

Cooper shook his head, feeling lower than a snake's belly. "I'm sorry. I felt as if I'd seen you before, and I couldn't resist trying to find out where. You're a very mysterious woman, Jess. I was intrigued, and I wanted to know more about you. But as for writing an article—or anything—about you, no, that never even occurred to me."

"And I'm supposed to give you a medal for that?" Her voice crackled with suppressed rage.

"What I did was despicable. But my only motive was wanting to know you better. Please believe me, Jess. I care about you."

"Care about me? That's a good one." She was throwing things randomly into the box. "So tell me, what did you learn?"

"Only that you were with the FBI. I never found out why you left and came to Branding Iron. That was what I really wanted to know."

She had gone cold and quiet, arranging the items in the box so that more of them would fit. To Cooper, her silence was even more unsettling than her anger.

"Suppose I tell you?" She spoke in an emotionless voice. "And after I tell you, I'll load my car, drive to Cottonwood Springs, and get a cheap motel room. You'll never hear from me again except about Trevor's school."

"And if I don't like those terms?" He began handing her things to put in the box. "I don't want you to leave, Jess."

"You have no right to stop me. I'm offering you my story. You can accept it or not. Either way, how can I stay here, knowing you invaded my privacy? How can I ever trust you again?"

Cooper didn't answer. He only knew that he'd lost something precious—perhaps for good. He battled the impulse to take her in his arms and beg her to forgive him. That wasn't going to work—not after what he'd done and not with a self-protective woman like Jess.

His only chance of winning back her trust was to listen to her story with respect and compassion and to abide by whatever decision she might make.

"All right," he said, picking up the loaded box. "Let's get these groceries into the house. Then, I'll be willing to listen to whatever you're ready to tell me."

"One promise first," she said. "I know you write articles for a living, and that you were researching me online. You have to promise not to use any part of what I'm about to tell you."

"I promise. But it never entered my mind to use anything I learned."

I just wanted to understand the woman I've come to care about. Cooper bit back the words that were on the tip of his tongue. She wouldn't want to hear them. She might even change her mind about telling him her story—a story he very much wanted to hear.

They sat on the sofa, warmed by the crackling fire and separated by the width of the center cushion. The setting was cozy. But as Cooper studied Jess's profile, it seemed as if she'd retreated to some cold, remote place inside herself. When she spoke, her expressionless voice came from that same icy distance.

"I joined the FBI out of college. It was all I ever wanted to do. I had to start at the bottom, mostly reviewing paperwork. But I was ambitious. I worked myself up through the ranks to become an agent. When a training program for hostage negotiators was announced, I was the first to sign up. With my psychology degree, it seemed to be a natural fit—and it was."

"So you were a hostage negotiator." Cooper spoke into her silence.

"Yes. Not that it was a full-time position. I was attached to a team of other agents, and we did our regular work. But when a situation called for it, and I happened to be in reach, I was brought in."

"Does that mean you were the one in charge?"

She gave a quick shake of her head. "Not at all. In a typical hostage situation, the person who calls the shots is a high-ranking official—FBI, police, or whoever is handling the crisis. Then there's a team of armed shooters—SWAT or trained snipers—whose job is to kill the suspect if the situation threatens to get out of hand. And of course there's a backup team of medics and social workers there to take care of rescued hostages and anyone injured."

A bitter smile tightened her mouth. "Finally, there's the negotiator—sometimes more than one. It's their job to stall for time, to try and defuse the situation just by talking. It's like walking a tightrope. One slip, and the boss sends in the guns, killing the suspect and maybe some hostages, too."

"I can imagine how that might burn you out," Cooper said.

"We were taught to walk away and not blame ourselves when things didn't go right. But that was easier said than done—especially . . . when there were children."

Cooper didn't miss the catch in her voice. Against his better judgment, he couldn't resist probing deeper. "Is that what happened to you, Jess?" he asked gently. "Is that why you decided to quit the FBI and take a job helping keep kids out of trouble?"

As soon as he spoke, Cooper realized he'd gotten too personal. Until now, he'd sensed that she was warming to him. But she'd gone cold again. Abruptly, she stood.

"I've told you enough," she said. "Now I need to get started packing."

"Damn it, Jess!" He blocked her way. "What do I need to do, get down on my knees and grovel? I apologized. I listened to your story and promised to keep it private. All I'm asking of you is to stay and let me be your friend."

He exhaled, forcing himself to be calm and rational. "Stay tonight and think it over, at least. Trevor will be home soon. He won't know what to make of you throwing things in the car and storming off like an angry sixteen-year-old. He saw enough of that behavior from his mother."

She gazed up at him, half yielding, half defiant. Her lips parted. Cooper was sorely tempted to kiss her. That might change things between them—but more likely, it would only make things worse.

Whatever she'd been about to say was interrupted by the wail of a siren from the direction of the main road, growing louder as it passed the ranch gate, then fading as it continued on down the lane.

Jess shook her head, her demeanor changing to one of concern. "That would be Buck, on his way to the McCoy place. I told you about them. Ed gets drunk and beats Ruth. After he passes out, she calls the sheriff to arrest him and take him to jail. In a day or two, once she's patched up, Ruth forgives him and takes him home—until it happens again."

"Can't something be done—legally, I mean?" Cooper asked.

"Only if she chooses to do it. According to Buck, the house is hers. She owned it with her first husband."

"So she could get a lawyer and throw him out."

"If she'd do it—and she should, for the sake of those poor kids. The situation is awful for them—Skip's not a bad boy, but he's so full of frustration because he can't protect his mother. And those poor little girls . . ." Jess shook her head. "This coming week I've got a routine conference appointment with Ruth. If she shows up, maybe I'll nudge her in that direction. At least I'll let her know what her options are—and give her the number of a pro bono lawyer in Cottonwood Springs."

She was looking up at Cooper, so fierce and passionate that she tore at his heart. It was a hell of a time to realize that he was in love with her.

"Stay, Jess," he said. "Stay through Christmas. Then your apartment will be ready, and you can move without all this drama. Please."

She was still for a long moment. Cooper held his breath. Slowly she nodded. "For now. Then we'll see."

Chapter 10

Not long after the siren's wail had faded, Cooper saw Trevor and Maggie coming through the ranch gate. Glory shot off the front porch and went bounding out to greet them, all wags and happy little yips.

"Back so soon?" Cooper asked as they came inside.

It was Maggie who answered. "When we heard the siren, Skip said he had to go home and be with his mom. He took his sisters and left. Abner needed a nap, so we stopped working and came home."

"Wait. Did you say Skip was there?"

Maggie nodded. She was still slightly out of breath. "He and his little sisters needed a place to stay because his stepdad was drinking. He wanted to help with the sleigh, so we let him."

Cooper's gaze turned to Trevor. "So Skip is your friend now?"

Trevor shrugged. "I guess so. I was still mad at first, but after he apologized about Halloween, I forgave him."

"What about Cody?"

"He moved away. So Skip doesn't have a friend either

now. Maybe we could have him over to hang out sometime. Things are pretty rough at his house."

"Maybe. We'll see." Cooper would need time to get used to the idea.

"Uncle Cooper, may I use your phone?" Maggie asked. "I need to let my mom know I'm here so she can come and get me."

"I've got a better idea," Jess said. "Why don't you stay for dinner? Then later, one of us can drive you home."

"I'll ask my mom if it's all right." Maggie skipped over to the phone, made a brief call, and turned around with a happy grin on her face. "She said yes!"

"Great," Jess said. "I'm making chow mein. If you want to help, I'll show you how it's done. Let me get set up in the kitchen. Then I'll call you. Okay?"

"You bet." Maggie glanced around the living room. "Uncle Cooper, you don't have any Christmas decorations up."

"No, I guess I don't." Cooper had lived without Christmas decorations since his divorce. On the holidays when he'd had Trevor, they'd usually taken a trip somewhere, like Hawaii. "I figure Christmas will come whether we have decorations or not."

A dismayed look crossed Maggie's face. "But at least you've got to have a tree. We've already got our tree up at home. My first mom—my birth mom—loved Christmas. We put all her special ornaments on our tree to remember her."

"That's nice for you, I guess. But I've never been that big on celebrating Christmas."

"You're a Scrooge, Uncle Cooper! Do you know who Scrooge was?"

"I do, and I'd say he had the right idea." Cooper was teasing her now, only half serious. "Bah! Humbug!"

"Well, maybe *you* don't need a Christmas tree. But Trevor deserves to have one—don't you, Trevor?"

"I guess it would be okay." Trevor had just emerged from the hall, where he'd gone to wash up in the bathroom.

"See, he doesn't even care," Cooper said.

"Care about what?" Jess stepped out of the kitchen, drying her hands on a towel.

"Uncle Cooper doesn't want to get a Christmas tree! That's just plain wrong. Tell him, Jess."

Jess's eyes met Cooper's—a flicker of challenge in their dark depths. "Heavens, Maggie's right. What's Christmas without a tree? I'll tell you what. After dinner, when we go to town to take Maggie home, we can stop at the tree lot and get one. My treat."

Maggie grinned, showing her missing front teeth.

"No way," Cooper protested. "If we're going to have a tree, I'll pay for it myself."

"Have it your way." She gave the little girl a victory wink. "Come on, Maggie, let's make dinner."

By the time they finished the meal and the cleanup, it was dark outside, and a chilly breeze was blowing. Cooper helped Jess into the Jeep and let Maggie and Trevor into the back. Christmas music was playing on the radio. At Maggie's insistence, they sang along as they drove to the Christmas tree lot on the south end of town.

Jingle bells, jingle bells, jingle all the way . . .

Cooper went through the motions, but he wasn't feeling the spirit. There were just two things he wanted for Christmas. The first was for his son to be happy here in their new home—a wish that was still hanging in the balance. The object of the second wish was sitting next to him in the passenger seat. She was laughing and singing, but he wasn't fooled. By looking into her past without her permission, he'd lost her trust. And he'd made her angry enough that all she wanted was to leave him.

It was too bad that Santa, or somebody like him, couldn't just slide down the chimney or knock on the front door and bring him the answers he needed.

The Christmas tree lot was set up in a fenced-off area next to the hardware store. Tonight it was a lively place, with Christmas lights strung overhead, Christmas songs playing on a speaker, and the fresh aroma of pine perfuming the air.

Customers, mostly families, strolled up and down the aisles between rows of trees. Two teenage girls, behind a long table, passed out miniature candy canes and served free hot chocolate in little Styrofoam cups. A couple of husky boys helped carry the trees out to vehicles and tie them in place.

The assistant manager, Hank Miller, stood by the gate, greeting people as they came in. A stocky, balding man in his late forties, with an artificial leg that gave him a slight limp, he was all smiles tonight. The tree lot had been his idea, and it was a rousing success.

Cooper remembered Grace telling him how Hank had lost his leg in a farm accident. After his wife and son left him, he'd become an alcoholic. It was Sam who'd gotten him into AA and found him a job at the hardware store—the job that had turned his life around.

"Come on! Let's find a tree!" Maggie gripped Jess's hand and tugged her down the rows. Trevor followed a little behind. Cooper hung back. He would pay for the damned tree, but the others could pick it out.

Scrooge. You're a Scrooge.

Guilty as charged.

"Look at this one!" Maggie pointed to a medium-sized tree. "What do you think, Trevor? It's going to be in your house."

"I guess it'll do," Trevor said. "Dad? You're the one buying it."

Cooper went through the motions of inspecting the tree, which was full, fresh, and not too big for the house. "It looks fine," he said. "Let's get it and go."

"But don't you want to look at more?" Maggie argued. "You have to look at them all and find the perfect one. That's part of Christmas."

"The tree is fine, Maggie," Cooper said. "You and Trevor both have school tomorrow, and it's getting late. We need to take you home."

Maggie pouted a moment, then tugged Trevor over to get some hot chocolate while Cooper paid for the tree. Jess stood at his elbow. "Good man," she said. "I knew you'd do the right thing and get a tree."

"No man could stand up to you and Maggie."

"You're going to need some decorations," she said. "I've got a box of them stored in the unit I rented for my furniture. I'll stop by after school tomorrow and pick them up. There's even a stand that holds water. We can decorate tomorrow night if you want."

"Or we can wait for a good time. Since Maggie was so keen on our getting a tree, she'll probably want to help. The tree will be fine outside for a few days."

They loaded the tree in the back of the Jeep, leaving the rear window down to accommodate the top. The piney aroma filled the space inside the vehicle, evoking Cooper's memories of boyhood Christmases, before his father left the family and his mother sank into depression. Both he and Grace had suffered scars from that time—hers worse than his because she was younger. Now Grace was happily married to a good man, with a child who needed her. But Cooper was still looking for his happy ending.

Would he find it here, with the woman beside him? Or had he already made too many mistakes?

"That's a nice smell," Trevor said. "I don't know if I've ever had a real tree before. Mom had one of those plastic ones that she put out every year. And with just you and me, Dad, we never even had a tree."

"Do you like it?" Cooper asked. "The tree, I mean."

"Yeah, I guess I do. It smells like . . . Christmas."

"See," Maggie said. "I told you that you needed a tree."

"Since you're such a smarty, you can help us decorate it," Cooper said. "Ask your mother to call me after school tomorrow and we'll arrange it."

"Goody! I love decorating trees!" Maggie clapped her hands as the Jeep pulled up to her house. The outside light was on, and Grace had come out onto the porch. Maggie scampered up the steps to her mother. Both of them returned Cooper's wave as he pulled away from the curb and drove off.

A cheerful Christmas song was playing on the radio as he drove back to the ranch. Cooper hadn't given much thought to Christmas this year, except for having it over with. Trevor had at least pretended not to care about the season. And with her house in ruins, Jess could hardly be in a mood to celebrate.

But it was as if the Christmas spirit was reaching out to surround them with its glittering promise—the promise that somehow things would be better, and that the gift of what each one wanted most would be under the Christmas tree, just waiting to be unwrapped.

The following week

Jess studied the woman who sat facing her. Ruth McCoy was dressed in an outdated polyester pantsuit, her light brown hair teased and curled at the ends. Her makeup had been carefully applied, but no amount of concealer and foundation could hide the swollen, discolored bruise that marred the left side of her face from cheekbone to chin. Years ago, she might have been a beauty. But tragedy, hardship, and abuse had taken their toll on her. She was fragile, broken in so many ways and so many places that, as it appeared to Jess, only the will to survive and her love for her children held the pieces together.

"So how is my boy doing?" she asked. "Is he behaving? Is he getting his work done?"

"Skip is doing all right," Jess said. "I have his file right here, with the updated reports from each class. His grades are passing, and there's no mention of his making trouble."

Ruth sighed. "Skip's a good boy—like his real father. But I worry about him. He's got a lot of anger inside because of the way Ed treats me. I'm afraid that one of these times it's going to explode."

"Ruth, there's no law that says you have to put up with abuse. The next time your husband hurts you—and he will—you could press charges against him. And while he serves time in jail, you could get a lawyer, clear his things out of your house, and move on with your life."

"You mean . . . divorce him?" Ruth's eyes widened in shock. "But divorce is a sin. Besides, I don't know how we'd live without the money Ed's construction job brings in. And what about my little girls? They need their father."

"Do your girls need to see him beating you, Ruth? What's that teaching them—that a husband has the right to treat his wife any way he wants, and she has to put up with it?"

A tear trickled down Ruth's cheek, leaving a thin trail of mascara. "I try so hard," she said. "I keep thinking that if I do everything just right . . ." She shook her head. "But it doesn't work that way, does it?"

"Not that I'm aware of. Do you have family or anyone who could take you in if you need shelter?"

"I've got a sister in Cottonwood Springs. We haven't spoken since I married Ed, but if I needed help, she wouldn't turn away her blood kin—especially the girls."

Jess shuffled through the Rolodex on her desk and found two business cards. "Take these. One's for a counselor in Cottonwood Springs. The other's for a divorce attorney. Neither of them will charge you for a first-time consultation. And if you need more help, it can be arranged." She pushed the cards into Ruth's hand. "I'm not saying you should use these. But they're a resource if you need them."

Ruth tucked the cards into her purse and rose from her chair. "Thank you." Her voice quivered as if she were holding back more tears. "I'll think on what you've said. But no promises. My children have to come first—and I need a man to help me take care of them."

She walked out of the room, leaving Jess to wonder whether she'd done the right thing, or just made more trouble for the poor woman.

After all, Jess asked herself, what business did she have advising someone whose path she'd never walked? She'd never given her trust to a man, let alone married one. And she'd never nurtured a child, let alone given birth to one. As for love, she barely knew the meaning of the word.

And here she was, telling another woman how to live her very difficult life.

After putting her files away, she slipped on her coat, gathered up her purse and keys, and headed out to her car. Tonight she'd promised to help Cooper, Trevor, and Maggie trim the Christmas tree. The stand and ornaments were in the trunk of her car. She'd also volunteered to pick up the two extra-large pizzas Cooper had ordered by phone from Buckaroo's, and to swing by Grace and Sam's to get Maggie. Sam and Grace had been invited, too, but they'd declined in favor of some private time together. After all, they'd barely been married six months. They were still newlyweds.

Jess was exhausted after a long day at work. But tonight was for the children, and she didn't want to spoil the holiday mood. She hoped that Cooper would feel the same way. If she saw any sign of his Scrooge face, she would take him aside and give him a piece of her mind.

Taking a longer route to Main Street, she drove to her house. She usually avoided the depressing sight, but she wanted to check on the progress of the repairs, which were going much too slowly to suit her. It was the insurance company who'd taken estimates and chosen the contractor—probably by low bid. And in this slow season they were taking their sweet time.

The cottonwood tree was long gone. The crushed roof of the house was covered in layers of plastic to protect the frame until the new roof could be added in the spring. A battered pickup with a shell on the back was parked in the driveway. As she pulled up behind it and opened the door of her Taurus, she could hear the sound of hammering. At least something was getting done.

She hadn't planned to go inside, but as long as someone was here, it might be a good time to check on what had been done since her last visit.

The front door was ajar. She stepped inside without knocking. The living room no longer looked like home. The furniture and anything personal had been hauled off to storage. The carpet was rolled up against one wall, the windows bare. Fading sunlight poured through the plate glass pane in front, which was cracked from corner to corner and would have to be replaced.

Why hadn't she just taken a wrecking ball to the place and started over? It would've made more sense.

A cardboard six-pack of beer sat on the kitchen counter. Half the bottles were empty. Not a good sign, but this was no time to complain.

The hammer blows were coming from down the hallway, probably from her bedroom, which had suffered the most damage.

Jess followed the sound to the open doorway. Standing there, she saw a hulk of a man in a sweat-stained gray tee hammering a slab of sheetrock onto a wall of exposed beams.

Jess cleared her throat. "Excuse me."

He stopped hammering and turned to face her. Below the bill of his paint-stained baseball cap, his pale eyes were bloodshot, his heavy jaw darkened with stubble.

"Is there something I can do for you, missy?" His voice was gravelly, his slow smile giving her a glimpse of tobacco-stained teeth. Something about the man, and the awareness that they were likely alone here, made her uneasy. But that was silly. He was a workman doing his job—that was all.

"Hi," she said. "I'm the owner of this house. I just stopped by to see how the repairs were going."

His manner became more deferential. "Sure. Okay. As you can see, there's a lot to do. We were hoping to save this wall, but the plaster was cracked. So we had to tear it out and replace it with this sheetrock. When it's spackled and painted over, you won't know the difference. We'll do the same to the ceiling. It'll be good as new. You'll see."

"What about the other rooms?"

"The other bedrooms won't need much, just some patching and paint. And the bathroom is done. Go on in and take a look."

The bathroom was across the hall, the door closed. Jess's FBI training kicked in. If the man had any ideas, that small room could be a trap. "I'll take your word for it," she said. "Right now I need to be going. I've got some people who'll be out looking for me if I don't hurry home. My name is Jessica Graver, by the way. You can tell your boss I was here."

"I'll do that. And if you see him first, you can tell him that Ed McCoy was working when you came by, and he treated you like the lady you are."

"I'll do that." Jess had gone cold.

Ed McCoy. I know that name. I just talked to your wife and saw what you did to her face. And I know your stepson, who's going through a struggle because of you. Get your gear and get out. I don't want you in my house.

The words flashed through her mind, but she left them unspoken. At least he was working. And any anger she might rouse in the man was bound to be vented on his poor wife.

Driving to Buckaroo's to get the pizzas, she tuned the radio to some cheerful Christmas music and forced herself to sing along. She'd be picking up Maggie in a few minutes, and she didn't want to dampen the little girl's excitement.

Still, she couldn't help remembering Ruth McCoy's bruised, stricken face and her own encounter with Ruth's abusive husband. What kind of Christmas would that family be having? Would they even have a tree, or presents?

Experience and training had taught her that Christmas was a time when dark emotions tended to surface. Suicides, robberies, murders, and domestic abuse all became more common. She'd sensed a violent streak when she'd faced Ed McCoy. The thought of where it might lead would worry her all through the holidays.

Having Maggie in the car helped to raise her spirits. The little girl chatted and sang all the way to the ranch. By the time they drove into the yard and saw Cooper, Trevor, and the dog waiting for them on the porch, Jess was ready to celebrate with her own small, borrowed family.

After leaving the pizzas in the warm oven, they unpacked the tree stand from the box Jess had brought, attached it to the base of the tree, and set it up in the corner of the living room. Trevor added some water to the reservoir in the stand. The aroma of fresh pine drifted through the house.

"Doesn't that tree smell heavenly, Uncle Cooper?"

"It does," Cooper conceded. "Kind of like being in a forest. Maybe we should leave it like this. It's so pretty and green. Why does it need a bunch of tacky old decorations on it?" He caught Jess's eye and gave her a private wink. So he was teasing with his whole Scrooge act, making it fun for Maggie. She couldn't help liking him for that.

"Stop it, silly!" Maggie gave him a play-punch above the belt. "It wouldn't be a Christmas tree without decorations— just a plain old tree."

"The tree can wait," Trevor said. "Right now, I'm starving. Can we eat before we decorate?"

"Good idea," Jess said. "I'll get the pizzas out of the oven. Trevor, you can get the sodas out of the fridge."

They sat in the kitchen, eating pizza off paper plates and sipping cold sodas. Jess could sense the warmth around the small, plain table—almost as if they were family. Not that they were anything of the sort. They were more like separate pieces of a jigsaw puzzle that didn't quite fit. But for now it was nice.

"How's the work on the sleigh coming?" she asked Trevor.

Trevor reached for a third slice of pepperoni pizza. "We're almost finished. Abner will be out of town, visiting his married daughter for a few days, so we won't be working. But when he comes back, we're going to turn the sleigh over and attach the runners. After that we can hitch up the horses and take it for a test run."

"But there's no snow," Jess said.

"I know. For now, while there's no snow, we'll have to use a ramp and put the sleigh on the hay wagon. We'll need your help with the wagon and the horses, Dad."

"Fine," Cooper said. "We'll just have to make sure the sleigh is securely fastened to the wagon—maybe by bolting it down. Is Skip still helping you?"

"Yup. He's a good worker, too. Abner's even offered him a job after Christmas, coming by to help out on the farm."

"That's good news," Jess said. "I know he and his family could use the money."

"He's a lot stronger than I am," Trevor said. "Abner has a bad back, so Skip does most of the heavy lifting. We'll need him when it comes time to flip the sleigh and put the runners on."

"You'll need me, too," Maggie said. "I'm the best at getting tools and things and handing them to you." She frowned. "But we still don't have a Santa. I've talked to my dad about it, and he says he's taking care of it. But I do worry. Dad could get busy and forget. And we can't just have an empty sleigh in the parade."

"Then I'd say leave it to him, Maggie," Jess said. "When Sam Delaney says he'll take care of something, it gets taken care of. That's why he's mayor. Now what do you say we finish off this pizza and get back to decorating our tree?"

"Oh, wow! Look at these little animals!" Maggie lifted up a carved and painted figure of a zebra and hung it on the tree. "And here's a lion—and a cheetah! Where did you get them, Jess?"

"They were my mother's," Jess said. "My father worked for the United Nations. He and my mother traveled all over the world. She collected these in Tanzania. I thought you'd enjoy seeing them."

Maggie picked up the figure of a small turtle, its shell inlaid with mother-of-pearl. "That one's from Thailand," Jess said. "And this pink kitten is from Hong Kong. The monkey is from India."

"Where are your mother and dad now?" Maggie asked. "Are they still traveling?"

"No. They died in a plane crash when I was about your age. I was raised by my grandmother. She passed away a few years ago."

"So you don't have any family at all?"

"None that I know of. Let's see what else is in the box."

The tree was beginning to look festive. They'd strung the lights first and added some shiny tinsel. Then Jess had opened her box of special ornaments. She hadn't hung them on a tree in years, but somehow this seemed like the right time and place.

Once the decorating was finished, it was time to take Maggie home. Cooper had volunteered to drive her. "You've got school tomorrow, Trevor," he told his son. "Do your homework. Then I want you in bed by ten."

Maggie buttoned her coat. "Can Jess come along when you take me home? Please, Uncle Cooper. We had such a good time. I want it to last a little longer."

"Jess has had a long day, Maggie," Cooper said. "She can come if she wants to, of course, but she's probably tired."

"Please, Jess." Maggie's expression would have melted a block of granite. "It won't take long."

"Of course, I'll come," Jess said. "Let me get my coat."

From the back seat, Maggie chatted all the way to her house. Cooper helped her out of the Jeep and made sure she was safely inside before climbing into the driver's seat again.

For the short time it took to drive back to the ranch, he would be alone with Jess. She'd been distant since their conversation about the FBI had ended with her almost walking out. She'd been willing enough to talk about her work, but when he'd asked her about the reason for leaving her job, she'd shut right down.

Whatever had caused her to leave, the memory was clearly painful. Cooper would be wise not to bring it up again. If she wanted him to know, she would choose a time to tell him. If not, it shouldn't matter. Right now, all he wanted was to spend more time with her.

As they drove down Main Street, the old-fashioned Christmas lights strung overhead glowed in the darkness. The holiday music on the radio—Johnny Mathis singing "I'll Be Home for Christmas"—was soft and mellow. Jess sighed and nestled lower in her seat.

"Tired?" he asked.

"Exhausted. But tonight was fun, wasn't it?"

"It was." Cooper chuckled. "Every celebration needs a Maggie." He passed the last traffic light and headed out of town. "I enjoyed seeing your little ornaments and hearing about them. You must've had an interesting childhood."

She sighed again. "Not really. My parents were gone a lot. And staying with my grandmother was no picnic. Forget the kindly white-haired grandma who greets you with hugs and cookies. Dorothy Graver was Professor of Religious History at a church-run college. She expected me to be a little lady at all times. As soon as I was old enough to go, she sent me off to boarding school."

"That sounds pretty grim," Cooper said.

"It was. But I struck a blow for freedom." She looked up at him, the dash lights reflecting a mysterious twinkle in her dark eyes. "Would you believe I got kicked out at fifteen for sneaking out of my room at night to have adventures? The headmistress caught me skinny-dipping in the lake—with a boy!"

"Jess, you little rascal!" He said it with a smile.

"Oh, it wasn't what you might think. It was dark, and we were just friends. We were only swimming. But my grandmother almost had a stroke. After that, she sent me to a place in Switzerland, for *difficult* girls. And those girls . . . oh, mercy me, that was an education."

Cooper made the turn off the highway, onto the dirt road that led to the ranch. He didn't want the drive to end. Jess was finally showing him her real self—and he was discovering that he didn't just love her. He *liked* her.

He found himself bursting with emotions. He wanted to empty his heart to her, to beg her to stay with him. But he knew better. The last thing he wanted now was to chase her back into her shell.

"You asked me once why I left my job with the FBI," she said. "If I tell you the story, you have to promise not to share it—not with Trevor, not with your sister, not with anybody. When you hear it, you'll understand why."

Cooper's throat tightened. That she trusted him with her secret was an unexpected gift. He would treat it with tenderness and respect.

At the end of the lane, he could see the ranch house. Travis's room showed a dark window. With luck, he would already be asleep. Slowing the Jeep, he drove quietly through the gate and turned off the headlights.

"I promise," he said. "And I'm ready to listen."

Chapter 11

The Jeep was warm inside, but the chill of memory was so intense that Jess felt a shiver pass through her body—the shock of the tragedy, the burden of self-blame, the interview with the reporter literally backing her into a corner, pummeling her with questions as cameras flashed. And then there was the photograph of her horror-stricken face as that woman attacked her—the one that had been published with the story in papers all over the country, exposing the shock and grief over her failure to anyone who wanted to look.

Tonight, sitting around the kitchen table, almost like family, she'd felt a yearning so powerful that it had almost brought tears to her eyes—the need to share herself with someone else. Was that the urge driving her now?

She wanted to move forward with Cooper. Still, in trusting him—a journalist—she was taking a fearful risk. Maybe she should just make an excuse, get out of the vehicle, and flee into the house.

"It's all right, Jess. Take your time." He was leaning into the corner of his seat, half facing her. His arm lay across the seat back. It was now or never, she told herself.

Taking a deep breath, she began. "It happened three years ago. My team was stationed in Reno. It was late one night when we got the call from a family resort near Lake Tahoe. A man was barricaded in one of the cabins with two kids—a boy of seven and a girl about nine. According to his wife, after the kids were asleep, she'd told him that she'd met someone new and wanted a divorce. He'd taken the news calmly, said they could work things out. But after she went outside to the vending machine for cigarettes, she came back to find her husband locked in with a gun, threatening to kill the kids and himself.

"When she couldn't talk sense into him, she called the local police. The police called us, a three-man SWAT team and one negotiator—me. There was no helicopter available, so we had to drive. When we got there we found three police cars, an ambulance with paramedics, and the father still inside the cabin with his children. As we were climbing out of the car, a news crew rolled up in a van. The place had become a three-ring circus."

Jess did her best to keep her tone calm and professional. Cooper listened in thoughtful silence. Jess could sense that he had questions. But he held them back, letting her tell her story.

"The wife was with the paramedics. They'd given her something to calm her down, but she became agitated again when she saw me and found out that I'd be the one negotiating with her husband. 'Not a woman!' she shouted. 'Floyd won't talk to a woman! Get a man!'"

"The police chief had someone sit with her in one of the cruisers. I took the phone that somebody had hooked up to the one in the cabin and began by introducing myself. The plan was to talk him into letting the two children go. Nothing else was to happen until they were safe. After that, if Floyd didn't surrender, the SWAT team could move in.

"Floyd was hostile. He kept repeating that he wanted to

talk with his wife. I kept telling him that as soon as he let the children come out, he could talk with her all he wanted. This was protocol—the way I'd been trained. You don't give the suspect anything he asks for until he does something you want. That's why it's called negotiation."

Jess paused to take a deep breath. Her unsteady fingers raked a lock of hair back from her face.

"Are you all right?" Cooper's voice was gentle.

"I will be. I'm just getting to the hard part, that's all."

"Take your time." His hand moved from the seat back to rest on her shoulder. Its warm weight lent her comfort and courage. She took a deep breath and continued.

"The standoff continued for more than two hours. Then the line went dead. A silhouette, outlined by a lamp, moved behind the window blind. Was he about to let the children go? Was he going to surrender? The SWAT team moved in close, to be ready if the police chief gave the order. I kept trying the phone connection, but it was no use. All I could do was pray in my heart that the children would make it out all right.

"The door latch turned. The door opened slightly. Nobody dared to breathe. That was when Floyd's wife came flying out of the police car, screaming, 'Don't come out, Floyd! They've got guns! They're waiting to kill you!'

"The door closed again. A moment later, before anybody had time to move, we heard two shots, then after a pause, a third shot. The SWAT team rushed into the house, too late, of course. Even before I saw the bodies, I knew they would all be dead.

"I remember that poor woman wailing, the paramedics trying to calm her. When she saw me walking away, she came rushing after me, screaming, 'This is your fault! You should've let me talk to him! I could've talked them out! I could've saved them all!'

"And the reporters—they were on me like vultures, snapping photos of the woman attacking me, shoving their microphones and TV cameras into my face.

"The next day I turned in both my report and my resignation. I just couldn't do it anymore." Her voice broke. "So now you know."

"Oh, Jess." His arms went around her, pulling her against his chest. "Damn it, I'm sorry. If I'd known what I'd be putting you through, I never would have agreed to listen."

Trembling now, she nestled against him. "The worst of it is the thought that maybe the poor woman was right—it really *was* my fault. I chose to follow protocol—to do everything by the book. And two innocent children may have died because of it. I never want to face a choice like that again."

"It wasn't your fault." His lips skimmed her forehead as he spoke. "You did your job."

"My job was to save those children. If I'd done it right, they'd be alive today."

"Don't torment yourself. All you can do is move on and maybe make things better for other children. That's your job now."

"Is it? Sometimes I wonder if I'm making any difference at all." Tears welled in her eyes and overflowed, trickling down her cheeks. Cupping her jaw with his fingertips, he used his thumb to stroke them away. "Don't," she said, drawing back. "Don't pity me, and don't feed me platitudes. I don't deserve them."

"Blast it, Jess—" He kissed her, not tenderly but with a fierce possession that set off a Fourth of July's worth of fireworks. Her response was a burst of need, hot and deep. Her hands caught his head and pulled him down to her, lips softening, molding to his, seeking what she'd wanted from the first time he'd touched her.

"Jess—" He pulled her against him, hands fitting her body to his. His breathing roughened, hardened, igniting swirls of heat in the depths of her body.

"We're not kids, Cooper," she whispered. "If we don't stop, we both know where this is going."

"I know." Still breathless, he eased her away from him. "But if anything happens, it's not going to be in this Jeep."

"Or in the house with your son." She gave a little laugh as she rearranged the front of her jacket. "I think we need to give this some time."

"You're right. It's too good to rush." He kissed her again, gently this time. "Come on. Let's go on inside and get some sleep. You've got work in the morning, and I've got deadlines on a couple of articles."

He came around the vehicle, helped her out, and escorted her to the house with one hand on the small of her back. Jess's pulse was still racing. Things were happening so fast. Part of her wanted to charge headlong all the way. But no, she and Cooper were sensible people. They would take things slowly, give their relationship the test of time. If what they'd found was for keeps, it would be worth the wait.

The porch light had been left on, as well as the light above the kitchen stove. Otherwise, the house was dark. Cooper checked Trevor's room and found him asleep. For a moment he was tempted to lure Jess into the living room for a cuddle session next to the Christmas tree. But that would likely end in frustration, and she had work in the morning.

Instead, he allowed her first chance at the bathroom, then gave her a chaste good night kiss. "Sleep tight. See you in the morning," he said.

After she vanished into her room, Cooper undressed and went to bed. At first, he was too elated to fall asleep. Jess in his arms, warm and willing, with the promise of more to come, was better than a dream come true. But he was tired. Fantasies became dreams as he sank into sleep.

Sometime after midnight, the wind howling beneath the

eaves of the house startled him awake. Unable to go back to sleep, he lay with his eyes open, gazing up into the darkness. As he listened to the incoming storm, Jess's tragic story drifted through his memory. Hearing it from her had opened the door to understanding this complicated woman. But one question remained.

When they'd first met, why had she seemed so familiar to him?

Had he seen her somewhere before? But that didn't seem likely. As far as he knew, they'd never been in the same place at the same time. If they had, he wouldn't have forgotten that stunning face.

So why should it matter now? He had fallen in love with her, and she seemed to return his feelings. Wasn't that enough? For some men it might have been. But Cooper was driven by curiosity. It was one reason he was good at his job. He knew that the question would chew on him until he found the answer.

She'd mentioned the photographers at the scene of the tragedy, the annoying flashes as they snapped their photos. What if he'd seen her in one of those photos?

Now that he'd heard Jess's story, he might be able to find out. He had a window for the date. And he had the location. Surely the local papers would have carried such a sensational story. It could even have gone national.

He would start with the *Reno Gazette-Journal*. With luck they would have archived editions going back more than three years. Since the hostage situation and shooting had been local, they would probably have a photograph or two.

And if he recognized her, then what? What was there to learn that he didn't already know?

If he didn't find answers now, the questions would keep him awake for the rest of the night.

As he rolled out of bed and wrapped his flannel robe over his pajamas, a slight misgiving tugged at his conscience.

Maybe this wasn't such a good idea. He'd just been gifted with the love of a wonderful woman. Why not be satisfied with that and let the rest go—or at least wait until tomorrow, when Jess would be out of the house?

But he was already headed out of the bedroom and moving down the hall.

Trevor's door was closed. So was Jess's. He would shut his office door and work quietly to keep from waking them. The blowing wind outside should cover any small sound he might make.

In his office, he closed the door behind him before switching on the desk lamp. Seated at the desk, he turned on his computer and brought up a search engine. In the search window, he typed in *Reno Gazette-Journal*. The site came up—so far, so good. But finding the date would be harder.

Jess had told him it was three years ago. But now it was December. The resort would more likely have had families there in the summer. Checking each edition would take time. Maybe he could do a cross search for *FBI* or *hostage*, or even Jess's name—the only name he had.

After several dead ends, he did a separate search for cabin resorts near Lake Tahoe. He came up with three possibilities. He ran each one through the newspaper archives. On the third try, he found a promising link and clicked on it.

As soon as the photo appeared, Cooper remembered where he'd seen the image—it had appeared in *Newsweek*, a magazine he subscribed to and usually read from cover to cover. It was hard to believe he ever could have forgotten it.

The picture, laid out here with others, was the kind of a once-in-a-lifetime shot every photographer dreams of—the perfect combination of light, angle, timing, and drama—the bereaved wife and mother springing like a wounded animal; the police officer, in silhouette, stepping in to stop her; and the light focused on Jess's stunning face, revealing all the shock, horror, and anguish of the moment.

The photo, Cooper remembered now, had been up for some major awards. No wonder Jess had wanted to leave her old life behind and lose herself in a small town where nobody knew her. And no wonder she'd almost cringed when Cooper had mentioned that she looked familiar.

Oh, Jess . . .

He clicked on the photo to expand it to full screen. How much courage had it taken for her to tell him her story, to open up and love him? If he had his way, he'd make sure she would never know that kind of pain again.

"What do you think you're doing, Cooper?"

Jess's cold voice came from behind him. He turned to find her standing in the open doorway, staring at the photo on the monitor screen. Her face was pale, her eyes narrowed.

Cooper knew he'd been caught at the worst possible time. He knew she'd be furious. All he could do was explain, apologize, and hope to heaven she'd forgive him.

Cooper switched off the image on the screen, then wondered whether he should have left it on. There was no way the situation wasn't going to be awkward as hell.

"Remember, at Grace and Sam's, I mentioned feeling as if I'd seen you before?" he began. "I couldn't remember where until you told me your story. Then I remembered seeing the photo in a magazine. I wasn't sleeping, so I thought I'd look for it online. I just wanted to make sure the woman in that picture was really you."

He'd told her the truth. But it sounded lame, he knew. And her angry expression told him that she wasn't buying his explanation.

"So why didn't you just ask me?" she demanded. "I'd have told you the truth. I'd even have found the photo for you. Why did you have to do this in the middle of the night, behind my back?"

"By the time I thought of it, you were asleep." It was true, but he sounded like a jerk—and felt like one.

"I gave you my trust, Cooper," she said. "I ripped open my soul and turned it inside out. I told you things I've kept to myself for years. And all I expected in return was the same trust and openness from you. Instead, I get up in the night for a drink of water, and here you are, checking out my story behind my back."

"I'm sorry, Jess. I don't know what to say, except that I never mistrusted you. I was curious, that was all. But I should have waited."

She drew herself up, lifting her chin and squaring her shoulders. "Well, it doesn't matter anymore. We're finished. I'm going back to my room to pack. As soon as my car's loaded, I'll be gone."

"Damn it, Jess, it's after midnight. Where do you think you're going?"

"I'll get a cheap motel room in Cottonwood Springs until my apartment's cleared out. You can keep the Christmas ornaments until you take the tree down. Then you can box them up and leave them with Grace. Unless it's in a professional capacity, I never want to speak to you again."

She turned and walked back down the hall. The next thing Cooper heard, through the wall, was the sound of her taking things out of the closet and dresser and tossing them into her suitcase. She hadn't brought much to the house. Packing wouldn't take her long.

Cooper's first impulse was to try to stop her. But no, Jess had every right to leave. And trying to keep her here would only make matters worse between them.

Everything he'd wanted had been within his reach. How could he have been such an idiot?

Knowing that any attempt to talk to her would be useless, he remained where he was, listening to the sound of suitcases closing and doors not slamming but closing hard.

Only as he heard the Taurus start up and drive away did he step out of his office. Trevor was standing in the open doorway of his bedroom, looking mussed and sleepy.

"What's going on?" he muttered. "Did you and Miss Graver have a fight?"

"Nothing like that. She just thought it would be better if she stayed somewhere else for a while."

"You had a fight."

"Yes, we did. Will you miss her?"

"I'll miss her cooking. It was a damn sight better than yours."

"Whoa, where did that expression come from?"

"From Abner and Skip. It's cowboy talk, Dad. This is Texas, remember?"

At least the kid appeared to be adjusting. But this was no time to discuss Trevor's language—especially when Cooper felt as if he'd just been kicked in the gut by a mule.

"Let's both get some sleep," he said. "You've got school tomorrow, and I've got work to do."

"What should I say if I see Miss Graver at school?"

"You just say 'Hello, Miss Graver.' And if she asks how we're doing, you answer, 'Fine.' Understand?"

"Got it." Trevor stepped back into his room, then paused. "You know, she wasn't so bad—for a cop."

"Go to bed, Trevor."

Trevor's door closed. Seconds later, through the wall, Cooper heard his son's radio come on—the volume turned low, as was the rule.

Cooper listened for a moment. A faint half-smile tugged at his lips. He shook his head.

Cowboy music.

The next day, Cooper buried himself in his work, doing his best to keep his mind off Jess. But that was easier said than done. Every time he saw the Christmas tree or even smelled it from the other room, he remembered watching her hang those precious ornaments. When he took a lunch break and warmed up the food she'd cooked, the pain of her leaving hit him all over again. When he walked into the bedroom, where she'd stripped the bed and piled the sheets for washing, it was all he could do to keep from pressing his face into those sheets and filling his senses with her womanly aura. At the sound of any vehicle coming down the lane his pulse leaped—but at least he'd known better than to jump up and look. Jess was a woman who guarded her trust. He had broken that trust. She wouldn't be coming back.

Trevor's return home provided a welcome distraction. Glory leaped off the porch and ran to meet him as he climbed off the school bus and came striding up the lane. From the front window, Cooper watched him approach, thinking how tall his son was getting. All too soon he would be a man.

Trevor paused outside the pasture, as if studying the cows, before coming inside.

"Dad," he said, "I think one of those cows is limping."

"Let's have a look." Cooper followed the boy outside to the pasture fence.

"That one." Trevor pointed. "See how her front leg stumbles a little when she walks, like it hurts? Do you think we should call Mr. Rankin? If we wait till his helper comes in the morning, she could get worse."

"Good call," Cooper said, feeling proud of his son. "Those purebred cows and the calves they're carrying are worth a lot of money. He wouldn't want to lose even one. But I don't recall that Judd Rankin ever gave me his phone number. We'll need to drive to his house. If he's at home, I'll let you give him the news yourself."

They piled into the Jeep, with Glory in the back, and drove out through the ranch gate.

The ranch's main gate was open. Close up, the house was impressive, not unduly large, but it looked as if it had undergone some extensive remodeling: a broad porch and timbered entrance with double doors in front and a built-on extension in back. The sight of it started Cooper thinking of changes he could make to his own simple house when he had the time and money.

A network of corrals, chutes, metal sheds, and a modern barn stretched behind the house. Cooper glimpsed cattle and horses in some of the pens. He recalled Abner mentioning that Judd Rankin had appeared out of nowhere after his parents died. There had to be an interesting story here. But that wasn't the reason Cooper had come today.

"Wow." Trevor climbed out of the Jeep, commanding the dog to stay put. "Now this is what I call a real ranch."

"Stick around long enough and we'll have a real ranch, too," Cooper said. "I see Mr. Rankin's pickup next to the house. With luck, we'll find him at home. Come on, let's ring the doorbell."

They rang the bell and waited for what seemed to be a long time. At last, they heard footsteps. Judd Rankin opened the door, a surprised look on his face.

"Hello," he said. "Is there something I can do for you?"

"Sorry, I would've called," Cooper said, "but I don't have your phone number. Trevor here noticed something about one of your cows. He wants to tell you about it."

Trevor described what he'd seen. "It looked like she might have something in her hoof," he said. "I thought you'd want to check her before she got worse."

Rankin frowned and nodded. "Thanks, Trevor. I appreciate your letting me know. I don't suppose you noticed the number on her ear tag, did you? That would make it easier to pick her out."

"I tried to make it out, but she wasn't that close," Trevor said. "It looked like 2022, but I can't be sure."

"That'll help. Good job, Trevor." He lifted the two-way radio that hung by a clip from his belt and spoke a few words into the transmitter. "I'm sending a couple of men over to check out that cow. If the problem's serious, they'll call me back. Meanwhile, if you've got time to stay, I've got some cold Mexican Cokes in the fridge."

"Mexican Cokes? That sounds almost illegal," Cooper joked, although he did know what the man was talking about.

"The Coca-Cola bottled in Mexico is sweetened with cane sugar," Rankin said. "The stuff sold here is sweetened with corn syrup. Some people like the Mexican Cokes better." He stepped into the kitchen and came back with a couple of glass bottles, already opened. "Here." He handed one to Cooper and one to Trevor. "What do you think?"

Trevor took a swallow. "Hey, it's good. I could get used to this!"

"I'm sorry you had to wait at the door," Rankin said. "I was working in my shop."

"Your shop?" Cooper was instantly curious. "Do you mind my asking what you do?"

"Not at all. I make custom saddles, everything by hand. It started as a hobby but it's grown into something bigger. That's why I need help with the ranching. Come on back. You might find this interesting."

Cooper and Trevor followed their host down a hallway and into a large, shed-like room with a high ceiling. The rich aromas of wood, leather, and various oils hung in the air. A long table was strewn with tools and leather pieces. Tanned hides hung like rugs along a sliding rack. Wooden saddle trees, each one labeled, sat on wooden sawhorses. A heavy-duty sewing machine stood along one wall. "I custom make them to fit the horse or the rider or both," Rankin said. "If the customer wants a fancy, tooled look, I can do that. But the main thing is a saddle that will be comfortable for hours and days of riding."

He turned to a saddle on a nearby stand. "This one's almost ready, just in time for Christmas. A movie actress ordered it for her husband, and no, I'm not allowed to share names."

"It's beautiful." Cooper ran a hand over the perfectly formed seat, the hand-tooled skirts and flaps. "I don't suppose you'd tell me what one of these would cost, either. But never mind. It's not a luxury I can afford right now."

Trevor had been wandering around the shop, taking everything in. "What's in there?" he asked, pointing to a walled-off section of the room.

"Just storage. Stuff that might or might not come in handy. I added the room to contain the mess."

"Can I look inside?" Trevor asked.

"Sure. The door's unlocked," Rankin said. "You'll want to turn on the light."

"Are you sure it's okay for him to be in there?" Cooper asked as his son disappeared into the room. "I don't want him to break anything."

"Sure. It's just junk. Spare parts, used tack, things like that."

A moment later, a rummaging sound and the jingle of brass bells came from the room, followed by a loud whoop from Trevor. "Dad! Come here! You've got to see this!"

Cooper burst through the door to find his son lifting a partial tangle of heavy leather straps, adorned with brass bells that jingled when he shifted the weight. "It's a double harness, Dad!" he said. "It would be perfect for our sleigh—so much better than that old hay wagon harness!" He turned to Rankin, who'd just come into the storage room. "I know this harness is worth a lot of money, Mr. Rankin. But could we, maybe, borrow it for Santa's sleigh, just for the Christmas parade? Then I promise we'll bring it back."

Rankin hefted more of the harness, which included two padded collars. "Hmmm. I'd almost forgotten I had this. I took it in trade for an orphan calf a few years ago. I'll tell you what, Trevor. You did me a favor by coming to tell me about the cow. I'll return the favor by letting you borrow the harness. Is that a deal?"

"Wow, yes!" Trevor pumped Rankin's hand. "Wait till I tell Abner and Skip and Maggie! Now we'll have a real Santa's sleigh!" He sobered, staring down at the tangle of straps and bells. "Now all we need is a real Santa."

"Trevor, this harness is too heavy to carry to your Jeep," Rankin said. "There's a flatbed cart outside the back door. Bring it in here. We'll load it and wheel it outside."

"Sure." Trevor was off like a shot.

"Great boy you've got there," Rankin said. "You must be proud of him."

"I am—more and more so lately," Cooper said, thinking the man might make an interesting interview. "You do amazing work. Where did you learn to make saddles?"

Rankin's eyes narrowed. "Prison," he said. "But that's a story for another time."

Jess lay awake in her room at the Budget Inn on the outskirts of Cottonwood Springs. Her end of the building was so close to the highway that headlights glared through the thin blinds every time a vehicle passed. The couple in the next room were having a noisy fight, the shower was rusty, and the mattress beneath her smelled like a baby in need of a change.

At least the woman at the front desk had let her pay by the week. But she'd only been here a couple of nights, and her endurance was already wearing thin. Maybe she could pay the tenants in her pending apartment to leave early.

Whatever she had to put up with, she couldn't go back to Cooper's place. His kisses had almost made her feel as if she'd found something special and lasting. But she should have known better. He hadn't even waited until she was out of the house to check her story and the photo. He had shown no trust in her at all, after she had trusted him with everything. She was so hurt and disappointed, she would never forgive him.

But the worst part of this mess was that Cooper, as a freelance journalist, was capable of using what he'd learned to do a "Where is this person now?" story that would make good second-section tabloid fodder. He'd promised not to use her story, but she'd already learned that Cooper's promises were nothing but lies.

Maybe it was time to look for a job in a new place. She would give the matter some thought once her move was settled.

Meanwhile she would try not to think about Cooper and how she had almost fallen in love with him.

Chapter 12

The following week

Since her move to the motel, Jess had discovered the pleasure of driving into Branding Iron early for a light breakfast at Stella's Bakery. Sitting at a tiny corner table, sipping coffee, feasting on a Danish, and chatting with Wynette between customers helped her get through the dreary days.

"So, how were your next-door neighbors last night?" Wynette asked with the tilt of an eyebrow.

"Well . . . at least they weren't fighting." Jess shook her head. "But I'm planning to pick up a set of earplugs on the way home."

"Good idea. You're going to get through this and be fine, you know. You're one tough lady."

"I hope you're right. Sometimes I have my doubts." Jess suppressed the urge to ask whether Cooper had stopped by the bakery. Even if he had, she'd instructed her friend not to tell her. To Wynette's credit, she hadn't asked why.

Nobody knew the reason Jess had moved out of Cooper's house—not unless Cooper had told them. But Branding Iron was a small town, and sooner or later the rumors would start flying. When they did, Jess knew she would have to be prepared.

"So, Wynette, are you ready for your bridal shower tonight?" she asked, changing the subject.

"Ready as I'll ever be." Wynette grinned. "I can't believe Buck's sister would do this for me. So kind. Are you coming?"

"I wouldn't miss it." The shower would be a nice break, as long as she could dodge any personal questions that might come up—but never mind that. Tonight was all about Wynette and her wedding. Her own problems could wait.

Jess had almost finished her coffee when Buck walked into the bakery. He looked rumpled, red-eyed, and exhausted, as if he'd been awake all night.

"Hi, honey." He leaned over the counter to give Wynette a quick peck, then turned toward Jess. "Hi, Jess. I saw your car outside and figured you might want to hear this."

Jess rose to offer him the single chair, while Wynette poured coffee into a porcelain mug. Shaking his head, Buck declined both. "I can't stay," he said. "But I wanted to tell you that I've got Ed McCoy locked up in the jail again. Ruth's pretty beat-up. Nothing broken, but she's got a cracked rib and a lot of bruising where the bastard worked her over. I'll be picking her up at the clinic and taking her home. Skip, her boy, is watching the little girls. He might not be in school today."

"I'll tell Skip's teachers he has family responsibilities," Jess said. "Blast that Ed. He needs to stay behind bars. But you know the old story. Ruth will show up tomorrow and take him home."

"Not this time," Buck said. "Ruth told me to file charges and keep him in jail long enough for her to get away. She's leaving him and taking the girls to her sister's house. While she's there, she says, she'll be talking to a lawyer."

Jess's throat tightened. This was what she'd told Ruth to do. "What about Skip?"

"As long as Ed's in jail, Skip should be all right in the house. If there's a problem, he says that Abner would take him in. The house belongs to Ruth. She wants to come back when it's safe. But she'll need a lawyer to make sure Ed stays away for good."

"So what's going to happen with Ed?"

"Right now he's sleeping it off. Once he sobers up, he'll be charged and get his bail hearing. I'll advise the judge to set bail high enough to keep him in lockup till his trial. That should give Ruth a few weeks to get everything in place."

"And the trial? What happens there?" Jess asked.

"Ruth will have to testify. The photos I took of her should help. Assuming he's found guilty, the sentence could be anything from time served to a couple of years. The important thing is keeping the family safe."

"In that case . . ." Jess took one of her business cards from her purse and scrawled the number of the motel on the back. "Take this, Buck. If anyone in the family needs help, will you give me a call?"

"Sure." He took the card. "Right now, I've got to go." He glanced from Jess to his fiancée. "Not a word about this, you two. I don't want anything getting out that could set that scumbag free. Understand?"

Jess nodded. Wynette crossed her heart over her pink smock. She loved a good story, but she knew how to keep a secret, especially where her future husband's work was concerned.

Jess left right after Buck did. She needed to get to her office at the high school in time to clear Skip's absence with his teachers. She wouldn't give them any details, of course. Telling them that he was needed for an emergency at home should be enough.

Skip was showing signs of becoming a responsible young man. But with his home life in chaos, he was walking a tightrope. Keeping the boy headed straight was her job, Jess reminded herself. She needed to support not only Skip but his mother.

What if Ruth had threatened to leave Ed because of what Jess had told her? Could that have been the reason Ed had beaten his wife again?

Could Jess's own words have set this current crisis in motion?

She drove up Main Street, toward the high school at the far end. The strings of lights that crisscrossed overhead lent an unnatural cheer to the bleak morning. But Jess wasn't feeling any Christmas spirit today. She had too much on her mind.

She passed the intersection with the street that led to her house. With Ed McCoy in jail, the contractor should have other people working on it. But she wouldn't have time to check until after school. Then she'd have three hours to kill before Wynette's bridal shower. Since it wasn't worth driving to her Cottonwood Springs motel room and back, she would do a little shopping, maybe get a snack, and spend the rest of the time in her office.

As she drove, images of the people whose lives she'd touched with a few well-meaning words clicked through her mind like an old-fashioned slide show.

She pictured Ed McCoy in his cell, waking up in a post-alcoholic rage. Did he know his wife was planning to leave him, or was he expecting her to show up and take him home? He'd controlled Ruth for years with threats and abuse. The idea of losing that control could make him even more dangerous than he already was.

She imagined Ruth, battered and broken, facing a crossroads in her life. Had she finally had enough? Or, as Buck drove her home, was she already having second thoughts?

And Skip, waiting at home with his frightened little sisters, doing his best to be a man. What was going through his mind? If his mother left, would he be all right on his own? Would he be safe in the house?

Whatever was about to happen, Jess knew one thing—if she were to turn her back on this troubled family, she would never forgive herself. With Christmas so close and the father in jail, someone would need to see that their needs were met. Maybe it would fall to her to be their Santa.

The bridal shower started at seven. Buck's older sister, Charlene, had married the assistant manager of the bank. Their nice home, on the outskirts of Branding Iron, included a spacious parlor with room for Wynette's many friends to come and wish her well.

Shower gifts were piled under the lavishly decorated Christmas tree in the corner of the room. Jess laid her wrapped gift—a set of luxury sheets—with the others before taking time to survey the room.

Most of the women were strangers to her, or mothers she recognized from school events but didn't know by name. Since she didn't attend church or make much effort to socialize, she felt a prickle of unease as she searched for a friendly face.

Wynette was surrounded by well-wishers. But Grace had just come in and was being greeted by the hostess at the door. As the wife of Branding Iron's new mayor, she'd be expected to mingle. But to Jess's relief, Grace crossed the room, pausing only for a few greetings, before coming over to hug her.

"Here you are," she said. "I was hoping you'd come."

"You know I couldn't miss Wynette's bridal shower," Jess said.

"Of course not. But I've been worried about you. Maggie

told me you'd left Cooper's place and moved into this trashy motel in Cottonwood Springs. Is it even safe there?"

"Don't worry. I know how to take care of myself. But yes, the motel is a dump. I even found a roach in the bathroom last night—got him with hairspray and threw him in the trash."

Grace shuddered. "You're a lot tougher than I am. I don't know how you stand living in a place like that."

"At least it's cheap. And I'll only be there until my apartment comes vacant after Christmas."

Grace sighed. "I know. But I was really hoping that you and Cooper . . ." She shook her head. "Cooper's one of the best guys I know. And I certainly didn't imagine the chemistry between you two. What happened?"

"Maybe you should ask Cooper."

"I did. He said that what happened was between the two of you, but he was guilty of being a complete jerk, and he could only hope you'd give him another chance."

"I'm not sure I can. Not anytime soon at least." Jess forced back a rush of emotion. She had shared the darkest piece of her soul with Cooper, and he had callously indulged his curiosity without a second thought.

Fixing her face in a smile, she changed the subject. "Say, that buffet table looks good, and people are already helping themselves. I'm starved. How about you?"

"I'm right behind you."

The buffet, with its array of miniature sandwiches, salads, drinks, and delicate pastries from Stella's Bakery, was as tasty as it was tempting. Jess filled her small paper plate before turning back to Grace.

"Go on now. You needn't babysit me. I know you have other people to greet."

Grace hesitated, then nodded. "If you're sure, I'll catch you later." She made her way toward a cluster of people on the far side of the room. Jess had spotted two women from the high school, both new in town, who looked slightly lost. They were happy to have her join them.

"Goodness!" Megan Smith taught American History. "I've never seen so many people at a bridal shower. Every woman in town must be here."

"Not quite," Jess said, thinking of Ruth and others like her who lived on the fringes of Branding Iron society. "But Wynette makes a lot of friends in the bakery. Before taking that job she was selling beauty products, so she met more women that way. And of course, everyone in town knows Buck."

"We've been trying to pick out people we know." Karen Carlquist worked in the school office. "But we don't recognize that beautiful dark-haired woman alone by the fireplace. Do you know her?"

Jess followed her gaze. "Oh, yes. That's Wynette's boss, Stella Galanos, or whatever her name is now. She owns Stella's Bakery. She used to work there, but she quit to marry a man who owns a Greek restaurant in Cottonwood Springs."

"The Acropolis, I'll bet! My husband took me there for our anniversary," Megan said. "It's fabulous—and expensive. So I take it Stella is Greek, too. She's stunning, like one of those Greek statues come to life."

"Yes, I always thought so, too," Jess agreed. But she'd just noticed something else about Stella. A year ago, when Jess had last seen her in the bakery, Stella had been wearing a spectacular diamond engagement ring. She'd had it on a chain around her neck to keep it safe while she worked. But today there was no sign of the ring, or any other ring, on her hand. Had something happened—a broken engagement or even a divorce?

This wasn't the time or place to be curious, but maybe the next time Jess saw Wynette at the bakery, she would ask.

* * *

By the time the guests had eaten, played a few giggle-inducing games, and watched Wynette open her mountain of gifts, exclaiming over every one, it was almost ten o'clock.

Jess hugged Wynette, thanked her hostess, put on her coat, and made her way down the street to where she'd parked her car.

Gusts of wind, which had been a light breeze when she arrived, now threatened to rip her coat off her body. On and off through the week, minor storms had been blowing in, bringing bursts of powdery snow, too brief and too light to stay on the ground. But this time the wind and the murky clouds stampeding in from the west were different. This weather meant business.

Her temporary, cockroach-ridden home was an hour away. But the Taurus was a big, solid car with new tires. She'd driven in worse weather than this, Jess reminded herself as she forced the car door open and braced it while she slid into the driver's seat. Released, the door slammed shut behind her, leaving her in sudden silence.

Only then did she realize how exhausted she was.

She'd slept poorly last night and been on the go all day. Between the rift with Cooper and the situation with the McCoy family, worry had chewed her nerves raw. All she wanted to do was sleep. But first she had to drive back to the motel. And even then, if her neighbors were going at it, she'd be lucky to get much rest.

She started the engine and switched on the headlights. The clouds blowing in could mean snow—even a rare Texas blizzard. But for now there was only wind. By the time the full storm blew in, she'd be at the motel.

She made it to the highway, wind battering the side of the car. Two huge semitrucks had pulled off the shoulder of the road to avoid the danger of being blown over. But her car was much lower. She would be all right.

A cardboard box flew across the road, hitting her windshield and blocking her view for a moment before it flapped away on the wind like a clumsy bird. Ten miles out of town, she could feel the need to sleep creeping through her body. Turning on the radio, she punched the Christmas music up to full volume and sang along.

"Jolly old Saint Nicholas, lean your ear this way. Don't you tell a single soul, what I'm going to say . . ."

Would Saint Nicholas really not tell, or would he be like Cooper Chapman and start digging for more information?

Ridiculous question. But it made her so angry that she turned off the radio with a click. So much for Christmas spirit. Maggie had called Cooper a Scrooge. Now she was becoming one, too.

Jess could see no other cars coming toward her on the road. She switched the headlights on high beam. Tumbleweeds from a nearby field flowed like a ghostly tide, bounding and rolling across the road. Slowing, she eased a path through them and continued on. She was getting sleepy . . . so sleepy.

The blast of a horn and the glare of lights in her eyes shocked her awake. She swerved hard right as a heavy truck flashed past her in the night. Shaking, she pulled onto the shoulder of the road. She must've dozed off and wandered over the center line. Only split-second timing—and luck— had saved her from a terrible accident.

She couldn't risk going on—not while she was a danger to herself and others. She would find a safe place to pull off the road and take a short nap before driving the rest of the way to Cottonwood Springs.

She crept along the edge of the road for another mile before finding a wide graveled area that marked the spot where a side road turned off toward a cluster of feed silos. Leaving plenty of room for anyone who might happen along, she pulled onto the far edge, locked the car doors, reclined her seat, and lay back.

Her position wasn't very comfortable, but she didn't plan on sleeping long—just long enough to take the edge off—maybe fifteen or twenty minutes. She would leave the parking lights on for safety. The car was warm inside. By the time it cooled, she'd be awake and ready to get back on the road.

She closed her eyes. Wrapped in her coat and lulled by the wind, she let sleep close over her like a downy quilt.

She woke to the glare of headlights from behind the car and a furious tapping on the side window. She turned toward the sound, struggling to sit up. The air around her was chilly, her limbs stiff and aching. Heavens, how long had she slept?

"Jess!" The familiar voice, raised to a shout, reached her through the glass. Half lit from behind and framed in snow, a face was visible. Cooper's face.

She lowered the window partway and raised her seat back. "What are you doing here?" she demanded, emotions clashing.

"Looking for you. I was worried, damn it."

"Why were you even looking? I thought I made it clear that I didn't want to talk to you."

"You did. But I've got things to say—things you need to hear. Grace told me you'd be on the road after the shower, so I waited by your motel, hoping we could go somewhere and talk. Finally, with the weather getting worse and no sign of you, I drove back to look for you. Thank God you're all right."

"I was just sleepy. So I pulled over to rest. What time is it?"

"Last time I checked, it was about eleven thirty. You must

be freezing in your car. Come on back and get in the Jeep, where it's warm. We can talk there."

"No." Her distrust kicked in—although she distrusted herself more than she did Cooper. "If you want to talk to me, get in my car, and plan to leave as soon as you're finished— or when I'm finished with you." She clicked the automatic button to release the lock. Cooper went around the car, brushing the snow off his coat before climbing into the passenger seat. Snowflakes glistened on his dark hair.

Jess started the engine and turned up the heat. "All right," she said, turning to face him. "I'm listening."

He exhaled, fogging the chilled window. "I just wanted to apologize," he said. "The first time I met you, I was intrigued—and attracted. I wanted to know more, not in order to exploit your secrets but to understand you. And the more I learned about you, the more I came to care about you."

Jess's gaze dropped to her clasped hands. She sensed what was coming, and she wasn't ready to hear it. "Don't," she said. "I don't want to be backed into a corner, Cooper. I know you're a decent man. But what you need is a sweet, uncomplicated woman with no dark past and no trust issues. There are plenty of those in Branding Iron. Just open your eyes and look around."

He was silent for a moment. Then he cleared his throat. "I'm not trying to back you into a corner, Jess. All I'm asking is that you take some time before you make a final judgment call. Give me a chance to prove that you can trust me."

"And how long do you expect that to take?" The tension in Jess's voice was almost painful.

"As long as you need," he said. "I've got plenty of time, and I'm willing to wait. And I promise that the story you told me won't go anywhere—ever."

Jess studied his face, etched in the reflected headlights from the Jeep. Such a handsome face, so strong and gentle. It would be so easy to give in to this man, to melt in his arms and forget the reasons why she'd packed up and fled his home in the middle of the night. But surrender wouldn't change what had happened. And it wouldn't make the anger and distrust go away. Maybe nothing would.

"I think it's time you were going," she said.

"All right." He shifted in his seat. "But I was hoping for some kind of answer."

"Fine. You deserve that much, at least," she said. "My only answer is that I need time and space—and don't ask me how much because I don't know. That's the best I can do. Take it or leave it."

"For now, I'll take it." He opened the door. A gust of windblown snow whooshed into the car. He pulled the door partway closed, gripping the handle. "The weather's getting worse. I'll drive behind you as far as the motel. You can't fault me for wanting you to get there safely."

"Thank you. I appreciate that. But don't call me. If I have anything to say, I'll let you know."

"Let's get going." He climbed out of the car, closing the door quickly. Jess put the Taurus in gear and pulled back onto the road. She drove slowly, half blinded by the flying snow. The road surface was already getting slick. She was grateful for the headlights that stayed behind her, far enough to avoid a glaring reflection in her rearview mirror.

Twenty minutes later, she reached the motel and pulled into her parking place. The Jeep lingered at the edge of the lot until she'd safely unlocked the door to her room. Then Cooper swung the heavy vehicle into a U-turn and headed back down the highway.

Jess watched the red taillights vanish into the storm before she went inside. The room was chilly but once she turned it on, the noisy space heater worked. Still wearing her coat, she sank to the edge of the bed, waiting for the air to warm.

The next-door neighbors were having some kind of party,

with loud music, raucous laughter, and occasional thumps and bumps, like bodies crashing into furniture. She had reason to complain to the manager, but why bother? She already knew that she wouldn't be able to sleep.

Sometime after 1:00 a.m., the noise next door faded away. Clad in her flannel pajamas, Jess lay sleepless in the bed. If she were home, or even at Cooper's, she might get up, make herself a snack, and curl up in a chair with a good book. But here there was no place to go and nothing to do. Nothing except lie here, listen to the rattle of the heater, and think about how her whole life had turned topsy-turvy.

She could have forgiven Cooper on the spot tonight. Why had she insisted that he prove himself? What had entitled her to demand such a thing? She wouldn't blame him if he threw up his hands and walked away from her.

None of this mess was Cooper's fault. It was hers. Why couldn't she simply let go of her fears and love him? Wasn't that what she really wanted?

Outside, the snow was still falling. If it kept up, the school district would probably declare a snow day. She would call in and check tomorrow morning. If school had been canceled, she would give herself a break—go somewhere nice for breakfast, do some Christmas shopping at the mall, even sit through an afternoon movie.

Maybe a day of total self-indulgence would lift her spirits and give her a fresh outlook on her own problems, which were nothing compared to what others were dealing with—like Ruth McCoy, who was struggling to keep her family safe and start a new life. Since she didn't have the address or phone number of Ruth's sister here in Cottonwood Springs, Jess could only hope for the best.

After a few hours of fitful sleep, Jess woke to a gray morning. Cracking open the blinds, she gazed out at a landscape thickly blanketed in fresh snow—snow that was still falling.

Using the room phone, she called the recorded message on the district line. The message confirmed that today would indeed be a snow day.

The students would be over the moon.

The Christmas parade and ball would be held the Saturday before Christmas—that would make it this weekend, just a few days off. After such a big storm, there should be enough snow to drive the sleigh on its runners. A real white Christmas. That would please Maggie and Trevor, and probably Skip, too.

A shadow of worry crossed her mind as she thought about the boy, alone in the house with his mother gone and his father in jail. But Skip was capable and independent. He would be all right. If anything went wrong, he would have both Abner and Cooper nearby to look after him. And she would check on him if he didn't show up at school the next day.

The TV in the room was broken, but the radio worked. After tuning it to a station that played Christmas music, Jess showered, washed her hair, and dressed in jeans, boots, and a red cashmere sweater. She took her time. The snowplows, what few the city owned, were still clearing off the main streets, and the mall didn't open until nine.

This had been a good idea, giving herself a small holiday. Maybe she could even find some good clothes on sale to amp up her meager wardrobe. And presents? That was a bigger issue. Cooper and his son had taken her in, but she and Cooper were barely on speaking terms, and Trevor had never warmed to her. Still, she wanted to get them something—maybe books, or something for the house. Or maybe she should just get a dozen boxes of gourmet chocolates and pass them out to all her friends. After all, she didn't have a Christmas tree or even a house to put it in. Her vacation plans had vanished when the tree fell on her house, and she wasn't even going to the ball.

Christmas. Bah! Humbug! She put on her hat, coat, boots, and gloves, turned off the radio, and went outside to scrape the snow off her car.

Faintly, from somewhere behind her, she heard what sounded like a ringing phone. But it was probably someone else's. And even if it was for her, she'd never make it back inside in time to answer.

Someone had plowed a path out of the parking lot. With her car scraped clean of snow, Jess climbed into the driver's seat, started the engine, and drove away.

Chapter 13

When Trevor looked out of his bedroom window, his jaw dropped. Snow, at least eight inches deep, was blanketing everything, and it was still coming down.

"Wow, awesome . . ." he murmured. Seattle got plenty of rain, and occasional light snow, but he'd never seen snowfall like this. This was real Christmas snow. If only he didn't have to go to school.

Glory, who now slept on the rug next to his bed, was waiting by the bedroom door. When he opened it, she went bounding down the hall to the front door, wiggling and whining until he let her out. With a happy bark, she dived off the porch and began romping in the snow.

Trevor's dad was seated at the kitchen table, drinking his morning coffee. "I take it you haven't heard the news on the radio," he said.

"News?" Trevor shook his head. The local station had music at night but nothing worth hearing in the morning.

"No school," Cooper said. "It's called a snow day."

"No school? You're kidding!"

"No kidding. But there are still chores to be done. Get some warm clothes on while I make you breakfast."

Trevor raced back to his room. He didn't have much in the way of heavy-duty winter clothes, but he could dress in layers, a vest over a sweater, and a coat over that, with extra wool socks on his feet and the rubber rain boots he'd worn in Seattle. His dad would have gloves and a wool cap he could borrow. For now, that would have to do.

As he dressed, he could smell bacon frying in the kitchen. He would eat, take care of the horses, and then maybe go over to Abner's and see if the old man needed any help. Abner had planned to be back from his trip last night, although the snow might have delayed him.

Skip was supposed to have come by to feed Abner's dog and check the place. But Skip hadn't been in school yesterday. Maybe he was sick. Or maybe he'd been needed to tend his little sisters. That happened sometimes. But surely he would show up later that afternoon when they planned to set the sleigh on its runners and try gliding it for a short distance. Even Maggie was going to be there. They'd planned to cushion the ground with straw, but snow would make everything perfect.

"We might need your help, Dad," he said as his father scooped two fried eggs onto his plate and caught the slice of toast that popped out of the toaster. "Abner has a bad back, so he won't be able to lift the sleigh off the sawhorses. And I don't know if Skip and I can do it alone. With all the hardware on it, that sleigh's pretty heavy."

"I'll be glad to help," his father said. "I've got an article that has to be finished today, but when that's done, which should be sometime this afternoon, I'll come over."

"Could you bring the horses?" Trevor slathered grape jelly on his toast and took a bite. "If you could bring them and help with the harness, we could take a real sleigh ride."

"I could try. We'll see how the weather's looking by then."

"We've got to do it soon. The parade's this Saturday. We can't just hitch up the team and go, Dad. We don't even have a driver. I thought Abner might do it, but he says it'll hurt his back. You said you've driven a hay wagon with a team. Could you do it?"

"It's been a long time. I'd offer to be your backup. But there's bound to be somebody better."

"How about Mr. Rankin? He's a real cowboy. I bet he'd know how to drive a team."

"Judd Rankin strikes me as a loner. He'd probably say no. Let's wait on that for now. Don't worry, you're not the only one working on this problem. It'll be all right."

Trevor cleaned his plate and gulped down the last of his hot chocolate. He was eager to get out in the snow, even if it was only to work.

"The snow shovel I found in the shed is on the porch," his dad said. "You'll need to clear a path to the barn. If you get tired, come find me and I'll spell you. Right now, I've got to get going on that article."

Glory was waiting on the porch. Trevor found the shovel and started scooping out a path, with the dog frisking around him.

Standing at the front window, Cooper took a moment to watch his son. There'd been times when he'd had his doubts about the move to Branding Iron and the purchase of the ranch. But so far things seemed to be working out. Trevor was maturing and becoming more responsible. He even seemed happy most of the time. It was as much as Cooper could ask for.

The Christmas tree stood in a shadowed corner of the liv-

ing room. Unlit now, it recalled the absence of the woman
who'd left him and driven off in the night. There'd been
times when having Jess here had felt almost like family.
He'd even pictured the Christmas they would enjoy together, the tree glowing, the fireplace warming the room as
they played music and opened presents.

He'd known all along that she wasn't here to stay—but
the way she'd departed, angry and hurt, had left him with an
aching hollow inside. He wanted her back, in his home and
in his arms—for Christmas.

Now that she'd given him a second chance, he would
guard his every word and every move. Whatever happened,
he couldn't risk losing her again.

Turning away from the window, he made quick work of
cleaning up breakfast. Then he went back down the hall to
where his overdue assignment waited. He would make every
effort to finish the article and send it off by midafternoon.
That would give him time to take the horses over to Abner's,
where they would probably stay until after the parade. Trevor,
Skip, and Maggie would be excited for their first real sleigh
ride. Cooper could only hope he'd remember how to hitch
and drive the team.

Cooper had mentioned to his son that other people were
working on the problem of finding a Santa and a driver.
What he'd promised not to mention was the conversation
he'd had with his sister the day before. Sam had found the
perfect Santa, and Grace was altering the old Santa suit to fit
him. Sam had also found an expert to drive the sleigh. But
all that was to be a surprise for Maggie and the two boys
who'd worked so hard to get the sleigh ready.

Cooper would be offering behind-the-scenes help with
getting the sleigh and horses safely to town. The sleigh
would be hauled the distance on a flatbed truck with a ramp.
The horses would travel in an enclosed trailer. Sam would
be responsible for bringing Santa. At the high school athletic

field, where the parade would start, everything would come together.

Hopefully, with everyone doing their part, Branding Iron's first Christmas parade would be a success. But he would think about that later, Cooper told himself as he took a seat and turned on his computer. Right now he needed to earn a living.

Jess had enjoyed her free day but not as much as she'd hoped. Her breakfast at a noisy mall restaurant—scrambled eggs, hash browns, sausage, and pancakes—had been more than she could eat. Afterward, as she'd strolled past glittering shop windows, mingling with crowds, hearing the blare of Christmas music, and inhaling a too-sweet mélange of pine, candles, and cinnamon buns, she'd felt like an alien life form that had landed here from another planet.

With school canceled for the day, there were children and teens swarming everywhere—girls trying cheap makeup and jewelry, boys playing games in the arcade, little ones tagging after their mothers, whining for toys and treats they saw.

What was wrong with her today? Most of the time she loved children. Today they just made her want to run and hide. Maybe it was because she'd barely slept last night—or because she was still conflicted about Cooper.

At least she'd found a few sales. At GAP, she'd bought a pair of jeans, a black sweater, and a leather jacket on clearance. And she'd also found some dressy boots with kitten heels. At the gourmet candy place, she'd bought a dozen boxes of assorted chocolates, already gift wrapped, to have ready for giving. As an afterthought, she'd stepped into a bookstore and picked up a copy of the bestseller she'd been planning to read.

Loaded down with shopping bags, she'd carried her purchases out to her car and locked them in the trunk. By now it was around noon. But she wasn't hungry enough to eat lunch, and it was too early to go home. Maybe she could find a good movie.

Leaving her car, she went back inside to the wing where the movie theaters were located. Most of the movies had already started or weren't scheduled to start until later. Of the movies that fit her time slot, the likeliest one appeared to be a romantic comedy with a Christmas theme—girl comes back to her hometown for the holidays and meets the boy she broke up with in high school. At least it didn't sound depressing. Jess paid for her ticket and found a seat.

Two forgettable hours later, the movie was over, and Jess had run out of excuses to stay away from the motel. At least she'd have something to read now. Or maybe she could nap and catch up on last night's lost sleep.

A light, powdery snow was falling. She brushed it off her car, climbed in, and headed back to the motel. She turned on the radio, hoping to get some weather news, but there was nothing on the local station except Christmas music.

By the time Jess pulled into her parking slot at the motel, she'd decided to leave her purchases in the trunk. They would be cleaner and safer there than in her motel room. There was nothing to take inside but her purse, the book, and the bag of fresh-baked pretzels she'd bought after the movie.

She was fumbling in her purse for her room key when she noticed the yellow Post-it note stuck to the number plate on the door. Pulling it off, she read the scrawled message.

Call Sheriff Winston's office. Urgent. It was followed by a phone number.

The note was damp, the ends curled, as if it had been on her door for a long time. Jess remembered the ringing phone she'd heard as she was leaving. She'd dismissed it from her mind, but what if it had been Buck, trying to reach her at the number she'd given him? The room phones had no voice messaging. When she didn't answer, Buck must've called the front desk.

Urgent. She stared at the word, worry forming a sour knot in her stomach. What was wrong? What had she missed? Nerves quivering, she hurried into the room, snatched up the receiver, and dialed the number.

"Sheriff Winston's office." Jess recognized the voice of Helen Wilkerson, the longtime receptionist who'd served under every sheriff for the past twenty years.

"Helen, this is Jess Graver," she said. "I just got a message to call this number."

"Yes, Jess. Buck isn't here, but I can tell you the reason he called you. Ed McCoy is out of jail. His cousin, the one he works for, posted his bail."

"Oh, no!" Jess felt her heart drop. "Do you know where he is?"

"Not anymore. Ed was cautioned to stay away from the house and from his wife. But that's no guarantee of anything. Buck wanted to see if you could locate Ruth and warn her that her husband is out. But that was this morning. I hope it's not too late."

"So do I. I'll do everything I can. Tell Buck he can reach me here at the motel—for now."

Pulse slamming, she ended the call. Images flashed through her mind—the brute of a man she'd met working on her house; his wife's bruised face, swollen eyes, and battered limbs. Had Ruth really left him this time? Or had she changed her mind and stayed home?

Either way, Jess needed to make her aware of the danger. When she'd counseled Ruth in her office, she hadn't thought to get the sister's address or phone number, or even her name. But surely Ed would know it.

Maybe he'd already found her.

Going on Ed's past behavior, if he knew she'd left—or even tried to—he'd be raging.

And what about Skip? There was no record of Ed's hurting his children. But Skip wasn't really his. And if he found the boy alone in the house, he could vent his anger on him.

Jess didn't have the McCoys' phone number. The closest number she had was Cooper's. She could ask him to go and make sure the boy was safe.

Without hesitation, she punched the number into the phone and heard the ring on the other end—once, then twice.

Please, please pick up . . .

But the only answer was Cooper's voice mail. Jess left him a terse message, asking him to check on Skip, then ended the call.

She was running out of options. But she had a card like the one she'd given Ruth, with the lawyer's number on it. Sharon Blackerby had retired from full-time practice, but still did some pro bono work, mostly for needy women and children. Sharon had worked with Jess on other cases. If Ruth had called her, Sharon should have a number where she could be reached.

Sharon answered on the first ring. "What is it, Jess? You sound worried."

Jess explained the situation as briefly as possible.

"Yes, Ruth called me," Sharon said. "She has an appointment tomorrow."

"But her husband could be coming to find her. She needs to know about this right away."

"Of course, she does. We might want to get a restraining order, or at least move her and the little ones somewhere safe. I'll call her at her sister's right now. Don't worry, Jess, I've got this."

"Thank you, Sharon. That frees me to go to Branding Iron and check on her son. She left him taking care of the house."

"Go. You can call me later."

Jess ended the call, gathered up a few necessities, and

hurried back outside. The parking strip along the front of the motel units had been salted, which served to melt the slush around the wheels of her car. She was about to open the door and climb into the front seat when she noticed it—the head of a nail sticking out from the tread of a sagging tire. Her heart sank.

No! Not now! Of all the times for this to happen—

She had her AAA card with her, but on a day like this, rife with dead batteries, slide-offs, and stuck vehicles, she'd be lucky to get a service truck here in the next hour. At least she knew how to change a tire on her own. But it would be a cold, wet, dirty job. And once she got the mini-tire in place, she'd have to find a shop to patch or replace the damaged one.

Meanwhile, with Ed McCoy out of jail, his whole family could be in danger.

With a sigh, Jess opened the trunk of the Taurus. Shoving her shopping bags aside, she raised the liner to get at the jack, the lug wrench, and the spare tire.

By midafternoon, Cooper had finished his article and emailed it off, with photos, to the editor of *Western Sportsman*. It was time to take the two horses, Spot and Dusty, over to Abner's to try them with the sleigh.

He couldn't help feeling uneasy. A lot of years had passed since he'd handled a team of horses. And pulling a sleigh on snow would be different from pulling a hay wagon. The big geldings were gentle and well-trained, but this would be a new situation for them. Even the brass jingle bells on the fancy harness might be enough to spook them. The parade situation, too, could be stressful, with so many people around. Cooper could only hope the man Sam had asked to handle the team was good at his job.

The horses would be left at Abner's until after the parade.

The mysterious driver would be responsible for trailering them to the high school, hitching them to the sleigh, and bringing them home to Cooper's barn. The hardware store owner, who had a low flatbed trailer for hauling lumber, would transport the sleigh. Cooper had offered to help him load and unload. Sam would be responsible for getting Santa to the parade and back.

The whole situation was a white-knuckle gamble. If everything went well, the Santa sleigh would give the children a magical experience and put Branding Iron on the map as a go-to place for pre-Christmas festivities.

But if even one thing went wrong, the whole production could fall apart. And no one would be more devastated than the three young people who were trying so hard to make it happen—Maggie, Trevor, and Skip.

In the barn, Cooper got the two horses into their halters and attached lead ropes. By now the road that connected most of the properties had been cleared by passing vehicles. But the shortcut between fields that led to Abner's place was still blocked by snow. Cooper had planned to walk the narrow lane, leading the animals, but he'd decided instead to hitch them to the Jeep's rear bumper and drive slowly ahead of them to break a path through the snow. As he drove, he could see the tracks where Trevor had gone that way a few hours earlier. With luck, the sleigh would be ready to move into position and hitch to the team. Then, if all went well on the first run, he could take the three youngsters for a short sleigh ride.

A few minutes later he pulled into Abner's yard and parked next to the barn. The older man, trailed by his big dog, came out to meet him. He was dressed for the weather in a red-and-green plaid mackinaw and a knitted cap of thick red wool.

"Bring the horses into the barn," he said. "I've got hay and water all ready for them."

Cooper went behind the Jeep and untied the lead ropes. Glory, who'd hitched a ride, jumped to the ground and ran to play with her friend. As the two dogs frisked in the snow, Cooper led the horses to their stalls. The sleigh still rested on the two sawhorses. There was no sign of Trevor or the other two children.

"Where are the kids?" Cooper asked. "Are they in the house?"

Abner shook his head. "Your sister dropped Maggie off about forty-five minutes ago. She and Trevor waited for Skip to get here, but he never showed up. Finally they decided to go to his house and look for him. I told them to come right back, so they should be here soon. I'd have gone myself but I can't walk that far and my old truck's on the blink."

Cooper tried to ignore the unease in his gut. He'd never been to the McCoy house, but he didn't like what he'd heard about Skip's home life, and he didn't have a good feeling about the situation.

"Which way did they go?" he asked. "I didn't see their tracks on the way here."

"There's another road that cuts off just past my property. That's where the McCoys live. Maggie said she knew how to get there. Otherwise, Trevor probably would have gone without her."

"They'll be getting cold," Cooper said, hiding his anxiety. "Point me in the right direction. I'll go and pick them up."

Abner gave him some directions. "I'm sorry," he said. "If I'd given more thought to it, I probably wouldn't have let them go. But they were worried about Skip. And you know kids."

"I know. It's not your fault, Abner. I'm sure they'll be fine. Just cold." Cooper climbed into the Jeep. Glory, seeing that he was about to leave, rocketed into the back.

Telling himself he was worried for nothing, Cooper drove out of the yard and headed up the snow-packed road.

Trevor had never seen the house where Skip lived. He'd known the family was poor. Skip's bike and his clothes had told him that much. He also knew that Skip's father worked construction on and off, and that when he drank too much, he tended to beat Skip's mother. She was a nice woman. He'd met her when she'd cleaned the ranch house before Trevor and his dad had moved in.

Now, as he and Maggie approached the small house, which was covered in dented aluminum siding with a sagging porch and a couple of snow-covered junk cars in the side yard, Trevor felt a fluttering sensation below his ribs, like the way he sometimes felt when he was about to be sick. He looked for the old brown Chevy sedan that Skip's mother drove. It wasn't here. Aside from the junk cars, only a battered heavy-duty Ford pickup was parked in the driveway. The single lines of packed snow behind the wheels told Trevor that the truck had arrived sometime after the storm and hadn't left since.

Maybe this was a bad idea, he thought. Maybe they should stop and go back to Abner's. But Maggie was marching ahead of him up the unshoveled walk, determined and fearless. It would be embarrassing to be shown up by a girl barely half his age and half his size.

By the time he caught up with Maggie on the porch, she had already rung the doorbell.

A beat of silence passed. Then, from beyond the door, came the sound of heavy work boots. The door opened inward to reveal the looming figure of a man, rumpled and unshaven, with narrow, bloodshot eyes.

"Please, sir," Maggie said. "We're looking for our friend Skip McCoy. Is he here?"

The man's annoyed scowl morphed into a grin. "Yeah, Skip's here, all right. Come on in. I'll tell him he's got company."

Trevor followed Maggie into the house. That was when they heard a frantic shout.

"Trevor! Maggie! Don't come in! Run!"

Trevor grabbed Maggie's arm and yanked her toward the open door. But he wasn't fast enough. The door slammed shut, blocking their escape. Looking beyond the big man, Trevor could see Skip, tied to a kitchen chair. His face was bruised down one side.

"Let them go, Dad," Skip pleaded. "They aren't part of this."

"They are now," Ed McCoy growled. "You two. Sit down over there where I can see you. Do exactly what I say. If I get what I want, nobody's gonna get hurt."

Keeping Maggie close, Trevor took a seat on an old-style kitchen chair with a metal frame and plastic seat. McCoy tossed Maggie a length of clothesline cord that lay on the table. "Tie your friend to the chair with this, girlie. Make it good and tight. If you do a good job, I won't tie you up, too."

"My name's Maggie Delaney." She faced him defiantly. "My father's the mayor, and I don't have to do what you say."

McCoy smirked. "You might want to think about that, honey."

His hand reached behind his back, pulled a .38 revolver out of his belt, and pointed it directly at the little girl. "Now, do as you're told, or I flip a coin to decide who gets shot first."

Hands trembling, Maggie wrapped the cord several times around Trevor's arms and upper body, binding him to the chair. She tied the knot in back, as tightly as her small hands could pull. Trevor suspected he could probably get loose, but as long as Ed McCoy had that pistol, he knew better than to try.

"Now sit still." Using the gun as a pointer, he directed Maggie to an empty chair. "Not a peep, any of you. I've got a phone call to make."

Keeping the pistol aimed at his captives, he picked up the phone from its cradle on the counter. Trevor heard just three beeps as he punched in the number. That must mean he was calling 911.

The dispatcher's voice—a woman's—came through faintly on the other end.

"This is Ed McCoy. I've got a message for Sheriff Smart-ass Buck Winston," McCoy growled. "Tell him I want my wife and daughters back in this house—now. And if they don't show up, I've got three kids here who might not make it past sundown!"

Chapter 14

When Cooper pulled up in front of the McCoy house, he didn't like what he saw. There was no sign of Ruth McCoy's Chevy. The only vehicle parked next to the house was a battered pickup, most likely belonging to her husband.

As he climbed out of the Jeep, he could see two sets of footprints going up the snowy walk—the familiar impression of Trevor's rain boots and Maggie's smaller tracks beside them.

There were no tracks coming out of the house.

Cooper hadn't meant to let the dog out of the Jeep, but Glory pushed past him and went racing up the walk. On the porch, she began barking and scratching at the door.

"Get that damned dog off my porch before I blow its brains out!" a voice bellowed from inside the house.

Alarmed, Cooper took a moment to call Glory back and shut her in the Jeep. Worry gnawed at him as he approached the house and stopped at the foot of the porch steps. Something wasn't right in there.

"Mr. McCoy," he called out, doing his best to sound reasonable. "My name is Cooper Chapman. I've come to pick up my son and my niece. I won't come in and bother you, but would you please send them out to me?"

There was no answer. Cooper waited a few minutes, his nerves crawling. He remembered seeing Ruth's bruised face when she'd come to clean the ranch house. Her husband was a violent man, and he was in there with Trevor and Maggie.

Cooper hadn't thought to bring a gun with him. If he forced his way into the house, and McCoy was armed, there could be shooting. He would need to play this as cautiously as possible.

"Mr. McCoy," he called again. "I know my children are in there. If you don't send them out now, I'm going to call the sheriff."

McCoy laughed, without humor. "I already called him myself. He should be here soon. Meanwhile, your kids are fine. You can have them as soon as I get my wife and daughters back."

The cold certainty slammed Cooper like a kick to the gut. This was a hostage situation. And before it was over, anything could happen.

"That's right, Mr. Chapman," McCoy said. "The bitch had me jailed, and while I was locked up, she took my little girls and skedaddled. Left me with this no-account bastard kid that ain't even mine."

So Skip was there, too. And it appeared he was no safer than the other children.

"Let them go, McCoy," Cooper said. "That's the only way this mess will have a good ending."

"The only good ending will be if my wife comes back and brings our girls—and if she withdraws the charge that sent me to jail. Otherwise, she's going to pay. If she doesn't, the whole damn town is going to pay. I've got these kids, I've got guns, and I've got enough dynamite to blow this house all the way to the moon. Get the picture?"

* * *

While Ed McCoy's attention was on the front door, Maggie edged close to Trevor, who was still tied to the chair. "Did you hear what he said?" she whispered.

"Yeah." Trevor was doing his best to be brave. "But that doesn't mean it's true."

"You don't think he's got dynamite?"

"Do you see any?"

"I don't know what dynamite looks like," Maggie said. "Maybe it's in the closet. I could ask Skip."

Trevor glanced toward the kitchen, where Skip, also, was still tied to a chair. His face was pale, his jaw tightly set, as if biting back any sign of fear. "It wouldn't make any difference," Trevor said. "Leave Skip alone. He's already in trouble for trying to warn us."

"If I could find the dynamite, I could pour water on it, so it wouldn't blow up."

"Don't get any silly ideas, Maggie. He'll tie you up, too."

"Maybe I could sneak up behind him and grab his gun. I'm good at sneaking."

Trevor sighed. "Maggie, just be quiet and do as you're told. My dad's outside. And the sheriff is coming, too. They'll find a way to get us out."

But would they? Trevor had seen true crime TV shows about hostage situations. Sometimes they ended with a rescue. Often as not they ended with people getting shot. But he wasn't about to tell Maggie that.

As Ed McCoy turned to check on them, Maggie slunk off and settled in a ratty-looking armchair.

"No more talking," McCoy snarled. "The next one of you makes a peep is going to be damned sorry."

When he turned his back again, Maggie stuck out her tongue.

* * *

The big tan SUV with the sheriff's logo on the door drove up and parked next to Cooper's Jeep. Buck climbed out, wearing a Kevlar vest and holding another one, which he tossed to Cooper. "Put it on. With the threats that lunatic is making, you never know what's going to happen."

"It's not me I'm concerned about. It's those kids," Cooper muttered as he pulled the vest into place. "Have you let Sam know?"

"Sam and Grace are on their way. And Cottonwood Springs is sending a three-man SWAT team, but their helicopter's in the shop so they're driving. They won't be here for at least forty-five minutes."

"A SWAT team? Good Lord, Buck, do you think it'll come to that?"

"Let's hope not. But better safe than sorry." Buck looked slightly ill. Cooper surmised that the young sheriff hadn't handled anything this serious before. The more experienced man would be Sam, the former longtime sheriff. But even Sam would never have faced a situation like this one, with his own daughter as a hostage.

"The first priority is getting those kids out safely," Buck said. "A trained hostage negotiator could make all the difference. But there's nobody available, not even in Cottonwood Springs."

That's where you're wrong.

Cooper's throat jerked tight. He had a decision to make—and he knew in a flash what the decision must be. He'd promised Jess that he would protect her privacy. But if her skills could save three innocent lives, he had no choice except to betray her secret.

Not even if it meant losing her.

"Find Jess Graver," he said. "She can do it."

"Jess? But she's a psychologist, not a—"

"She can do it, Buck. She's had the training and experience. I left her at her motel last night, but she's angry with me. I don't even have her phone number."

"I do. She gave it to me when Ed was arrested. But we've been playing phone tag. When Ed was bailed out, I left a message at the motel. She called back and got dispatch. The last I heard she was going to find Ruth and warn her that Ed is free. That's all I know."

"So Jess doesn't know what's happening here."

"Not unless she's called dispatch again. But she was worried about the boy—Skip. There's a chance she'll show up here."

"So for now, all we can do is wait and hope." Cooper mouthed a curse.

Damn it, where are you, Jess? I need you. We all need you.

It had taken Jess twenty minutes to replace the flat with the small emergency tire and another half hour to find a shop that would patch the leak without making her wait. An extra fifty dollars had persuaded the attendant to drop everything else and do what she needed. Now, with four sound tires under her car once more, she was headed down the highway, about halfway to Branding Iron.

The asphalt surface had been scraped and salted, allowing most of the snow to melt. Jess pushed the speed limit, anxiety pumping adrenaline through her body. All her instincts told her that something was wrong—and whatever it was, she needed to be there.

Traffic on the road was light today. Jess gunned the engine to pass slower vehicles, urgency making her reckless. When she heard the wail of a siren behind her, her heart sank. The last thing she needed today was a speeding ticket. Muttering, she pulled onto the shoulder of the road and waited.

To her surprise, the vehicle, marked with the logo of the Cottonwood Springs Police Department, sped on past her, red lights flashing. It wasn't the usual police cruiser but a white van, outfitted to carry a crew and needed equipment to the scene of a serious emergency.

A serious emergency.

Her heart slammed like a wrecking ball as she swung the Taurus back onto the road, switched on her headlights, and floored the gas pedal. Only when the powerful car had closed the distance behind the van did she ease off and follow. Maybe the emergency had nothing to do with her or the McCoy family. But given the timing, she had to believe that the boy she'd promised to protect was in grave danger—if she wasn't already too late.

The McCoy house remained silent as Cooper and the sheriff waited for more help. Once or twice Cooper thought he saw movement behind the warped venetian blinds, so he knew the two of them were being watched. But like them, Ed McCoy was waiting for whatever was to happen next.

Cooper's thoughts dwelt on the three young hostages—Trevor, who was just beginning to discover his own strength; spunky little Maggie; and Skip, the boy he scarcely knew. All of them had to be terrified, and with good cause. He would trade places with any one of them in a heartbeat, even give his own life. All that mattered was getting the three youngsters to safety. Then Ed McCoy could blow himself to hell for all he cared.

The thought vanished as Sam's pickup came roaring up the road, tires spraying snow as he swung the big vehicle around and parked next to the sheriff's SUV. Sam switched off the engine and leaped to the ground. His expression made it clear that he was taking charge. He was more experienced than Buck and had infinitely more to lose.

On Buck's face, there was nothing but relief.

Cooper strode around to the passenger side of the truck and helped Grace to the ground. Her face was drained of color, her expression stoic. Cooper knew that she loved Maggie like her own flesh-and-blood daughter. She would do anything to save the little girl.

Neither of them had been raised with much affection, but now Cooper took his sister in his arms and hugged her tight and hard, each of them drawing strength from the other. When they parted, they saw that Sam was fastening on an oversized Kevlar vest, probably his own from his old job.

The adults were armored. The children unprotected. Maybe Grace was thinking of that, too, when she declined the vest that Buck offered her. "I'll just stay out of the way," she said.

Buck had handed Sam a bullhorn. Sam's deep voice boomed as he spoke.

"Ed, this is Sam Delaney. So far, no harm's been done. Let those children go now, and we'll work a deal with you. Otherwise, we've got a SWAT team on the way, and you'll have to deal with them."

"Go to hell, Sam." Ed McCoy didn't need a bullhorn. "I don't care if you've got a whole damned army out there. As long as I've got your little girl and the two boys, nobody's gonna touch me. Now, bring my wife and kids, and don't take too long about it. Then we'll talk. Otherwise . . . *kaboom!*" He laughed, a chilling sound.

"We're doing everything we can, Ed, but it's going to take time." Sam lowered the bullhorn. "At least we know what we're dealing with. If the man isn't crazy, he's making a good show of it."

"Sam, we've got one option," Cooper said. "Jess is a former FBI hostage negotiator. We're trying to locate her now."

"Jess? A hostage negotiator?"

"That's true, Sam," Grace said. "I don't know the whole

story, but she was with the FBI for years. She's our best chance of getting those children back without a fight."

"I've got dispatch trying to track her down," Buck said. "Since she was involved with the family, we're hoping she might show up here."

"And what about Ruth?"

"She took the girls and went to her sister's. But Ed would be able to find them there. According to what Jess told dispatch, the lawyer promised to find them a safe place."

"And the boy? What was he doing in the house?"

"You know Ruth," Buck said. "She's a good mother. She wanted him to stay in school, and she needed somebody to look after the house until she could come home. But she would never have left him if she'd known Ed would be released so quickly."

Sam muttered an oath. "So we couldn't produce her even if we wanted to."

"Not unless she gets worried about Skip and comes on her own—that, or unless Jess knows how to reach her."

"So right now, all we can do is wait," Sam said.

Buck nodded. "That's it. Wait and pray."

Christmas lights blurred in Jess's vision as she followed the police van through Branding Iron. The traffic had slowed their progress, but the siren was still blasting, urging people and vehicles to let them pass.

When the van passed through town and took the road south, Jess knew that her worst fears had come to pass. There was only one place the police could be headed and only one reason they could be going there.

By now, the sun was low in the sky. In the west, sooty clouds were flowing along the horizon, threatening another storm. The night would be dark and cold and long.

As the van swung onto the turnoff road, the siren's wail

ceased, but the red light atop the vehicle continued to blink. Jess knew where the team was going but she still didn't know what to expect. She only knew that it would be bad.

At last the McCoy place came into view. Jess could see three vehicles out front. The sheriff's SUV was here as expected. And the sight of Sam's pickup wasn't really a surprise. But what was Cooper's Jeep doing here?

Buck waved the van to a parking place. Jess parked some distance behind the other vehicles, giving them plenty of room to back out. Cooper was first to see her climb out of her car. He strode toward her, his face a mask of distress. His hands caught her shoulders, as if bracing her, but he made no attempt to pull her close.

"What is it? What's happening?" she asked.

He told her, in a voice ragged with strain. "Ed McCoy's in the house. He's got Skip and Trevor and Maggie. He's got at least one gun, and he's threatening to dynamite the house and everyone in it if his wife doesn't show up with their little girls."

Jess willed her limp knees to support her. She could see Grace standing behind the open door of the pickup. The SWAT team, already in their gear, was climbing out of the van. Sam appeared to be briefing them.

Buck had spotted her. Leaving the others, he sprinted to where she stood with Cooper. "Thank God you're here, Jess," he said. "We need you."

Her surprise was no more than a flash. Of course they would know about her—Buck and Sam and Grace. Cooper would have told them. With precious lives at stake, how could he not have told them?

A tremor, as real and as physical as an electric shock, passed through her. It was as if a set of gears connecting her mind and her body had meshed and begun to turn—familiar gears, still working smoothly after all this time. This was what she did, Jess told herself. It was who she was.

But never before, in all the years at her old job, had a situation been as personal as this one.

Her gaze met Cooper's. Their contact was brief, but she saw the hope in his eyes, the trust mingled with fear and uncertainty. She couldn't say more to him now. If she did, she would break.

Jess turned to Buck. "I'll do everything I can. But I'll need help."

"You've got it," Buck said. "Sam's the one in charge—thank heaven for that. He's already planning on you."

"I'll need to talk to Sam and to the SWAT team. But first—" She reached into her purse, found Sharon's card, and handed it to Buck. "This is Ruth's lawyer. Have dispatch call her and let her know what's happening. We need to get Ruth here, as fast as we can."

"And the little girls?"

"Not unless their mother insists on it."

Sam turned as she approached. He looked as if the weight of worry had aged him by ten years. If Jess's efforts failed, it would be his call to post a sniper or send in the SWAT team to kill Ed McCoy—and risk the lives of three precious hostages, including his own daughter.

"Here. Put this on." He passed her a protective vest. "The team's setting up a direct phone line so you can talk to him." He gazed toward the house, his throat moving as he swallowed. "Thanks, Jess. This can't be easy for you."

"It isn't easy for any of us, Sam. And you can thank me when there's something to be thankful for."

While she waited for the phone line to be set up, along with a chair, a folding table, and a notepad with a pen, Jess took time for Grace. As she walked toward her, Grace opened her arms. For a long moment, the two women held each other.

"We argued before I took her to Abner's." Grace was fighting tears. "I wanted to take her Christmas shopping, but

Maggie insisted that she had to be there to try out the sleigh. I gave in, but I wasn't very pleasant about it. What if those cross words are the last ones she ever hears from me?"

"You mustn't think like that. We'll get her back, Grace. We'll get them all back."

A ghost of a smile tightened Grace's lips. "You know, I keep thinking of that old story, 'The Ransom of Red Chief,' by O. Henry. Surely you've read it."

"I have." Jess remembered the tale of the inept kidnappers who snatch a young boy for ransom—a boy who makes such a pest of himself that they end up paying the boy's father to take him back. "That would be Maggie, all right. She's one spunky little girl. She'll get through this. You'll see."

"Jess, we're almost ready for you." Sam was calling her.

"I'm coming." Jess squeezed her friend's hand, then hurried to the table that had been set up for her next to the van. She willed her mind to shut out all distractions. She had to believe she could get those children safely out of the house. Anything less was unthinkable.

Trevor felt as if he'd been tied to the chair forever. His legs ached from sitting and his arms hurt from being pulled behind his back. He could probably get loose if he had to. Maggie wasn't much good at knots. But then Ed McCoy would tie him up again, so tightly that he couldn't move. McCoy would probably slap him around for good measure.

From where he sat, Trevor could see Skip in the kitchen, also tied to a chair. His head was down, and he appeared to be dozing. Except for the bruise on his face, there was no way to know how long he'd been there or what his stepfather had done to him before tying him up.

His friend had it harder than he did, Trevor reminded himself. Being threatened and tied up by a stranger was bad enough, but being held captive by a member of your own family—that had to be worse.

"Do you know what this place needs, Mr. McCoy?" Maggie was still unbound, and she wouldn't stop talking. Trevor was afraid the man was going to hit her or worse.

"This place needs a Christmas tree," she said. "You know, if you let us go, my dad will get you a nice big one, for free. He'll even buy you some decorations to hang on it."

"Shut up, little girl," McCoy growled. "Your yammering is making me want a drink, and I need to stay sober."

Maggie fell silent but only for a moment. "Mr. McCoy, do you really have dynamite?" she asked.

"Wouldn't you like to know?" He sneered at her.

"Can I see it? Will you show it to me?"

"Be still, Maggie!" Trevor hissed. "You're going to get us in trouble."

"It looks to me like we're already in trouble," Maggie said. "Maybe we should sing some Christmas carols. What's your favorite, Mr. McCoy?"

McCoy's lip curled. "Little girl—"

He didn't finish because just then the telephone rang.

"Ruth? Damn it, you bitch, if you don't get your butt home this minute, you're gonna wish you had."

Jess took a breath and spoke in a chatty tone. "Ed, this is Jess Graver. Remember me? You were working on my house when I stopped by."

"Sure. I never forget a pretty face. But why the hell are you calling me now?"

"I'm right outside, and I'm calling to help you. I know you want your family back together. We're doing our best to make that happen."

That last part was a lie, but it was what Jess had been

trained to do. Tell the suspect anything he wants to hear, even if it isn't true. All that matters is saving the hostages.

"So where's my wife? Is she with you?"

"She was in Cottonwood Springs. But she's on her way back here now. She says she still loves you and wants to work things out. She'll be here soon, so you can let those children go."

"Uh-uh. When I see her and hear her say it, that's when I'll let those kids go. And if she takes too long, you know what I'll do . . . *Kaboom!*"

Buck had come to the table. He picked up the notepad, scrawled a message on the first page, and laid it down where Jess could see it.

Lawyer can't locate Ruth. Kids are with sister but Ruth went out and hasn't come back. She'll keep trying.

Jess nodded. It was a setback, but she would just have to deal with it. She took a moment to think.

"What's goin' on?" McCoy demanded. "Is my wife there?"

"Not yet. But she called. Your little girls can't wait to see their daddy again. But she can't let them see hostages in your house. You'll need to let them go."

There was silence on the other end of the line.

"How are the children, Ed? Are they all right? Do they need anything?"

"They're fine. The little redheaded brat's been talkin' my ear off. Some damn nonsense about me needin' a Christmas tree. Now she's singin' 'Jingle Bells.'" He put a hand over the phone but Jess could still hear him. "Shut up, you little bitch, before I knock your block off."

He was losing patience. That worried Jess. "You know, Ed, you don't have to keep her. You've got the boys. Letting Maggie go now would buy you some points with the judge."

"Judge? Hell, missy, what law have I broke? Skip lives here. And the other two kids knocked on the door and came in on their own. It's not like I snatched 'em off the street. And my wife's bound to withdraw the charges for slapping her into line, just like always. I deserve to be as free as a bird."

"Then prove it. Ruth is on her way, with the girls. If she finds everything as it should be—you in the house waiting with open arms—think how happy she'll be."

Silence.

Jess's thoughts flew back to the last time she'd done this job, her decision to hold back the man's wife, and the awful conclusion. Ed McCoy was violent and unpredictable. If Ruth didn't come, and he learned that he'd been lied to, the same thing could happen here.

"Let's bargain, Ed," she said. "What do you want in exchange for letting Maggie go now? Food? We can get you some pizza or doughnuts. We can get you a car—a nice one, yours to keep—if you want to leave. Name your price."

More silence. Then an outburst. "I just want some *peace*! All right! You can have the little hellion!"

He put the receiver down. A moment later, the front door opened far enough to allow a small figure to squeeze through before it slammed shut again. Then Maggie was running, running down the steps, down the sidewalk and into her father's arms.

After the tearful reunion with her mother came the questions.

"What did you see in there, Maggie? Where are the boys?"

"Tied to chairs. I think Trevor could get loose but he doesn't dare. Mr. McCoy has a pistol. That's the only gun I saw."

"What about the dynamite? Has he really got some?"

"I don't know. I asked to see it and he wouldn't tell me."

The leader of the SWAT team stood close by, listening. "We could position snipers outside the windows—take him out when we get a clear shot."

Maggie burst into tears. "Oh, please don't shoot Mr. McCoy. He isn't a bad man. He's just really, really sad."

Sam's eyes met his wife's. He nodded. "Let's give it a little more time," he said.

Jess glanced toward Cooper. One child was safe. But his own son's life was still in peril. She wanted to put her arms around him and tell him everything would be all right. But that reassurance could be as false as the lies she was telling Ed. The situation was highly charged and growing more dangerous by the minute.

McCoy was back on the phone. "Okay, I gave you something you wanted. Now get my wife, damn it."

Jess gave Buck a questioning look. He shook his head. There was no sign of Ruth McCoy.

"She's on her way. But the traffic's heavy on the highway at this hour. All we can do is wait."

"She'd damn well better be here soon, or all hell's gonna break loose. I'm gonna hang up now because I got to use the can. Call me soon as she shows."

As the bathroom door closed, Skip raised his head, instantly alert. "I saw how Maggie tied you," he said to Trevor. "If you can get loose, do it. Do it and run! Hurry!"

For an instant, Trevor was tempted. He could feel the slight give in the cord that held him to the chair. Yes, he could probably get loose. But what would happen to Skip if he left? Alone, with no witnesses, what might a crazed Ed McCoy do to his stepson?

"Can I untie you, too?" he asked.

"No. There isn't time! Hurry, blast it!"

"I'm not leaving you alone with him, Skip."

Skip's curses purpled the air. "You're out of your freakin' mind, Trevor Chapman."

"My choice," Trevor said. "You're my best friend, and I'm not going without you."

Skip turned his face away, as if to hide his emotions. Just then the bathroom door opened. Ed McCoy strode out. Scowling, he walked behind Trevor, bent, and tightened Maggie's loose knots, ending any chance of escape.

Time crawled at a leaden pace, ten minutes, then fifteen and twenty, without a word from Ruth. As Cooper watched the woman he loved battle for his son's life, every second was agony. If she were to fail, as she had the last time, she would be shattered. Not only would he lose Trevor—he would lose her as well.

With the phone on speaker, he could hear Ed McCoy becoming more agitated, and more erratic. The threat of *kaboom* was spoken more and more often. Was it a bluff, or did he really have dynamite in the house, ready to be lit and detonated?

Mindful of the need to let the professionals do their job, Cooper had stayed out of the way, even taking a moment to calm Glory and give her water from a bottle in the Jeep. But as the tension mounted, he moved closer to the house, as if driven by the need to be near his son.

More minutes ticked past. Then, suddenly, everything seemed to happen at once.

An old brown Chevy came tearing down the lane, swung into the yard, and screeched to a halt. The door flew open, and Ruth leaped out. But it was a different-looking Ruth than Cooper had seen before—her hair freshly coiffed and tinted, flattering makeup and a becoming pantsuit. She'd done what almost any woman might have done when turning a corner in her life: She'd gone to the mall and gotten a makeover. No wonder no one had been able to reach her.

It was Buck who got to her first. He steadied her as she stumbled forward in her new high-heeled boots. "I didn't know," she gasped. "I didn't know Ed was out of jail until I called my sister. What's happening? Where's my son?"

"Take it easy, Ruth." Buck gave her a rapid-fire update on what had happened. "Jess has been stalling, hoping you'd get here. Ed wants to talk to you on the phone. Can you do that?"

"Certainly. But what do I say?"

"You'll need to stay calm. Tell him you're coming back. Tell him you love him. Tell him anything he wants to hear—anything that will help us get those boys out."

Ruth nodded. Jess motioned her over to the table and spoke into the phone. "Ed, your wife is here. She wants to talk to you."

"Well, it's about time," Ed growled. "Put her on."

Jess seated Ruth in the chair and handed her the receiver. Ruth looked shaken, but she was a tough woman, Cooper reminded himself. And, like him, she would do anything to save her son.

"Hello, Ed, honey." She spoke into the phone. "I'm here. I've come home. Now our family can be together again."

A blind slat moved. "You sure have. I can see you out there, gussied up like you just won the lottery. You're probably gettin' ready to troll for a new husband. But that's fine. I've been plannin' a little show to welcome you home. Now that you're here, we can start. Just sit back and watch."

The line went dead. Ruth glanced around with startled

eyes. At a nod from Sam, the SWAT team, weapons at the ready, began closing around the house.

"There!" One of the team saw Ed racing out the back of the house, heading for the car he'd left in the yard. The three men gave chase, shooting at the tires to stop him.

"*No!*" Suddenly Cooper realized what was going on. Shouting, he charged the house. He had to get to the boys.

Chapter 15

Hurling himself against the front door, Cooper felt the lock splinter and give. With another shove, the door crashed open.

He saw no dynamite. But that didn't mean it wasn't there—in a back room or hidden in a closet. Given the way Ed had gone racing out the back door, Cooper had to assume that the house was about to blow up. He had seconds, if that, to get the boys out.

The two boys were lashed to chairs, about ten feet apart. Both of them looked scared—clearly they knew about the danger. There was no time to untie them. He would have to carry—or drag—them out.

"Take him first." Skip nodded toward Trevor. "He didn't have to be here."

"No," Trevor said. "We're not leaving you here, Skip."

"I'll take both of you." *If the house goes, we all go.* Cooper didn't voice the thought. He dragged the two chairs together, tilted them backward, and tried to take them using one hand for each. But the weight was awkward, the progress slow, too slow. He imagined the fuse burning its way to the detonator, the explosion that might or might not happen. He could take Trevor, who was lighter, then go back for Skip.

No, this is the only way.

Then, suddenly there was a voice, a pair of manicured hands pushing his away. "I've got Skip. You take your son." It was Ruth, seizing Skip's chair, dragging him toward the broken door. "It's about time I put my boy first."

Cooper shoved her out ahead of him, then snatched up Trevor's chair and followed. They stumbled onto the porch and down the front steps, crashing into the front yard and rolling clear as the house exploded in a deafening roar of flame that rained debris around and on them.

Cooper had flung himself over his son's body to protect him. When he raised his head, the explosion was over, but his ears were ringing. Trevor, now lying on his side, was moving beneath him but Cooper could hear only the lingering vibrations of the blast. Shingles, chunks of timber, broken glass, and sharp-edged slices of siding were scattered all around them. The air reeked of smoke and explosive residue.

Sitting up, Cooper felt wetness trickling down his temple over his cheekbone. He ignored it. His hands fumbled with the knotted cord that held Trevor to the chair.

A few feet away, Ruth was doing the same. Her elegant coiffure was flattened and coated with plaster dust. Her new outfit was smudged with dirt and spotted with blood from a cut on her cheek. But she gave him a smile and a thumbs-up. She and her son were alive.

Two figures were running across the yard, dodging their way through the scattered debris. Sam and Jess appeared to be shouting something like *Are you all right?* But Cooper still couldn't hear them. He nodded and pointed to his ear.

Seconds later, Jess was kneeling beside Trevor, her deft

fingers untying the knots that Cooper's shaking hands couldn't manage. As she pressed a handkerchief to Cooper's head wound, Trevor rolled free and sat up.

"Can you hear me, Trevor?" Cooper's own hearing had started to return. Hopefully, when he'd covered Trevor with his body, he'd blocked the force of the sound from the boy's ears.

"Yeah. I can hear fine." As Trevor's lips moved, the sound was slightly blurred, but Cooper could make out the words. His hearing was coming back.

Trevor turned to Jess, who was still putting pressure on Cooper's head wound.

"That was cool, talking on the phone like you did. I knew you were some kind of cop. I bet you could tell a lot of stories."

"Not anymore," Jess said. "That part of my life is behind me—I know that now. Come on, Trevor. You and your dad need medical attention."

Cooper noticed the paramedics' van parked beyond the other vehicles. Buck must've called them. Skip and Ruth were on their feet. Sam was helping them in that direction.

"Where's Ed?" Cooper asked. "I saw him run out of the house."

"He's under arrest," Jess replied. "The SWAT team caught up with him in the backyard. Buck's taking him to jail right now, to be held for trial. Charges of kidnapping and attempted murder are serious enough to warrant a long sentence. But my guess is that he'll end up in a psychiatric facility. A sane man doesn't do what Ed did today. I only wish that I could've talked him into freeing his hostages and surrendering to the police."

"You did everything you could," Cooper said. "But Ed wasn't in his right mind. He'd planned that explosion ahead of time. Nobody could have stopped him."

"As long as he never hits Skip's mom again, I don't care where he goes." Trevor, who appeared unhurt, strode ahead to catch up with his friend. Leaving Cooper and Jess behind.

Cooper's head wound still stung but the bleeding had stopped. He slowed his steps to let Trevor gain some distance from them.

Jess matched his pace, walking beside him in silence. This brush with death had made him even more aware of how much he loved her. But he'd betrayed a confidence that he'd promised to keep. Her past would be gossip fodder all over town.

Had he lost her? Was she about to tell him that she was leaving Branding Iron—and him—as soon as she could make the arrangements?

Steeling himself, he waited for her to speak. But Jess didn't say a word.

As they walked, he felt something soft and cool brush the side of his hand. Slender fingers stole between his, seeking and clasping, nestling into his palm.

Cooper's heart contracted. His hand tightened around hers. No words were needed.

As they crossed the muddy distance to the vehicles, snowflakes began drifting down, like a lacy white curtain against the twilight sky.

Branding Iron's first annual Christmas parade took place as scheduled, at ten in the morning, on the twentieth of December, the last Saturday before Christmas.

Not everything went well. The band teacher was down with the flu, so the Branding Iron High School band, with no one to lead them, sounded woefully out of tune. And the Cottonwood Springs band arrived so late that they had to run down the street to catch up with the rest of the parade. The chilly wind tore streamers of crepe paper off the hastily constructed floats, and Tex Morgan, the TV star who'd grown up in Branding Iron, was a no-show. Sam, Grace, and Maggie led the parade without him, waving and tossing candy from a red convertible.

But never mind all that. Everyone agreed that the Santa Claus sleigh was magnificent.

From the prancing horses with their jingling harness bells, to the beautifully finished sleigh, gliding along the snow-packed street, it was perfection—as was Santa Claus himself.

Jess had joined Ruth on the sidewalk to watch the parade. Ruth had brought her two little girls. They were jumping up and down, laughing and waving.

"That Santa is great. But who on earth is he?" Jess asked.

Ruth grinned. With her hair fluttering in the wind and her cheeks rosy with cold, she looked like the pretty, lively woman she'd been before she married Ed McCoy. "Look at him. Can't you tell? Look at those eyes. Listen to that laugh."

Jess shaded her eyes from the bright sun. "Oh, my goodness! It's Abner! He's perfect!"

"He agreed to do it early on," Ruth said. "But he and Sam wanted to keep it a secret. They wanted him to be the real Santa for the children. And look at him. He's about as real as Santa can be."

Jess didn't need to ask how her friend knew about Abner. The kindly man had offered Ruth, Skip, and the little girls a place to stay until she could collect the insurance on the house, sell the land, and find another home to buy. To repay him, Ruth had scrubbed his house from top to bottom and she was spoiling him with the delicious meals she cooked.

Abner was playing Santa as if he'd done it all his life, his laughter booming as he flung small bags of candy onto the sidewalk for the children, making sure no child was missed.

"But who's that driving the team?" Jess studied the rangy figure dressed in jeans and a sheepskin coat, his weathered

Stetson worn low to shadow his face. Oblivious to the cheering crowds, he was controlling the team with the skill of a man who understood horses.

"I can't recall ever seeing him before," Jess said. "Do you know him, Ruth?"

Ruth's expression had changed, as if a shadow had fallen across her pretty face. "Yes," she said. "I know him."

"I know him, too!" Trevor, trailed by Skip, had joined the two women. "His name's Judd Rankin. He's renting our pasture for his cows. He didn't really want to do this—he doesn't like being around a lot of people. But Sam talked him into it—they were friends in school. Sam wanted to make sure the horses wouldn't spook, and Mr. Rankin was the only one he trusted to handle them. He's cool—a real cowboy." Trevor turned to his friend. "Come back to the field after the parade. He'll be helping my dad load the horses. You'll get to meet him."

Ruth turned to her son, almost too abruptly. "I'm sorry, Skip, but we need to leave. Your sisters are getting cranky, and I have to start dinner."

"Aw, Mom . . ." Skip protested. "Can't I stay? I can always hitch a ride home."

"Not this time. I said you could go to the Christmas ball tonight. That's enough." Ruth hiked her purse strap onto her shoulder and took each little girl by a hand. "Come on, let's go, while we can get out ahead of the traffic."

Jess watched Ruth walk away with her children, headed for the side street where she'd left her car. It struck Jess as odd that she would leave so suddenly, especially when her girls hadn't seemed cranky at all.

But never mind, Jess told herself. She'd had enough drama in the past week. She didn't need to borrow any more trouble. Instead, she would enjoy the day and look forward to tonight.

Especially tonight.

* * *

Branding Iron's second annual Cowboy Christmas Ball was an even bigger success than the previous year's. Branding Iron's citizens turned out in their western finery to enjoy homemade food, entertainment for the kids, and dancing to country music. Abner's Santa was as good as the real one, people said, although he was looking tired by the evening's end. There was also talk of maybe, next year, putting aside enough money to hire a real live band.

Not everyone in Branding Iron had come to the ball. In a modest ranch house south of town, Cooper and Jess lounged on the sofa in front of a crackling fire. In the corner, the Christmas tree, now with a growing stack of presents underneath, glowed softly in the darkened room.

Taking advantage of the rare time alone, they'd feasted on pizza from Buckaroo's, wrapped a few gifts, and settled back to watch a Batman video. About halfway through the movie, he'd leaned over and kissed her, and the rest of the movie was forgotten.

Now they lay back against the cushions with their stocking feet on the coffee table, drowsy and slightly giddy.

"This was a good idea, not going to the ball," he murmured with his lips against her hair.

"Anyway, I didn't have anything to wear." She snuggled against him, nibbling at his earlobe. She smelled of pizza and Christmas tree. "I really ought to be going. Trevor should be getting home soon. Didn't you say Sam was dropping him off?"

"That's the plan, after he drives Abner home. I don't think either Trevor or Sam will be surprised to find you here with me. But you can't drive all the way to Cottonwood Springs tonight. You're wiped out. Your bed here is made up and ready. I even laundered the sheets and put them back on, in the hope that you'd need them again. Come on—the cockroaches can get along without you for a night." He gave her a stern look. "The roads are slick and there are drunken idiots driving at this hour. You're staying, even if I have to tie you to the bed."

She giggled. "Now that sounds interesting."

"I'm not kidding, Jess. I want you back here, at least until your apartment's ready. We'll have Trevor around to make sure we don't misbehave."

"What will Trevor have to say about that?"

"Are you kidding? He thinks you're cool. And he's been whining about my cooking ever since you left. He'll be happy to have you back. So what do you say?"

Her only answer was a kiss.

Epilogue

Christmas dinner was spectacular. Abner's house was the only place with room for a table long enough to seat eleven people. The table—actually two tables rented from the school lunchroom, set up end to end and covered with cloths—was set with matching china and glassware that had belonged to Abner's late wife. The Christmas tree place cards had been contributed by Maggie.

And the food . . . Trevor had never seen such mouth-watering food, not even at the Cowboy Christmas Ball. Ruth had baked the ham and prepared the mountain of mashed potatoes and gravy, but his Aunt Grace had brought a stuffed turkey and fresh, hot rolls. Jess had made some vegetable dishes, and Cooper had all but bought out the bakery, bringing an assortment of pies and a tub of vanilla ice cream.

As the guests took their seats and waited for Abner to bless the food, Trevor's gaze moved around the table. Three months ago, the only one of them he'd known was his father. Now they were all like family—and all of them had helped him survive a hard time in his life.

Abner was the grandfather he'd never had, the sleigh a

lesson in hard work, responsibility, and devotion. Ruth, who had a new job with the school district and was shopping for a new home, was teaching him her own lesson in moving on and starting over. She and her children were survivors, stronger for what they'd been through.

Skip had given him the joys of forgiveness and friendship. Maggie had shown him what a single small person could accomplish and been a shining example of courage in the face of danger.

His Aunt Grace and Uncle Sam had taught him the importance of community and service to others.

Cooper and Jess were glowing with love. But they were taking things day by day, giving their relationship time to grow. Trevor no longer feared that his father would abandon him for a woman. Together, they were teaching him trust, even as they learned to trust each other. Trevor couldn't help hoping that they would get married. Jess was becoming his friend—and hey, how cool would it be, having an ex-FBI agent for a mother?

Abner cleared his throat to get Trevor's attention. People were joining hands around the table. He slipped one hand into Jess's, the other into Skip's, and bowed his head.

With his new family, he gave thanks.

Please read on for an excerpt from CALDER GRIT by
Janet Dailey!

**During the summer of 1909, a battle rages in Blue Moon,
Montana, between immigrant homesteaders and cattle-
men determined to keep the range free. In a fierce struggle that echoes the challenges of today, history is made.**

*As the countryside explodes in violence, the Calder patri-
arch has the power to stop the destruction, though some
believe Benteen Calder is only stoking the flames for his
own gain. One man courageously straddles the divide . . .*

That man is Blake Dollarhide, the ambitious young owner
of Blue Moon's lumber mill. When Blake's spoiled half
brother takes advantage of the innocent daughter of a home-
steading family, Blake steps in as Hanna Anderson's bride-
groom to restore her honor and give her unborn child his
name. But Blake doesn't count on the storm of feelings he
develops for sweet Hanna. When the war between the fac-
tions rages anew, everyone wonders if Blake will stand by
the close-knit community he serves, or the wife he took in
name only . . .

A marriage of love is more than Hanna ever dreamed of. For
her family, surviving the rugged trip west, claiming a parcel
of land and planting their first crops on the vast prairie are the
only things that matter. Which is why the unexpected passion
she feels for her husband is all the more poignant. But even
as she longs to trust the strong bond growing between her
and Blake, Hanna knows it will take courage and grit to overcome the differences between them. And even greater
strength of will to put down roots in this wild new country.

*The epic tale of the settling of the American West comes
to vivid life in this inspiring saga of love, hope and
endurance.*

CHAPTER 1

Blue Moon, Montana
July 4, 1909

Hanna stood next to her stern-faced father, one foot tapping out the beat of the polka. Couples whirled around the rough plank floor to the music of the old-time accordion band. She would've given anything to join them. But Big Lars Anderson had already turned down three cowboys who'd asked to partner his daughter. Hanna would've said yes to any of them, just to get out there and dance. But Big Lars had made his position clear. Those rough-mannered men from the ranches, even the polite ones, weren't fit company for an innocent girl.

As if being guarded like a prisoner wasn't bad enough, her mother had forced her to dress like a twelve-year-old, in a white pinafore, with her long, wheaten hair in two thick braids. But even the girlish costume couldn't hide the breasts that strained the bodice of her gingham dress. She was almost seventeen years old, with a woman's body and a woman's mind. When would her parents stop treating her like a child?

As the music flowed through her limbs, Hanna gazed at the deepening sky, where the sun was just setting behind the rugged Montana mountains, turning the clouds to ribbons of flame. It was so beautiful. How could she complain after such a glorious day—a celebration of America's freedom in her family's new home?

As she breathed in the fresh, free air, her memory drifted back to the tiny apartment in the New York slum, where she'd helped her mother tend the babies that just kept coming. Her father had worked on the docks, barely making enough to keep food on the table. When her older brother, Alvar, had turned fourteen, he'd gone to work there, too. In the desperation of those years, the American dream that had brought her parents from Sweden had been all but lost.

But then the news had traveled like wildfire through the tenements. Thanks to the passage of the new Homestead Act, there was free land out west. All they had to do was get there on the train, build a cabin, farm the land for five years, and it would be theirs, free and clear.

Now the dream had come true. Hanna's family and their neighbors had claimed their parcels of rich Montana grassland. The fields had been plowed; the wheat was planted and growing. On the anniversary of America's independence, it was time for friends and neighbors to celebrate an Independence Day of their own.

The festivities had begun earlier that afternoon with picnicking, races, games, and now a dance, with fireworks to end the day. It was the homesteaders, like Hanna's family, who'd planned the event; but the whole town, as well as the folks from the big cattle ranches, had been invited. That included the woman-hungry bachelor cowboys who'd shown up hoping to dance with the daughters of the farm families.

So far, the cowboys hadn't had much success. The immigrant fathers had guarded their girls like treasures. They wouldn't trust rough-mannered ranch hands anywhere near their precious girls.

But the girls, even the shy ones, were very much aware of the men.

"That cowboy is looking at you." Hanna nudged her friend Lillian, who stood on her left. Lillian, an auburn-haired beauty, was only a little older than Hanna, but she was already married, which made all the difference in the way she was treated.

The cowboy in question stood on the far side of the dance floor. He was taller than the others, with black hair and a hard, rugged look about him. Hanna knew who he was—Webb Calder, son of the most powerful ranch family in the region. And yes, he was definitely looking at Lillian.

"Does he know you?" Hanna asked.

Lillian shrugged and glanced away, but not before Hanna had noticed the color that flooded her cheeks. She was married to Stefan Reisner, a humorless man even older than Hanna's father. Lillian wasn't the sort to play flirting games with men. But it was plain to see that Webb Calder had made an impression on her.

As if to distract Hanna, Lillian gave a subtle nod in a different direction. "Now *that* cowboy, the one in the blue shirt and leather vest. He was just looking at *you*."

Hanna followed the direction of her friend's gaze. Something fluttered in the pit of her stomach as she spotted the rangy man standing at the break between the wagons that surrounded the dance floor. He was hatless, his hair dark brown and thick with a slight curl to it. His features were strong and solid, and there was pride in the way he carried himself—like a man who had nothing to prove.

But even though he might've been looking at Hanna earlier, he wasn't looking at her now. His gaze scanned the dance floor and the watchers who stood around the edge. He started forward. Then, as if he'd been called away, he suddenly turned and left.

Blake Dollarhide swore as he made his way among the buggies and wagons toward the open street. The Carmody brothers, who worked at his sawmill, had been warned about picking fights with the homesteaders. But with a few drinks under their belts, the two Irishmen tended to get belligerent. If they were making trouble now, Blake would have little choice except to fire them. But before that could be done, he'd probably have to stop a fight.

With the dance on, Blake had hoped to get a waltz or two with pretty, blond Ruth Stanton, whose father was foreman of the vast Calder spread, the Triple C Ranch. It was no secret that Ruth had her eye on Webb Calder, who would inherit the whole passel from his father, Chase Benteen Calder, one day. But there was no law against Blake's enjoying a dance with her. He might even be lucky enough to turn her head.

Taking anything away from Webb Calder would be a pleasure.

Ruth had been free for the moment. Blake had been about to cross the floor and ask her to dance when he'd heard shouts from the direction of the street. A quick glance around the dance floor had confirmed that the brothers weren't there. Dollars to donuts, the no-accounts had started a brawl.

Blake broke into a run as he spotted the trouble. The two Carmody brothers, small men, but tough and pugnacious, were baiting a lanky homesteader who'd probably left his friends to find a privy. The confrontation was drawing an ugly crowd.

"Pack your wagon and go back to where you came from, you filthy honyocker." Tom Carmody feinted a punch at the man's face. "We don't need you drylanders here, plowin' up the grass to plant your damned wheat, spoilin' land what's meant for cattle. Things was fine afore the likes of you showed up. Worse'n a plague of grasshoppers, that's what you are."

"Please." The man held up his hands. "I don't want trouble. Just let me go back to my family."

"You can go back—after we show you what we do to squatters like you." Tom's brother, Finn, brandished a hefty stick of kindling. Readying a strike, he aimed at the homesteader's head.

"That's enough!" Blake's iron grip stopped Finn's arm in midswing. A quick twist, and the stick fell to the ground. Finn staggered backward, clutching his wrist.

"I warned you two about this," Blake said. "I'm sorry to lose two workers, but I can't have you stirring up this kind of trouble. Any gear you left at the mill will be outside the gate."

"Aw, they was just funnin', Blake." Hobie Evans, who worked for the Snake M Ranch, was the chief instigator against the homesteaders. He'd probably goaded the Carmody brothers into targeting the lone farmer, hoping others would join in and give the poor man a beating to serve as an example.

"Don't push me, Hobie. This is a peaceful celebration. Let's keep it that way." Blake glanced around to make sure the farmer was gone and his tormentors had backed off. "Before I had to come out here, I was planning to dance with a pretty lady. For your sake, you'd better hope she's still available."

Blake strode back, past the wagons that ringed the dance floor, intent on seeking out Ruth. But in his absence, something had changed. Webb Calder was on the dance floor with the pretty, auburn-haired wife of one of the farmers. Ruth was on the sidelines, looking stricken.

Blake nudged the cowboy standing next to him. "What's going on?" he muttered.

"Webb got Doyle Petit to talk the drylanders into lettin' us dance with their women. My guess is, soon as this dance is over we can start askin' 'em." The young cowboy grinned. "I got my little gal all picked out—the one in white, with the yellow braids. She's right next to that big farmer—he's her pa. See her?"

"I see her." Blake gave the girl a casual glance. She appeared to be a child, almost, in her white pinafore, with her hair in schoolgirl braids. But then he took a longer look and the bottom seemed to drop out of his heart. He swore under his breath. She wasn't a child at all, but a stunning young woman with an angel's face and a body that even the girlish pinafore couldn't hide.

"Ain't she somethin'?" The cowboy asked. "What do you think?"

"I think you'd better be damned fast on your feet," Blake said. "Otherwise, somebody else might get to her first."

Somebody like me.

As the music faded, Webb Calder escorted the pretty redhead back to her husband. A few words were exchanged. Then Webb turned back to the waiting cowboys. "All right, boys. You can invite the young ladies to dance. But remember your manners. Any Triple C boys not on their best behavior will answer to me."

There was a beat of hesitation. Then the eager cowhands broke ranks and walked across the floor to ask the fathers' permission to dance with their daughters. Blake had decided to hang back and let the lovestruck cowboy enjoy a dance with his dream girl. But when he looked across the floor, he saw that someone else had already claimed her.

Seen from behind, the girl's escort was almost as tall as Blake, but a trifle broader in the chest and shoulders. He was dressed in city-bought clothes, his chestnut hair neatly trimmed to curl above the collar of his linen shirt.

Blake mouthed a curse. As usual, his half brother, Mason, had seized the advantage and run away with it.

Whirling blissfully around the dance floor, Hanna gazed up at the man who held her in his arms. The smile on his handsome face deepened the dimple in his cheek. His green eyes reflected glints of sunset.

"You looked like an angel, standing there in your white dress," he said. "Do angels have names?"

"My name's Hanna Anderson, and believe me, I'm not an angel," she said. "Just ask my parents."

He chuckled. "But you're an angel to me because you just saved me from a very boring evening. So that's what I'll call you—my angel."

Hanna had never heard such flattering talk. Who was this charming stranger? Certainly not a cowboy. He was too well dressed and too well spoken for that. "I'm Mason Dollarhide," he said, answering her unspoken question. "I run the Hollister ranch south of town. It may not be the biggest spread in Montana, but it sure is the prettiest. Almost as pretty as you."

"Now you're playing games with me," Hanna said. She wasn't a fool. But after what seemed like a lifetime of scrubbing, tending, washing, mending, working in the fields like a man, and never being made to feel attractive or desirable in any way, she let his words wash over her like the sound of sweet music.

Missing a step, she stumbled slightly. His hand, at the small of her back, tightened, drawing her so close that she could feel the light pressure of his body against hers. Heat flashed through her like summer lightning, making her feel vaguely naughty. Did he feel it, too?

"I would never play games with a precious girl like you." His voice had thickened. "I'd wager you've never even been kissed. Have you?"

"That's none of your business," Hanna said, although she hadn't been kissed, except by a neighbor boy when she was ten.

He chuckled. "Feisty little thing, aren't you?"

"I just don't like people forming ideas before they know me, that's all," Hanna said.

The music was drawing to a close, but his hand—smooth, with no calluses—didn't release hers. "I'd like to get to know you better, Hanna," he said. "Why don't we walk a little, where we don't have to raise our voices over the music?"

Hanna glanced back over her shoulder. Her father was talking to Lillian's husband. Lillian was nowhere in sight. Neither was the rugged cowboy who'd danced with her. Hanna felt the gentle pressure of the stranger's hand against her back, guiding her off the floor. She didn't resist. Nobody would miss her if she stepped out for a few harmless minutes.

They made their way among the wagons. He stopped her next to an elegant-looking buggy that was parked outside the circle. "This is my buggy," he said. "Get in. I'll take you for a ride."

He offered a hand to help her up, but she stopped him. "No. I can't go for a ride with you."

"But why? It's a beautiful evening. And I've got the slickest team of horses in the county."

"You don't know my father. He'd punish me, and he'd probably find a way to damage you, too. He's a good man, but you don't want to cross him. Let's just stand here and talk."

"All right." He nodded, leaning against the buggy. "So, is your mother here, too?"

"No, she took the wagon home early with my brothers

and sisters. I wanted to stay for the dance, so my father remained with me. We were planning to ride home with a neighbor."

"I could offer you both a ride. Maybe if he got to know me, he'd let me see you again. I'm not one of those cowhands that might take advantage of a sweet girl like you. I've got my own ranch—at least it'll be mine when my mother passes away."

"Don't bother asking. My father would never accept." Hanna was beginning to feel uneasy. What if her father were to catch her out here, alone with a man? "I'd better go back before he comes looking for me."

She turned to go. Mason blocked her path. "Wait." His hand cupped her jaw, tilting her face upward. "Lord Almighty," he murmured. "Angel, I feel like I just stepped into heaven. You're the most beautiful thing I've ever seen."

Hanna's heart broke into a gallop as he bent closer. His lips were almost touching hers when an angry voice shattered the spell.

"Damn it, Mason, let that girl go. Her father's fit to be tied. If he finds her out here with you, he'll skin you alive!"

Hanna turned. The tall cowboy she'd noticed earlier, the one with the blue shirt and leather vest, stood a few feet away from them. "Get inside and find your father, miss," he said. "You can claim you went to the privy. If he asks, I'll tell him I saw you coming from that direction. Meanwhile, I need to have words with my brother, here."

Hanna gasped, shocked that a man would mention bodily functions to her. But at least he'd come up with a good excuse for her father. Hot faced, she fled back toward the dance floor, weaving her way among the buggies and wagons. That was when a cry went up from somewhere out of sight.

"*Fire!*"

Turning, Hanna saw a distant column of smoke rising against the twilight sky. The prairie was burning.

Chapter 2

"Come on!" As the fleeing girl vanished from sight, Blake leaped into his brother's buggy, yanking Mason in behind him.

"What the hell—?" Mason sputtered.

"My horse is tied at the saloon. There's no time to get him." He grabbed the reins and released the brake. Around them, people were piling into buggies and wagons, some already racing toward the fire.

"It's my rig, damn it! I'll drive!" Mason snatched the reins away and slapped them down on the backs of the two matched sorrels. The buggy shot ahead, careening around a wagonload of settlers.

A narrow column of gray smoke rose to the west—a grass fire, judging from the color. Not too big yet, Blake calculated, but in this torrid July weather the dry prairie grass could flame up like tinder. Uncontrolled, the fire would race across fields and pastures, destroying everything in its path, including animals, homes, and even human lives.

Some of the settlers looked confused, maybe not understanding what needed to be done. But when they saw the ranch folks and townspeople rushing with breakneck urgency toward the smoke, they joined in. A prairie fire was everybody's problem.

The buggy swung off the road and cut across the open grassland, jouncing over the rough ground. Blake could see the fire now, and the burned skeleton of the tar paper shack where it must've started. Coming closer, he could smell the acrid smoke and hear the hiss and crackle of burning grass.

Fires didn't start themselves. Blake had his suspicions about who'd set this one. But nothing mattered now except putting out the blaze. And with no source of water nearby, that was going to be a dangerous challenge.

By the time Mason pulled the team up behind the wagons and buggies, Webb Calder had already taken charge of fighting the fire. The men he'd ordered into a line were beating back the flames with horse blankets and anything else that could be found. Those without blankets flailed at the flames with shovels or scraped away the grass to act as a firebreak.

Grabbing a wool blanket out of the back of the buggy, Blake vaulted out and raced to join the line. The smoke reddened Blake's eyes and stung his throat as he beat the fire's encroaching edge. The shortness of the grass kept the flames low, but the heat was searing, the fire spreading before the wind as fast as a man could walk. The dry blankets were losing the battle with the licking flames. Only water had any chance of quenching them before the blaze burned out of control.

Now more settlers were arriving. The men and older boys jumped off the wagons to fight the fire with whatever they had.

Some of the wagons carried water barrels that had been filled in town. As Webb began shouting orders, the women on the wagons took the blankets one by one, wet them in the barrels, and returned them to the men. As Blake passed his blanket up into a waiting pair of hands, his eyes met those of the girl he'd caught with Mason—the girl with the golden braids.

Her indigo eyes were reddened from the smoke. Stray locks of hair clung to her flushed face. Her white pinafore was wet and smeared with soot from handling the charred blankets. But even so, with smoke swirling around them, Blake was struck by her innocent beauty.

For an instant, their gazes met and held. There was a flicker of recognition before she turned away, dunked the lower part of the blanket in the water barrel, and passed it, still dripping, back down to him. Grasping it, he raced back to the fire.

The water-soaked blankets made a difference, but the flames were still burning. Glancing down the line, Blake glimpsed Hobie Evans and the Carmody brothers beating at the fire. If somebody had started it, Blake's money would be on those three. But of course they'd be here, helping, to avoid any suspicion.

Webb Calder moved up and down the lines, stepping in where help was needed. Webb's father, Benteen, who was well into his fifties, was on the fire line, too. Overcome by smoke, he suddenly doubled over, coughing. Webb seized his father's shoulders, guided him away from the flames, and left him with Ruth Stanton, who'd come in the buggy with Benteen's wife. Blake was grateful that his own parents and sister had left the celebration and gone home early. His father, Joe, was younger than Benteen, but even he had begun to show his years.

By the time the fire was out, the fighters were filthy and staggering with exhaustion. The homesteader who'd lost his house and most of his wheat crop stood apart with his wife and children, gazing at the destruction. The woman was in tears, the little ones wailing.

Damned shame, Blake thought as he walked back toward

the buggy, keeping an eye out for his brother. His eyes were red and sore from the smoke, his clothes filthy, his good boots charred. Neighbors would help the family rebuild their shack and see that they had food and clothes, but it was too late in the season to plant and harvest a new wheat crop. And no wheat to sell meant no money.

Blake had nothing against the recent settlers. Their arrival had been a boon to the town and to his family's lumber business. The drylanders bought cheap green boards to frame their tar paper shacks, while the high-quality, seasoned lumber from the Dollarhide sawmill went to build solid homes and new businesses in the growing community.

Joe Dollarhide, Blake's father, had seeded his fortune with his own early land grant and the wild horses he'd broken and sold in Canada. Now the family business combined land, cattle, and lumber. The lumber mill was Blake's responsibility, and he had ambitious plans for it—new sources of timber and more efficient ways to get logs to the mill, as well as the construction business he wanted to start. In this fast-growing town, there was money to be made. And Blake was determined to rake in his share of it.

Blake's father tended to measure his family's wealth against the Calders, who ruled like Montana kings in their big white mansion. The Triple C had more land and more cattle than all the other ranches combined. But with the beef market in a slump, the Calders could barely afford to pay their hired help. Ranchers all around Blue Moon were having to let their cowhands go. Some, like Mason's friend, Doyle Petit, had even sold off their grazing land to the wheat farmers.

But the Calders were different. If they were struggling financially, they refused to show it. They carried themselves with pride, gave generously to the community, and refused to complain in public or to sell so much as an acre of their land. Despite the rivalry between his father and the patriarch of the Calder family, Blake had nothing but respect for Benteen and Lorna Calder.

Their son Webb, however, was a different story—a story that had started back when Webb, the biggest boy in the one-room school they'd shared, had bullied the smaller Mason so cruelly that on some days, the younger boy would go home in tears. When Blake had tried to interfere, Webb had given him a black eye and a nosebleed. Of course, neither of the brothers told their teacher or their parents. There was nothing more shameful than a snitch.

All three were men now. Blake would bet that Webb Calder wouldn't even remember how he'd tormented the smaller, weaker Mason. But Mason had neither forgotten nor forgiven.

Blake found Mason waiting in the buggy. He'd lost track of his half brother while the fire was raging, but the dust that coated Mason's clothes, and his dirt-streaked face suggested that he'd been helping to shovel a firebreak.

Mason grinned. "Good thing you showed up. I was just about to drive off and leave you."

"You know better than to do that, little brother." Blake hauled his tired body onto the buggy seat. "But I'll tell you what. When we get back to the saloon, I'll buy you a drink."

"Done. I've got a powerful thirst. I may need more than one." Mason swung the team in an arc and headed the buggy back toward town. The homesteaders' wagons departed in the opposite direction, leaving men behind to make sure the fire didn't flare up again. Blake found himself scanning the crowd for the girl in white, but he didn't see her. Not that it mattered. Why should it? He didn't even know her name.

Driving back toward the road, they passed the Calder buggy. Webb was driving the matched bays, with Ruth beside him on the front seat. Benteen, looking pale and drawn, sat in the back with his wife.

Mason slapped the reins to get ahead, leaving the Calders

in a cloud of dust—something Blake wouldn't have done, but he'd long since learned that Mason had his own way about him.

"Webb was quite the hero boy today," Mason said as he slowed the team down. "He was strutting around like the biggest rooster in the coop."

"He did all right." Blake didn't much care for Webb either, but, unlike Mason, he kept his opinions to himself. The Dollarhides didn't need enemies—especially enemies as powerful as the Calders.

"Hell, it's not like we don't know how to fight a fire," Mason said. "We all knew what to do. We didn't need Webb to boss us around. I think he was mostly doing it to impress that sodbuster's redheaded wife."

"The one he was dancing with." It wasn't a question.

"That's right. The pretty one. Webb was all over her at the dance, and with her husband right there. If Webb had got his teeth kicked in, it would've served him right." Mason maneuvered the buggy back onto the dusty, rutted road. "And poor Ruth, having to stand there and watch. Her face said it all. A classy girl like that deserves better than Webb."

"If I could convince her of that, she could have me."

Mason chuckled. "You and half the other single men around here. But did you see the goings-on back at the fire?"

Blake shook his head. "I guess I was in the wrong place. Or maybe I was too busy fighting the fire to notice."

"You'd have noticed if you'd been there. It happened when the fire was almost out. As the wind changed, the fire started toward the wagons. The redhead—the wife—tried to stomp it out, and her skirt caught on fire. Webb tackled her and rolled her on the ground to put it out."

"Was she hurt?"

"It didn't look all that bad. But then Webb scooped her up in his arms and started for his buggy. That old man she's married to stepped right in front of him and snatched her away. He looked mad enough to kill. And of course Ruth saw it all."

"Ruth needs to show Webb the door and give the rest of us a chance," Blake said.

"But she won't. She wants to be a Calder. And she's got Webb's mother backing her. Hey, brother, there are other good-looking ladies out there—like that little angel with the golden braids. She's the one I've got my eye on. I just need to find a way around her father."

"Good luck with that." Remembering those innocent eyes, Blake felt a stab of something he didn't fully understand. The thought of Mason with that girl, winning her with his usual charm, then most likely breaking her heart, made him want to grind his teeth.

"How's your mother?" Blake asked, changing the subject.

"Fine. Spinning her little webs as usual." Amelia Hollister Dollarhide, Joe's first wife, had inherited her father's ranch and expanded it into her own empire. Blake, the son of Joe and his second wife, Sarah, was a year older than Mason. There was a story behind that incongruity. But most people either understood or knew better than to ask questions.

"And how's Dad doing?" Mason asked. "I've been meaning to come up to the house and see him."

"He's slowed down since that stallion broke his leg this spring. But otherwise he's doing all right. And Sarah's the same. They miss you. You know you'd be welcome anytime."

"Sarah was like a second mother to me. You can tell her I said so. But I didn't see our little sister at the dance. I was looking forward to watching the cowboys battle to lead her to the floor."

"Kristin isn't much for socializing—or cowboys. She's got her own way of thinking, whatever that is. But she misses you, too. We got used to having you around in the old days. Now it seems everything's changed."

"I know." Mason pulled the buggy up alongside the saloon, where Blake's buckskin horse was still tied to the rail. "Mother's grooming me to take over the ranch—a waste of time if you ask me. She'll probably live to be a hundred, and she won't let go of the reins as long as she's got breath in her body. Her only ambition for me is that I marry a rich woman. Do you know any of those around here?"

Blake chuckled. "Only your mother. Now what do you say we get that drink I promised you?"

The Andersons' nearest neighbor, Stefan Reisner, paused his wagon outside the shack that was Hanna's family home. His wife, Lillian, lay in the wagon bed with wet cloths on her blistered legs. The burns would heal, but she was in pain. Stefan was anxious to get her home. He was stopping only to drop off Hanna and her father.

Hanna had ridden in the wagon bed next to Lillian, cradling her friend's head and giving her sips of water. "I could stay with her the rest of the way," she said. "It's not that far to walk home."

"I can take care of her." Stefan sounded almost angry. "Just get out so we can go."

Big Lars had already climbed off the rear of the wagon. As Hanna moved back to join him, he turned and held out his huge hands to help her to the ground.

"I'll come to see you, Lillian," Hanna called as the wagon rolled away. Stefan didn't look back. She hoped he wasn't angry at Lillian. It wasn't Lillian's fault that her skirt had caught fire or that Webb Calder had been there to save her.

As Hanna walked toward the house with her father, she could smell the rabbit stew cooking in the kitchen. Her mother came rushing outside, wiping her hands on her apron. "We saw the smoke. Are you all right?" Inga Anderson had been a pretty girl in her youth, but twenty years of work, worry, and childbearing had aged her before her time. Her blond hair was streaked with gray, her face creased, her body shapeless beneath her worn gingham dress.

"We're fine. I'll wash up." Big Lars was a man of few words. Walking to the barrel, he filled a tin dipper with enough water to splash the soot off his face and out of his sparse, light brown hair.

"And you." She looked Hanna up and down, shaking her head. "I was hoping that pinafore could be passed down to Britta, at least. But it'll never come clean. We might as well tear it up for rags. Why can't you be more careful, Hanna? We don't have money for nice clothes. We need to make them last."

Hanna untied the sash of the pinafore and slipped it off, uncovering the threadbare calico dress beneath. She could see that the pinafore was ruined. And new clothes cost money the family didn't have. "I'm sorry, Mama," she said. "I needed to wet down blankets so the men could fight the fire. The blankets were dirty. What could I do?"

"I suppose you could've taken the pinafore off and put it out of the way. But that might be asking too much of a young girl with other things on her mind." Inga held up the pinafore, examined the soot stains, shook her head again, and rolled it into a ball. "So, did you have a good time at the dance?"

"It was . . . all right."

"And did you behave yourself?"

"Of course, Mama." Hanna knew better than to talk about the handsome, well-dressed man who'd almost kissed her. As for the news about Lillian's accident and the rancher who'd rescued her, that would be best passed on by her father.

"Let me wash up, and I'll set the table." She dipped enough water into a shallow basin to get her hands and face clean. Her hair would have to be brushed clean at bedtime.

Mason Dollarhide.

Hanna's lips shaped his name as she set the table with the tin plates and the few chipped, mismatched dishes that had been salvaged from their old home. When Mason Dollarhide had told her his name, he'd mentioned that he had his own ranch, so he wasn't one of those common cowboys her mother had warned her about. She wasn't fool enough to think she was in love, or that she had any future with such a man. But the memory of his pretty words caused her pulse to skip a little.

What if he had kissed her? Would his lips have felt like warm velvet touching hers? That was how she'd imagined her first kiss. There next to his buggy, with his hand tilting her face toward his, she'd been ready to let it happen. But then the other man had come—his brother—and sent her running back to her father like a scolded child, her face burning with shame.

"Hanna, didn't you hear me?" Her mother's voice broke into her musings. "I said, go outside and call your brothers and sisters to supper. For heaven's sake, what's got into you?"

With a sigh, Hanna obeyed. Daydreaming was a waste of time, she admonished herself. Her life was here with her family, plowing and planting, washing and mending, tending the animals and the younger children—all for a future in this land where nothing was won except by hard work. For now, at least, she would have to put away her secret longings and try to be content with her lot.

Blake and Mason had enjoyed two whiskeys each and were about to leave the saloon to go home and clean up when Mason's friend, Doyle Petit, walked up to their table and sat down without an invitation.

"Doyle." Blake gave him a nod. He didn't especially like the young man who'd inherited his father's cattle ranch and sold every stick and pebble of it to the wheat growers. Doyle was awash in money—some of which he'd spent on the county's first automobile. He was keen to make more, even if it meant taking advantage of other people's bad luck.

Blake pushed his chair back from the table. "You're welcome to stay and visit with my brother. But I was just about to climb on my horse and head home."

"But I came in to talk to you, Blake." Doyle's clothes were spotless. When the fire had needed fighting, he'd clearly been somewhere else. "Stay a minute," he said. "I've got a business proposition for you. I'll buy you a drink while you listen."

Blake sighed. He already knew what his answer would be, but it wouldn't hurt to know what Doyle had on his mind. "All right. But I've already had enough to drink. Just keep it short." He left his chair pushed clear of the table, to make his getaway easier when he decided he'd heard enough.

Settling back in the chair, Blake waited for Doyle to begin his pitch. Four cowboys who'd been at the fire were sitting at the table behind him. They were talking and laughing, making a lot of noise, but Blake willed himself to ignore them. He didn't plan to be here much longer.

"Here's what I'm thinking, Blake," Doyle said. "You sell a lot of cheap green lumber to those drylanders. But it's a long drive for their wagons, out to your sawmill. I aim to start a lumber business here in town—buy the lumber from you, haul it to a lot I've staked out behind the general store, and sell it at a profit. I'm betting the drylanders will be glad to pay a little extra for the convenience. Mason thinks it's a great idea. You even said so. Didn't you, Mason?"

"I did. But it's not up to me. It's up to Blake."

"So what do you think so far, Blake?" Doyle asked.

Blake shrugged. "As things stand now, you can buy all the lumber you want from me, Doyle. And once you've paid me, I don't care what the hell you do with it. So what do you need me for?"

"Just this. If we're partners, you can give me a better deal on the lumber and lend me one of your wagons to haul it. That way we can sell it cheaper, sell more, and still make a profit."

"A profit for you, not for me. No thanks, Doyle. I'm not interested. You can buy all the lumber you want, but not at a discount." Blake shifted in the chair, preparing to stand.

"No, wait." Doyle took a small notepad and a pencil out of his vest and began scribbling. "I've thought this all out. Let me show you some figures."

As Blake waited, knowing it was a waste of time, bits of conversation from the cowboys at the neighboring table broke into his awareness. He'd seen them come in, and he recognized a couple of them. They worked for the Calders.

"Can't say I think much of them sodbusters, but glory hallelujah, they brought some good-lookin' gals with 'em." The speaker was a big, bearded man named Sig Hoskins.

"I'll say," another cowboy responded. "That redhead's a pretty one. But it looks like Webb Calder's already staked his claim to her, even if she's married to that old geezer."

"Hell, that won't stop Webb. When he wants somethin', he goes after it."

"Webb can have her," Hoskins said. "The one I want is Yellow Braids. Now there's a fine little filly for you."

Blake had been listening idly while Doyle scribbled on his pad. But the mention of Yellow Braids caught his full attention. He glanced at Mason. Either his brother hadn't heard or he didn't care.

"I'll bet you that little filly ain't never even been rode." Hoskins's voice rose above the buzz of conversation and the clink of glasses. "Twenty bucks says I'll be the first one to get up her skirt. Anybody want to raise me?"

Blake's blood had begun to boil. Forgetting Mason and Doyle, he stood up, turned around, and grabbed Hoskins by the front of his vest.

"Take this for your twenty bucks, you sonofabitch!" he muttered. Then his fist slammed into the cowboy's jaw.

Letting the man fall, he turned away, stalked outside to his horse, and rode off into the dusk.

Hanna bowed her head while her mother said grace. The prayer included words for the Gilberg family whose home and wheat field had been destroyed by the fire. Tomorrow Hanna would be sent trudging across the fields with a basket of food—as much as Inga could spare, and then some—as well as a bundle of hand-me-down clothes for the little ones, clothes she'd put aside from her own children.

At dawn, Hanna's father and older brother, Alvar, would gather their tools and any scraps of building material they could find to set up a shelter for the family. Others would do the same. It was what good neighbors did—and who could say which of them would be struck by the next disaster?

The stew, made from the skimpy meat of a rabbit Alvar had snared that morning, along with some vegetables from Inga's garden, was a treat for the hungry family. Served with plenty of fresh biscuits, it was just enough for the seven of them. The parents ate sparingly to make sure there would be plenty for the children. Alvar, barely eighteen, and Hanna did the same. The younger children, Britta, almost thirteen, Axel, ten, and Gerda, eight, filled their plates. There would have been one more child at the table, but the baby boy, born after Hanna, had only lived a few days. Much as Inga loved her blue-eyed, flaxen-haired brood, Hanna knew that her mother still mourned the little one she'd lost.

The children ate in silence, as was the custom. But for the parents, the evening meal was a time to catch up on the events of the day.

"I was talking with Stefan on the way home from the fire," Big Lars said. "He told me that somebody found a broken lantern in that burned shack. That means the fire was started on purpose while the family was in town."

"Are you sure?" Inga had gone pale. Hanna knew what her mother was thinking. If she and the children hadn't gone home early, with Alvar driving the wagon, their place could have been the one that was burned.

"That fire didn't start itself, Inga. Some cowboys at the dance almost beat up Ole Hanson. They left after a man stopped them. Ole thinks they might have gone to start the fire. Those cowboys hate us. They blame us for the bad cattle market. It isn't true, but they don't care, as long as they've got somebody to punish."

"We could be next," Inga said. "Anybody could be. And maybe next time it won't be just a fire. They'll start hurting people, even killing them."

The younger children had stopped eating. They were staring at their mother.

"We'll just need to keep our eyes open," Big Lars said. "Keep the shotgun loaded and handy. Watch for any strangers coming around. If you see anybody you don't know, assume they're an enemy."

"So the cowboys and ranchers are our enemies now?" Hanna asked, thinking of the handsome man who'd almost kissed her.

"Yes," her father said. "We can't trust any of them. Remember that."